two
equals

Book Three

marta Szemik

MyLit Publishing

ISBN-978-0-9878772-5-3

To my Mom

CHAPTER 1

He should have killed her.

I couldn't understand why Xander thought the witch ought to live—not after she'd stolen my body in her scheme to destroy both the human and vampire races. The memory of her theft four years ago still sent chills down my spine. She'd almost killed me.

After my soul had been switched with hers, I'd never felt the same. My body responded to emotions in unexpected jolts and shivers. I'd want to cry, but tears wouldn't flow until a day later. Delayed laughter at a joke escaped my throat when I was alone. Tardy reactions to the life I was supposed to enjoy tortured me.

Xela was the only one who could explain why I'd changed. Part of me had never returned to my body, and I wanted to know why.

Today, I waited on the porch, counting the minutes. Every day, after my children's training, my friend and one-time protector Xander went out into the woods to see the witch. He'd kept it a secret for almost four years, and rightly so, as now that I knew about her, I was determined to find their hideout.

I sat on the front steps with my eyes closed and welcomed the cooler morning breeze. With spring ending, the summer heat wave loomed, ready to blast the Amazon and dry up its burgeoning rivers. *Four minutes since Xander left,* I thought, tapping out the seconds with my wiggling fingers. My right knee bobbed, and the heel of my sole thumped on the deck, sending dull wooden echoes through the clearing. The force under my hand on the knee couldn't stop the nervous habit.

My strategy to follow him without taking food and hygene supplies had to work. I hadn't asked him about Xela nor mentioned his trips and made sure he overheard I had plans with William. This time, I would succeed and find the witch's hideout. Xander wouldn't catch me the way he had on the two occasions I'd tried before. I should have known better than to extradite information from him. Anything could alert a shapeshifter.

Was Xander afraid I'd kill her? Why did he want her alive?
Woody musk fused around me and I opened my eyes.

"He's going to catch you," my husband, William, warned stepping out of the house. He must have put the twins to bed quicker than I expected. William handed me a glass of water.

"It's been a week since I followed him last." I took a sip of water.

"And you think that will make him less suspicious?"

"I'll be careful." The breeze cooled my fingers around the glass.

He raised his brows. "You're trying to outsmart a shapeshifter."

"You think I can't?" I retorted.

"I'm not getting involved in your quarrels, but he's still your best friend. He trusts your promise."

I hadn't told William I'd crossed my fingers behind my back when I made the promise to my best friend after my first failed attempt. Childish, yes; unwarranted, no. How could he believe I would stop searching for the witch? Didn't he know me? She tried to steal my life. My only option was revenge, after gaining answers I sought.

"He's hiding a witch who wanted to kill me," I reminded him, eager to justify my betrayal.

"He must have a reason." William sat in the wicker chair behind me and leaned forward, cradling his glass in his hands. "Come on, Sarah, it's Xander. He'd never hurt you." He sipped from his glass. "And I don't like you getting too close to her. It's as if you're still drawn to her."

I didn't realize my fingers had tightened around my glass until it shattered. The slit in my palm reminded me of the blood I'd lost when in Xela's body. She'd cut her chest to let her soul escape and push mine away. My spirit had taken over her empty host. I never felt I'd gotten my full self back when Eric, the evil-bender, bent the witch back to her own body, returning mine to me.

William entered the cabin and came back seconds later. "Just be careful, Sarah, please," he said as he bandaged a slit that would heal in minutes.

"I will." I kissed him. "I'll say goodnight to the kids, then go."

"I'll be waiting."

William began to sweep up the broken glass, and I rose and went inside. In their room, I inhaled the lavender soap aroma that wrapped my children's bodies like a blanket. It soothed my soul. I'd never forget the mixture that my own and William's scents conjured when mingled with their natural honey and lemon smell. Both children slept with their mouths slightly open, exhausted from their daily training. The tricks Xander and Mira, demonic shapeshifter siblings, taught them got more difficult to master each day.

I often wondered whether we were pushing the twins beyond what three-year-olds should be able to do. I'd find them sleeping in the middle of the hall; up in the trees, their limbs dangling off supporting branches; even in the emerald pond, floating on their backs. Crystal and Ayer weren't regular twins.

We didn't have a name for what they were. Another mystery I'd lost sleep over at night.

The kids were developing abilities beyond my understanding. Mira and Eric taught the twins the defence moves when they weren't gathering the lingering souls from the hereafter. They'd promised me that once it was time, I would be reunited with my mom and my aunt before they passed on. I hadn't seen their ghosts since they'd helped me after Xela stole my body.

I looked at my watch. Xander had a ten minute lead, and it was time to follow him through the forest. His daily ritual of bringing food to the witch was as predictable as the sunrise and sunset. He'd leave right after the training, and in the evening when the twins went to sleep. Twice a day, my best friend split his duties between watching over me (which I no longer needed) and uselessly talking to the witch.

Did Xela trick him the way she had tricked me? Part of me didn't like the jealousy swirling though my body. After all, I had William and the twins. I was happy—happier than I'd ever imagined—raising my children, preparing them for a future I knew would be nothing short of difficult.

Should I listen to William and leave Xander and the witch alone? Perhaps, but I was drawn to Xela more than I wanted to admit. The connection between us after our soul switch lingered in my bones.

I missed the adventure, too, and longed for the day we could finally be rid of the warlock. We had no doubt the battle would be fiercer than the one in the underworld against hundreds of seekers. But Aseret had last attempted to attack over a year ago. His efforts to locate us were futile. Each time he tried, Eric would twirl his finger and magically tie Aseret back to the underworld. The warlock could send seekers to capture us again, but they had no chance against us. Their fears weakened them, and William could wring their necks before they even blinked their orange eyes. We were safe, but I didn't want to feel such strong security. I knew as soon as we relaxed our guard, Aseret would step in.

Xander's tracks on the forest floor were difficult to follow, but I eventually closed on him, remaining far enough behind that he wouldn't detect my presence. Xander in a wolf form slowed his jog and shifted back to human. He must be nearing the place where Xela was held captive. The sun covered with stray clouds hung high enough not to affect my sight. I inhaled his aroma of a wet dog and shivered at the stench.

He froze and scanned the forest. Was he hunting?

I stopped when my best friend disappeared. *Crap!* Did he sense me? I ducked behind a bush. My ears perked up, sensitive as a hare's. His footfalls were soundless and I peeked through the branches. Xander wasn't there.

I rose and followed his scent, letting my nose find the way. Xander leaped in front of me and I jumped back, startled.

"What are you doing?" Xander stood with his hands on his hips, brow furrowed. He was controlling his anger; green shade hadn't infused his face yet.

"You're sneaking off to see her again," I accused, holding my chin higher, but shame for breaking my promise made my cheeks burn. The contained revenge for the witch brewing inside me rushed through my body.

"First, I'm not sneaking. Second, it's not your business, Sarah." Xander squared his shoulders.

"She tried to kill me." I widened my eyes for emphasis, and crossed my arms at my chest.

"It wasn't her."

"What?" I blurted as resentment burned in my veins. How could he dare defend her? "Then who? Why are you keeping her locked away? She should be dead."

"You assume too much, Sarah." Xander strained to sound calm.

"She stole my body and pretended William, my other half, belonged to her!" The echo of my voice flowed through the woods.

"Like I said, she's no longer your business," Xander said stubbornly.

"Xander," I said, my tone now more reasonable, "I just want to understand. We're friends."

He relaxed as well. "No one can understand, because *I* don't understand."

His answer wasn't satisfying. "Then let me help you figure out whatever you're trying to figure out," I pleaded.

He shook his head, the door closing again. "It's not a good time. Go home, Sarah; be with William, be with the kids."

I lowered my head.

"You don't want to be with them?" he asked.

I looked at him. "No, it's not that."

"Then what is it?"

"I miss you, and Mira."

"We're still around."

"Not the way you used to be." I bit my lip; my complaint sounded so childish. "You used to care more. You had my back."

Xander sighed. "We still care, but at that time you didn't know who you were. You needed our protection. Now you can hold your own and William can take care of you. I thought William was everything you'd wanted."

"He was, and he is." I cleared my throat. "It's just a little hard to get used to all the changes so quickly. I mean, I'm married!"

"Mr. Perfect isn't Mr. Perfect?" He chuckled.

"Stop it!" I showed my fangs. "You know he is, but I'm having a difficult time adjusting. Everyone cares about me so much. I'd always had only you and Mira and now, I have a family. A real family."

"They always cared. You just didn't know it."

"And my children are trying to explore their demonic side." I threw my arms up.

"You're not telling me something. I know when you lie." Smirking, Xander leaned against a tree. It was as if he'd turned the tables around on me and now I was beginning to amuse him.

"Well, it's complicated for me, too." I shuddered. How could I tell him the witch he's been hiding was still connected to me and it felt like she hadn't returned my entire soul to my body?

"Fine, then why is it so difficult for you to accept the children's training?"

"Because I don't understand their demonic side," I exclaimed. "I know how to be human and a vampire, but the demons . . ."

"First off, they're not *demonic*." He rolled his eyes. "Besides, you know us."

"You're shapeshifters."

He raised his brows. "We're a little more than that, aren't we?"

"Yes," I admitted. "And that's what I want to understand. What would make a strong shapeshifter like you want to keep the enemy alive?"

"There are things in this world you still don't understand."

His dismissal angered me. "Bull! You're keeping a shield between us."

"Sarah, I have to keep a shield between us." He stepped forward until he stood only a foot away from me.

"Why?" A hint of his testosterone oozed toward me, and I held the air in my lungs. His scent danced inside me.

"Because if I don't, I'll do something we'll both regret."

The lump in my throat cleared with difficulty. This wasn't the first time in the past year that Xander had almost crossed the line of our friendship. At one point, he and William had had a falling out after Xander stumbled upon me naked in the bathroom and made a comment about my perky front. They hadn't spoken to each other for a month. Although it was an honest mistake, Xander apologized. Eric convinced us to let it go, that it wasn't Xander's fault. I trusted Eric more than I trusted my own instincts. After all, he was the only one who recognized me after my body had been switched for the witch's.

"Xander, I'm with William." I whispered with a difficult breath.

"I know. Believe me, I know." His shoulders lowered, Xander brushed my cheek with the back of his hand.

"Then why?" I held my gaze locked with his.

"Because I'm a man." He licked his lower lip.

"And that's supposed to make me feel better?"

"I can make you feel better." He lifted my chin, rubbing his thumb on the dimple below my lip.

"Xander . . ."

I wanted to pull away but couldn't. A magnetic force held me close to my best friend. Stepping back would feel like falling off a cliff, death.

"I've known you all my life, and you bear the closest resemblance to someone I'd known well. Your curves are identical, your smile, the way your eyes light up when you say my name." He tucked a loose strand of hair behind my ear with his other hand.

"That's because you're my best friend. I trust you. I . . . I care about you but not in the way you want me to."

"I know, Sarah." He sighed. "I care about you too, and not in the way you may be thinking right now, but our friendship is the closest thing to love I may ever have."

"Why can't you find someone?"

His laugh was bitter. "I already found her, but we cannot be."

"Who?"

"It's complicated."

"You know you have a friend in me forever, right?" I leaned in to comfort him, even though I knew shouldn't have.

"I know," he whispered, burrowing his face in my shoulder, nestling his nose in my hair.

The cologne he wore today smelled more attractive than other days. There was a hint of the woody musk I loved to smell on William, along with a sweet aroma of raspberries and the tartness of a rose.

Xander lifted his head, bringing his face inches away from mine. I'd never looked at his mouth the way I did today. The pull toward him was more than magnetic; it was magical. His lungs expanded against my front as his chest pressed into mine.

Xander's eyes mellowed, and his lip swelled, inviting me. I refused to breathe, afraid that if I did, my next breath would be shared with his.

"Shit!" He pulled away.

I shook off the pheromones that drew me closer to him, shivering like a wet dog. What just happened?

"I'm sorry about this, Sarah." He backed against a tree.

"What was that?" My hand flew to my mouth then my head. I paced in a circle wondering how my feelings for Xander could have been so strong. I cared for him, but this was more than caring. This was love, lust and desire all combined into one.

He held up his hand. "I'll fix things, I promise."

"What do you have to fix now?" I froze, my forehead wrinkling.

"Look, if I show you where Xela is, do you promise to keep your distance?"

I nodded like an eager kid.

"And you won't question why I'm keeping her?"

I nodded again, stepping from one foot to the other.

"Nor hurt her?"

"Yes, yes, yes. I agree to it all." I grinned.

"Pinky swear?" He held out his hand, hesitant.

I didn't laugh. This was the most important promise Xander could make.

"Pinky swear." I hooked my finger into his.

"Close your eyes."

"Why?"

"Because even if I take you to her, I don't want you to see where she is."

"Fine." I shut my eyes, keen on seeing Xela. If I could face her just once, perhaps she'd answer my question as to how I'd changed. This was progress, and much more than I expected after Xander discovered my trail on him.

A ripping sound drew my gaze, and I opened my eyes long enough to see that Xander had torn the sleeve off his shirt. I closed them again as he tied the sleeve around my head, covering my sight.

"And don't use your senses. I'll be confusing you anyway."

"You know you don't have to do that," I said.

"You'd be surprised what kind of trouble acute senses can get you into."

I exhaled. "Okay." But I crossed my fingers behind my back.

Fur tickled against my leg. Xander had shifted into a wolf and sidled up beside me, indicating that I should sit on his back. The dip just above his hinds was a perfect seat as he carried me through the forest. The cool wind wrapped around my limbs. Leaning forward, I burrowed my face in his fur and tightened my grip. He sped between the trees at his fastest sprint, sometimes circling back the way we'd come. I tried not to use my senses, but that was like asking a human not to breathe. My senses were part of me and not something I could turn off, not anymore. And Xander knew that.

He leapt over a creek, then a second one, much wider. At one point I thought he'd jumped over a gully; perhaps he did. After a while, his sprint turned into a trot, then a walk. Xander shook his torso, wriggling me off his back. Breaking bones and cracking ribs told me he'd shifted back, and I removed my blindfold. We continued as two humans on foot.

Twenty minutes later, we stood in a valley deeper in the Amazon than I'd ever ventured. I'd never been to the Grand Canyon before, but this place was exactly what I imagined that geographical wonder to be, except here, the forest didn't thin into pink rock cliffs. It expanded, the greenery as luscious as it was in my corner of the jungle. I looked up, shielding my eyes from the sun directly above us. A stream of fresh water gurgled nearby, and my stomach grumbled.

"We'll get food on the way back," Xander told me, stepping toward a rock the size of a minivan.

I nodded when he turned back at me.

"When you see her, don't listen," he continued. "She'll try to sway you, and if she does, I'll have to sedate her."

"Okay," I said cautiously.

"And wipe that smirk off your face. You look like you've just won a prize." He paused, then added. "Trust me, you haven't."

Xander pushed aside a boulder to reveal the dark opening of a cave. We stepped into the endless abyss. As my sight adjusted, Xander lit the end of a branch he'd retrieved from beside the entrance. I smelled gasoline. The torch cast pervasive shadows on the walls. Chills ran up my spine—not from fear, but adrenaline. I felt the way I had four years ago, when I fought against Aseret, then tricked Xela to get my body back. Anxiety rushed through me, mixed with nerves and excitement of the unknown. My passive life before I met William and knew who I was had long been gone, and I craved danger and someone to challenge my strength all the time.

Xander led me ten steps down into the cave before pushing open a wooden door. Rusted hinges squeaked, sprinkling copper-colored dust in an arc along the cave floor. In one corner of the misshapen almost octagonal room, black roses bloomed on a low bush with one red flower in the midst of its leaves. The aroma from the blossoms hit me as soon as we entered; their intense scent reminded me of the rosy scent I'd smelled on Xander. Walls lined with shelves held pots and clear jars filled with skeletal ingredients and gooey liquids; dried herbs hung from the ceiling. The burrow reminded me of Mrs. G's hill, but this one felt lonely. Even with the heat streaming from a fireplace, the chills never left my spine. Anyone living here was meant to be isolated from the world.

"This was her house?" I asked.

"No, this is a replica of where she lived in the underworld."

I shook my head. "I don't understand why you would do this, Xander."

"I . . . I have my reasons," he stuttered. Xander's voice never shook. His eyes darted from me to a darker corner of the room.

He stepped in front of me, blocking my view, probably wary of me, fearing I'd kill the witch.

"I promised I wouldn't do anything," I assured him.

"Sometimes promises are broken." He raised his brows.

"I can see how much this means to you." I turned in a circle, examining the room again, "This promise holds true, Xander. I won't touch her."

He rolled his eyes but didn't lecture; I wondered whether he knew I'd crossed my fingers behind my back.

Xander stepped aside, clearing my view of the witch. I took two steps forward.

"Far enough." Xander's arm flew in front of me.

Near the back end of the room, Xela sat in a wooden chair, her arms chained behind her. The shadow of a webbed root penetrating the ceiling in front of her concealed her body. Beside the chair sat a bowl filled with leftovers. Xela's head had fallen forward.

"She's sleeping," I said in a low voice.

"No, sedated."

"Why?"

"I can't explain everything, but I'm not hiding her to spite you." Xander turned to face me again, his eyes suddenly mellower and the tautness in his jaw softened.

The smell of black roses filled the cave. A new rush of endorphins swam through my veins. My sight blurred.

"I've never met another woman like you," Xander whispered.

Xander's breath caressed my face. I wanted to push him away and punch him the way I'd normally do, but I couldn't. Something held me in this gloomy room, and part of me felt as if I was in a different time and space. The Xander with me today wasn't from today; he was happier, with shining eyes. He looked like he was in love and carefree. His skin glowed like a teenager's who just hit puberty. Each inhale was deeper than the previous and his breath contained hope and vigor. The burden of his shapeshifter duties was gone.

The pull toward him increased. I wanted Xander to place his arms around me, and as if on command, he did. Part of me felt like it'd travelled back in time as well. My soul watched from the side as my body reacted to his. His eyes sparkled, and I didn't want to take away his happiness. He pulled me in closer, tightening his hands on my hips before running them up both sides of me to my arms, and finally framing my face. My front felt glued to his hot body, which responded to my rushing pulse. I leaned in, needing him to do things to me that only William had done.

William.

"Take me back," I whispered, pushing away from his chest with difficulty. "Take me back to William."

Xander's eyes bulged, and he jumped back.

A cackling laugh echoed through the cave. Xela lifted her head, unable to contain her mirth.

"Stop that!" I yelled, feeling my ears press against my head.

"Ah, what's the matter? William ain't enough for you?" she taunted.

I sprang forward, ready to rip her heart out, but Xander stopped me midway. My fists pounded on his chest, but I may as well have been hitting rock.

"You can't stop me, Xander," I hissed.

"You can't hurt her." Xander pleaded in a forceful voice. He tightened my wrists in his hands, and I felt like I'd been imprisoned with supernatural cuffs.

"Oh, the poor boy misses his witch." She laughed again.

"What is she talking about?" I asked.

"I can't do this. You have to leave, Sarah. Please." His pain-filled eyes pleaded more than his words.

"What are you doing to him?" I yelled toward Xela over his shoulder. "Why do I feel empty and different? You stole my rage!"

"I don't think she stole your rage." Xander pushed against me, backing me toward the door. My feet pushed against the earthen flooring, mounting dirt behind my heels.

"Why are my emotions out of whack? I know you did it! It's all your fault!"

Xela only laughed. The pitch increased until the shelved jars began to crack, one after another. Soon, my eardrums would burst, and I couldn't shift them the way Xander could his.

I pulled my hands to my ears, turned on my heel, and darted out of the cave. The witch's laugh followed us.

I stepped out in the sunlight and stomped my foot. "Ugh! She's not going to answer me, is she?"

"Calm down, Sarah."

What was that in there?" I turned to face Xander and touched my lips.

He grinned. "Me trying to kiss you?"

"You've tried before; it's no big deal," I said, concentrating on the blooming daisy at my feet.

"No big deal?" he exclaimed.

"The problem was, this time, I wanted to kiss you as well." I lowered my head. It had never occurred to me before to kiss Xander. I considered him like a brother. But today, the lust inside me grew, and Xander seemed more like a man to me than a brother.

"Really? I hadn't noticed." He smirked.

"You knew this was going to happen?" When he nodded, I added "Then why did you let it?"

"It was the only way for you to understand why I cannot let anyone come here. I didn't want to push it this far, but you gave me no choice. Xela's magic is powerful, and we haven't been able to contain it." Xander paced between me and the opening of the cave.

"We?"

"Mira and me. You should have seen her face when I tried to kiss *her*." He shook his head at the memory.

"Ew! Your sister?" I burrowed my face in my hands.

"Could *you* control your lips in there?"

"No." Blood rushed to my cheeks as I squeezed my eyes shut, still unable to look at him.

"Maybe I shouldn't have stopped. That way it'd make your trip worthwhile." He took my hands away from my face.

"Don't do that again," I warned.

"Fine, but you need to understand," he walked back to the cave entrance and pushed the boulder to cover it, "it wasn't me in there. The closer you get to this cave, the more powerful she is. You need to stay away."

"Fine." I spat a bit harder than I meant.

"Pinky swear?" Xander pulled out his hand.

"Pinky swear." I sighed but crossed the fingers of my other hand behind me again. The unexplained connection I had to the witch would bring me back, even if I didn't want to admit it out loud. Part of me craved the unknown and the rush I felt when Xander came so close to me. I wanted him as much as I wanted William, and I couldn't forget what had passed between me and my best friend.

The witch's laugh roamed through the valley, circling back to our ears again.

"Don't pay attention to her." Xander lowered his head.

"You're asking a lot."

"I know."

"It seems that she's sucking the life out of you, and I don't like it." I stepped forward to take his hand to comfort him. The contact flowed over my skin like satin, and my pulse raced. Xander took my other hand, and the feeling intensified. Every time I touched him, his life vibrated with mine. My heavy breathing raised my chest higher. All I wanted was to give in to the warmth oozing from Xander and let him fulfill the tingling urges near the bottom of my pelvis.

Xander's lips hovered above mine, then he whispered, "We'd better go, before I get slapped for you kissing me."

Startled, I jumped back, straining to concentrate on something other than my hot best friend. Xander released my hands, and I sped away through the trees toward the stream I'd heard earlier. I dove in feet first and sank below the cool water, letting it chill my heated body.

Xander waded into the river up to ankle depth, his pants rolled to his knees. He offered his hand. "Don't worry, I won't let it happen again," he said as he pulled me up, "if you promise not to come here."

"Fine." I shook the lust off my body. *That was some magic.*

"You're soaked."

"Really?" I said sarcastically.

"Hop on and close your eyes." He shifted into a wolf.

I swung my leg over his back and gripped his fur, pressing my body along his back as he took off. Xander's heat warmed my limbs through my drenched clothes. My eyes stayed open as he galloped through the forest, across fields, and over gullies, memorizing the way to the cave, careless about my promise. If I knew Xander the way I thought I did, he'd know I didn't mean it. He'd know I wouldn't be able to stay away. Did he want me to break it? Did he want me to come back despite saying he didn't?

As we left the boundary of the valley, I heard Xela's laugh inside my head for the first time: *"I'm still here, Sarah. I'm still here."*

CHAPTER 2

After an hour long gallop, we returned to the clearing in the Amazon. The glade was one of my favorite places, along with the tree house and the emerald pond. Living anywhere else wouldn't be the same. With the rain season nearing its end, the jungle gorged on streams and rivers filled to capacity. Most of the sun spots that once speckled the grass from above as if viewed from under a strainer were gone. William had pruned the overhanging branches, but their leaves tripled in size during the rainy season and stole most sunny patches.

At the side of the cabin linen curtains fluttered in the windows of our bedroom. The logs extended beyond the original walls that had been burned by the seekers when they captured me. The extended space allowed for the twins' rooms to connect to our master suite through a shared bathroom. The layout of rest of the cabin remained the same, only larger, to accommodate the entire family and frequent guests: Mira, Eric, and Xander. We'd enclosed the lab, separating it with a glass wall from the kitchen and open living room. William's mother, Willow, used the space to produce serums, most of which revived dead blood, and were sent to our distribution centre in Mexico. The potency of the serums increased with each new trial.

William sat on the front porch of our rebuilt cabin. When he saw us, he closed the book he'd been reading and narrowed his brows. "You're all wet. What happened?" William darted inside and returned with a towel in his hand. He held it wide and wrapped me into his arms.

"Don't ask. I don't even understand what happened."

Xander laughed. "She followed me again and got her dose of punishment."

"Shut up!" I scolded. I didn't want Xander to be the one to tell William about our *almost* kiss.

"And so you threw her in a lake?" William coaxed.

"No, she took care of that herself." Xander folded his arms at his front, obviously waiting for me to own up to what happened.

William returned his attention to me. "You're shivering." He rubbed my arms.

I tightened my jaw, trying to stop the jittering teeth. I wasn't ready to share what I'd heard in my head. The hope that I'd imagined it was too much to ask for: but I was sure Xela had invaded my mind. Xander probably thought my shakes were for a different reason. "Perhaps I'm a little cold," I fibbed, biting my lip. "I need Eric. Now." The towel fell to the grass.

I felt William's gaze burn into my back as I stomped away; he'd know something was wrong.

"What's the matter?" William called to my back. Then he growled, "What the hell happened, Xander?"

"Nothing." Xander raised his arms in innocence.

"This doesn't look like nothing to me."

I turned back in time to see William pointing to me, feverish anger burning his face.

"She tried to kiss me," Xander blurted.

"What! Why?" William stalked toward Xander

Xander shrugged and took a step back. "It's complicated."

I rolled my eyes. Everything lately was complicated to Xander.

"Not when you're talking about kissing my wife, shifter," William hissed at my best friend. A couple more steps and he'd be at Xander's throat.

"William, it's not Xander's fault, and it's not about the kiss," I interjected.

He spun to look at me. Pain washed over his eyes. "So there *was* a kiss?"

"No."

"Almost," Xander whispered.

William's gaze found Xander again before he ran back to my side.

I threw a dirty look at my best friend. *You'd better shut it if you don't want a fight!* Aloud I said, "It was Xela's stupid magic trick. Where are the kids?" I perked my ears, trying to hear their faint laughter.

"At the lake with our parents. I warned you not to get close to the witch. Sarah, what's going on?" He touched my shoulder as I stepped onto the porch.

"I don't know yet. I think Xela's messing with Xander. I'll be back in a moment."

I dashed to our bedroom and opened my jewelry box where my ruby ring nestled. The gem shined as I held it between my fingers, examining its shape against the lamp light. It was the same. No one had stolen it. My only affirmation of my identity rested in my palm. This ring had helped me trick Xela into revealing herself in my body. The ruby showed others who it truly belonged to; no one could mistake me for someone else when I wore it.

I came back outside. "I have to talk to Eric. Everything is fine," I added as I met William's concerned gaze.

Xander stretched his legs out on the patio chair.

"And you'll tell me whatever 'is fine' when you're ready?"

"Yes." The ring slipped onto my finger. It fit the same way it had the first time I wore it, conforming to it perfectly. I closed my eyes, then opened them. "Who do you see?"

"You."

"Good." I exhaled.

William narrowed his brows. "She's not going to steal your body again. Never."

He stepped forward and took me by my shoulders. My husband pulled me in to his chest, and I closed my eyes, inhaling his sweet musk. The comfort of William's embrace slowed my pulse, my heartbeat adjusting to run in sync with his calm thumps. The beating in our chest always remained the same, and this constant in my life soothed my worries. My gaze shifted higher. I missed seeing the love on William's face when he wasn't preoccupied with work.

In my head, I heard, *"Never say never!"* followed by bellowing laughter.

I jumped back. "Eric! Mira!"

"He can't hear you. He's bending," William said.

"Xander, can you get them? I need Eric as soon as possible, and I cannot leave here," I pleaded, hearing giggling, and turned toward my returning children.

"Done." Xander tilted his head back to look skyward. He squeaked in Harlow's tongue—one of his gifts as a shapeshifter that I admired. A moment later, a similar sound resonated from above the canopy. Xander's falcon could find Mira and Eric, hopefully quickly.

"Let me know when they're here."

He nodded.

With a smile on my face, I rushed toward the end of the path to greet my kids. Crystal crushed into me when I crouched; Ayer jumped into William's arms.

"What's wrong, Mama?" She placed her hands on my face.

"You're so good at that." I kissed her forehead.

"Where are you going?" she asked.

I opened my mouth, then shut it again, confused. "What do you mean? I'm not going anywhere."

Ayer came to my side and touched my face. "Don't be shcared, Mama. She won't hurt you."

"Who?"

"The lady with the black hair," Crystal answered.

I stood and held my breath. Everyone stared at the twins, including my in-laws and my father who neared the end of the path. The ruffling leaves in the treetops above the clearing seemed loud.

Xander stepped forward.

Fearing what I'd hear, I asked. "You've seen her?"

"No, but I know." My daughter smiled.

"How do you know?" Xander asked. "Was she old? Wrinkled on her face? Messy hair?"

"No, she was booful."

Xander's expression mirrored the one I'd seen in the cave—a younger version of my best friend in happier times and I wondered whether his connection to Xela had more depth than he ever cared to share.

"But you haven't seen her?" he asked with almost frozen lips.

"No, I just know," Crystal answered. "Who is she?"

Xander's breathing became shallow, and he turned around, running his fingers through his hair, seemingly lost in thought.

I crouched, taking the kids' hands into mine. "Do you remember when we talked about bad people?"

"Demons and seekers," Ayer supplied, then cocked his head to the right. "I'm not shcared."

Willow fluffed the towels, hanging them on the porch railing. My father and Atram sat on the steps, watching their grandchildren with intent. Both had kept busy letting the air out of a blown-up mattress.

"I know, baby. I just need you to always be on the lookout, and if you see someone odd, you need to let us know."

"Don't worry, Mama. Look, we can do this!" Ayer pulled his hand free and glanced at Crystal as if in confirmation. The children took a step back, and red flames shot out of their palms, rocketing toward the forest. The flames impacted a tree. William raised his arms to catch its trunk before it fell on the house.

"When did this happen?" I whirled toward my husband.

"This morning." William grinned with pride.

"What does this mean? Is the red flame a power from the underworld?"

Crystal took my hand and my nerves calmed. "It's okay, Mama."

"Let's not jump to conclusions." Willow knelt beside the kids. "Are you guys hungry?"

Before she could take them inside for snacks, wind gusted through the clearing. The air spun, opening a vortex in the middle of the field. Freshly mown grass flew in circles, and I smelled lavender and lilac. When the whirling stopped and the dust settled, Eric was walking toward us, hand in hand with Mira.

The twins ran up and knocked Mira and Eric to the ground. They rolled together on the grass, tickling one another and giggling so joyously. I laughed as well. My twins and the siblings didn't have to speak to understand one another. I wished I could communicate with my children the way the siblings did, without having to speak. I only had that ability with Eric. The siblings and Eric exposed the children to all the magic and power they knew. My best friends' unconditional love and devotion in training Crystal and Ayer would never be forgotten. For their own protection, my twins had to know and understand who they were and their role in this world, even when we weren't sure of it ourselves.

"Whoa! Who took down that tree?" Eric exclaimed. Then he rustled Ayer's hair.

"Me, me!" The twins bounced up and down, their hands up, each trying to be louder than the other.

Eric held his own hand just above his head. The twins had no problem reaching it to give him a high five.

"Want to see, Auntie Mira? Want to see?" A blue flame materialized in Crystal's hand.

"Perhaps we can find a tree farther away from the house?" Eric extinguished the flame in her hand with his palm.

"Are we ready for snacks yet?" Willow tried again.

"Why don't we pack for tomorrow, too." William nodded to his mom. "Once the blood donation papers are signed at the prison, we can concentrate on these two little bugs." He rubbed Ayer's head, the way Eric had done a minute ago.

"We're no boogs. I hate boogs," Crystal complained.

"I know. You have your mama to thank for that." William laughed and motioned the kids toward their grandparents. "Snack time."

"Yeah!" The kids dashed inside to devour pudding while we stood in a circle in the clearing, arms crossed.

"Sarah, you knew the kids would need to master the use of darker powers." William put his arm around me.

Flustered, I crossed my arms at my front. "They're three years old!" I spat, feeling as if I were about to assume Xander's green shade indicative of angry frustration. I didn't want them to master the underworld.

"We don't know when they're supposed to begin their work, but it could be anytime. They need to be ready," William said.

"They're three!" I felt the pressure of my fangs on my lower lip. "I don't think it's time yet."

"Sarah, you're forgetting although they look like normal kids, they're not human children. They probably won't age like human children, just like you. You wanted to talk to me?" Eric shifted the subject.

"Yes, later." My gaze focused on the ground. I needed privacy for what I was going to share with Eric, especially with Xander hanging over my shoulder.

"Whatever she tells you, Eric, I hope you can help, because she hasn't been herself today." William stared at me with concerned eyes as he spoke. I recognized the look. My husband knew I wanted to speak with Eric about something I couldn't tell anyone else. But that was only because I didn't understand why Xela invaded my mind and I didn't want to worry them.

I avoided his gaze. "It's not funny," I grumbled.

"It wasn't meant to be, honey. I want to help, and you won't let me."

"I don't know what it is I need help with. Yet." I found his pleading expression but couldn't find the strength to explain Xela to my husband, and I headed toward the cabin.

William followed me. "I hope our life will be clearer once the prophecy is fulfilled."

"To hell with the prophecy!" I growled, turning back from the porch.

"Mama, what's hell?" I heard Crystal call from inside the cabin, then William's father, Atram, hushed them and offered another spoonful of pudding.

I threw my hands up, looking to William for support.

"Let's eat first, talk later," Mira suggested.

William continued to watch me, then Eric, and me again. His cheek twitched. I thought I saw him turn to a vampire for a moment, and I rubbed my eyes. I waited for an opportunity to sweep Eric away. If I tried to talk to him in my mind, William would notice. Guilt swept through me as I realized I was going to share private information for the first time with someone other than William, but I had to know I hadn't imagined what I'd heard—in my head, and from the kids.

We sat at a dinner table set for ten. The aroma of tomato sauce and parmesan cheese wafted through the cabin, but nothing tasted right. A bitter film covered my tongue, and no matter how many sips of juice I took, it wouldn't wash away. The idea that Xela could get inside my mind bothered me. My need to figure out why grew stronger. I looked at the ruby ring still on my finger; I didn't want to take it off. The stone was my only affirmation of who I was. The events from four years ago haunted me at night, but today, for the first time in four years, my enemies haunted my mind during the day.

I'd kept my guard up while raising the twins. It had proven challenging, especially since everyone around me seemed cooler and more likable than a mother who made new rules to protect her kids. But I loved them more than anything. I'd die for them.

"I love you, Mama." Crystal kissed my cheek, as if she understood what I'd been feeling. She touched my hand, soothing my angst.

Ayer jumped down from his seat beside his sister and came to my other side for a squeeze. He pressed his cheek against my bare arm. "We'll love you no matter who you awe," he added.

"I love you too, but I'm a half-breed vampire. You know that, right?"

They nodded and looked into each other's eyes as if they knew some mystery I didn't. My twins had a way of knowing the future before it happened, but the way they shared it through ambiguous words mystified me, reminding me of aged warlocks.

"You will fix everything." Crystal smiled.

"What's everything?" I asked.

"Soon," she whispered, then hopped off her chair and trotted over to the rock wall near their bedroom William had built them for their first birthday. The twins began climbing, tilting their heads back toward the vaulted ceiling with its exposed beams.

I moved my spaghetti around the plate.

"You're not eating." William noted. The concern from his face transferred into his voice in a low tone.

I turned to my left, whispering to my husband, "I think time is up."

"For what?" He narrowed his brows.

My whisper caught my father's attention at the end of the table, but he didn't stir. He kept his gaze locked with Atram's at the other end of the table. I had everyone's attention, but I guessed no one wanted to step on my toes today.

"It's been too quiet. Things aren't right. I can feel it in my bones." I joined my hands to crack my fingers.

"Has anything odd happened today?" Eric asked from across the table. One of Mira's hands was on his lap, under the tablecloth, the way it has always been when they sat side by side.

My family's answers came one after another: "No," "Nope," "All okay."

"Are you kidding me?" I rose abruptly and walked over to put some dishes in the kitchen sink.

"What?" they asked in unison.

"Something is off. The kids are gaining greater and stronger powers and . . ."

"What?" William asked.

I looked up at the kids, both near the ceiling at the top of the wall now.

"Sarah's right." Eric's hush drafted chills up my spine.

"You know something?" Mira turned toward him.

He shook a warning with his head. "He's on the move," Eric said before wiping his mouth with a napkin. "The souls are scattering, looking for a place to hide."

We avoided using Aseret's name in front of the children and wanted to ensure he had no connection to them, or as little as we could control.

"The mark on the children is beginning to imprint. You can't see it yet, but their wrists heat up more than the norm. They will be imprinted soon, just like we have." He held out his wrist, where the water mark glowed at his will.

"Please tell me they'll be marked with the water mark." I shut my eyes.

"Nothing is ever guaranteed Sarah," he whispered.

"Are you saying it could be the sphere? My children could be connected to the underworld?" I felt my brows rise.

"Don't jump to any conclusions, Sarah. All I know is that once the children get their mark, they'll be able to bind Aseret," he said calmly. "When you come back from the prison tomorrow, it will be time to test the children's strength."

"They're three!"

"They're more than three, Sarah," he said solemnly.

I stared at him a moment. "What does that mean?"

"We will see tomorrow. Those are my instructions. Now, I think you and I need to talk." He raised his brows.

He knows!

I do, I heard him say in my head. At times like these, when the children stared from me to William with their round eyes, I was thankful I could still communicate with Eric telepathically. It was the only way I knew how to protect their innocence. It didn't matter how many times my father and William's parents tried to distract them, my three-year-olds were brighter than many adults. And William could read my face as well as I could read his, so anything I shared with Eric through my mind, he'd know.

"Let's go to the pond," Eric said.

"I'll be back soon." I kissed William on his cheek, then jumped up the climbing wall to hug Crystal and Ayer.

William followed me. "Don't shut me out," he whispered, holding onto the beam with one hand to hover just above me.

I vaulted to the floor and began clearing the table. "I won't. I love you."

"I love you too."

"Leave these." Willow took the dishes out of my hands. "Go."

Eric had already left.

"Thank you, Willow."

"He loves you and only you," she whispered as if to clear any possible doubts.

I smiled. "I know, Mom. I know."

* * *

When I arrived at the emerald pond, Eric sat on the bench at the entrance, his elbows resting on his knees. The crickets chimed their concert, light bugs dancing in the air in time with the chirping. Moisture from the fluorescent pond hung in the air. It had been a while since I enjoyed a swim with William in water where our bodies became invisible, one of the few perks of being a half-breed vampire.

"Any more news about the bodies?" I asked.

Eric shook his head. He'd been working with Mira on reuniting the lost souls from the hereafter, and I knew I'd be the first one to know when my mother's and aunt's bodies were found.

"I think Xela's back," I blurted without giving him a chance to reply. "I can hear her in my head. She's taunting me."

His brows rose. "Are you sure?"

I shook my head sideways and sat beside him on the carved out tree trunk. "I don't know what to believe. Is it even possible? When I saw her in the cave, even though she was tied up, I felt her freedom more than mine. I don't know how Eric. I know she's contained, but it doesn't feel like it to me." My hands trembled and I heard vibrations in my voice.

Eric placed his hand on mine. "If what you're saying is true, then Xela is scheming again, and I wouldn't be surprised if Aseret was behind it. I thought there was something odd about her when we switched your souls. I have a feeling her soul is able to leave her body to roam the ghost realm, perhaps do Aseret's bidding in that form. Your mother isn't answering me, either," he continued. "I think she's gathering other souls to fight against Aseret."

Now my eyebrows went up. "My mother?"

"And your aunt."

"They can't." I threw my hands forward and stood. "It's too dangerous. He'll steal their energy."

"I don't think we have much say in this. I've been assigned to clean up Aseret's chaos, but I can't do it if the spirits don't answer."

The leaves ruffled. Eric's head darted toward the bushes at the same time as mine did.

"It's not your mess, Eric." Mira stepped through the trees, her body a dark silhouette against the black backdrop of the forest. "I'm the one who opened the hereafter. It's my fault your mother's soul lingers and cannot move on," she said me. "She's fighting to keep her essence because of me."

"I don't understand." I shook my head. "Why would you do that?"

"It's not your fault, sugar. A lot happened that day." He took Mira's hand, pulling her to sit onto his lap.

"I shouldn't have pushed Aseret out of the way." Her eyes glossed over.

"You saved your brother." He whispered.

"When?" I asked.

"When we bound Aseret to the underworld."

"Good job," I whispered. "Sorry; I didn't mean it."

Eric shook his head. "You're right. We failed. Aseret found a way to free himself and even Castall, the most powerful warlock of all, couldn't get rid of him last time. Unfortunately, the magic that holds him to the underworld now is temporary."

"He's been rebuilding an army. He knows the prophecy threatens him. I'm sure he fears your children," Mira added.

"I know they're part of the prophecy, but I just can't see it." I shrugged. *They're three,* I wanted to add but didn't.

"You don't have to see it. The keepers are ensuring that the children's powers are kept as invisible as possible, to protect them."

I stood up to pace the narrow path. "The twins seem to grasp it more than I do."

"They understand it better than any of us. Now, what are we going to do about Xela?" Eric asked. "You're sure you heard her in your mind?"

"Yes." I felt a little weird sharing my fears with Eric and Mira before I'd told William, whom I trusted more than anyone else, but I didn't want to worry him for nothing, and I wanted to figure this out before alarming him.

"She's up to something. Xander had better do his job, and not give in." Eric gave Mira a meaningful look, one I'd seen before: to keep Xela in the cave and nowhere near me.

"I still don't know why he's keeping her." I grunted.

"Xander and Xela had met before. When he's ready, he'll tell you all about it. I'm sure," Mira soothed, using the voice that had the power to mesmerize animals on me. She took a deep breath in before continuing. "Xander asked us not to involve you. He feels bad that she almost killed you. He's been hurt in the past, very hurt, and he wouldn't want you to be her victim again."

"Xela hurt him?"

Eric and Mira remained silent, but they didn't have to answer. I read their faces, and more anger boiled in my veins toward the witch. Not only has she tried to kill me, she was the source of my best-friend's internal turmoil.

"Fine. I'll wait, but he better not let her loose."

"He won't. In the meantime, I'll chat with the souls," Eric said. "You let me know if the witch threatens you again. We'll talk to Xander, have him make sure her soul's not escaping."

Better you than me. I don't want to be anywhere near him and that cave.

Ah, so he tried to kiss you too?

I tried to kiss him. I crossed my arms.

Interesting. Eric stretched, then pulled his shirt off. "Anyone in the mood for a swim?"

Mira bit her lip. Eric's torso, scarred from the battles he'd fought in his time, made him sexier than if his flesh were flawless. The white marks defined him like a map of accomplishments, a reminder to his opponents what they had to deal with, although I'd never seen Eric take off his shirt in a fight.

Eric's "anyone" meant Mira, and I wasn't in the mood to be a third wheel. For the first time since I'd known my best friend, she was happy and in love, living the life she was meant to with her soul mate, my watcher.

As I left, I heard a splash in the pond, and spray hit my back. I shivered.

On my way home, I tried to determine why Xander would keep the witch in that cave, which led to recollections of when I posessed her body. I'd never shaken off the pain of swapping our hosts four years ago. At that time, living without my body estranged me from others. Only Eric recognized me; everyone else fell for Xela's trick.

The loneliness I'd experienced while in Xela's figure still haunted me. William sensed it, I could tell. Everything he did for me took on the form of an apology. Or perhaps it only seemed that way. Maybe I wanted everyone to be sorry, but I wasn't brave enough to admit it.

My conciliatory nature since the children's birth had begun to bother me. I missed my rage, my quick thoughts and sharpened senses. The time when I'd denied my abilities seemed to be so long ago, and I began to forget why I'd ever reject my traits. Now, it seemed I was reverting to my old ways, wanting to be sensed by the underworld again. The idea brewed inside me. Was I inviting the underworld to haunt me? Did I want it to haunt me? The dark pleasure I'd felt when I'd almost kissed Xander roamed within me, and I liked it. The joy of quickened pulse when I didn't follow any rules spread through me like a toxin. I needed the frenzy of a black witch controlling me when I was near Xander, more than air. Could the need to seem perfect and good be abandoned? The idea intrigued me and tingled my senses.

Before I reached home, Xela's laughter thumped in my head. When I touched the doorknob, I heard, *"I'm ba-ack!"*

CHAPTER 3

The tour of the Huntsville prison ended in the execution room. I wanted to close my eyes as the vampire sank his teeth into the inmate's neck. The prisoner didn't twitch, and I wondered what her crime was. She seemed to enjoy the puncture, smiling with her eyes, face slack from blood loss. In her drugged state, her body swayed in the vampire's arms as if she were dancing. For all she knew, the handsome young male sucking on her neck had courted her. In truth, he was draining her. The toxins meant to calm and disorient her flowing through her veins would have no effect on the vampire; to him, they were a harmless by-product in the form of a bitter taste. And she wouldn't turn; her heart would stop before she had a chance to feed. She would be dead.

The inmate smiled as the rhythm of her pulse slowed. Her eyes mellowed, the lids closing. There was nothing romantic about the way the vampire sucked the human dry, unlike in movies. Finally, her heart gave its last beat, and the vampire dropped the woman onto the metal bed beside him, licking the blood from his lips. I pitied anyone on death row and leaned on my father for support.

"It's done." The warden pulled the curtain across the glass window, sheltering those of us in the viewing room from the satisfied vampire who probably dreams of human death.

The warden's pasty skin reminded me of a drag queen in makeup. Hunch-backed, he wobbled more than walked to my side. "Mrs. Mitchell," he cleared his throat to get rid of his usual grunt, "you're saying this potion you've developed will allow the vampires to feed on dead blood?"

"Technically the blood won't be dead, but yes, we don't need to kill the prisoners this way any longer."

"You want us to kill them the old-fashioned way?" He tilted his head up, looking at me from below.

"Yes. No. That's not what I meant. Whatever laws humans make for their kind, vampires will not have to be involved." I paused. "We'll survive on your donations."

The donations were not for me: I hunted animals to feed. But for the vampires who weren't vegan, the alternate arrangement would spare human life; I understood their need for blood. It was odd to speak of myself as not being one of the humans, the way I had always tried to be. But I wasn't a human; I was a half-breed vampire with a priority to raise twins and nurture human-vampire relations.

"Donations from us?" The warden's unibrow rose.

"Yes, and in return, the vampires agree to continue their services and protection against demons."

In the past four years, we've been able to introduce the human and vampire races to one another. My father and William's, Ekim and Atram, had worked hard with the governments to ensure a swift transition. William introduced them to the human authorities. With a little help from Mira and Xander's parents and their magic, persuading the public to see the world in a new light proved less difficult than we thought it would be. Vampires publicly protecting and saving human life from frequent demonic attacks helped with the inevitable changes.

"I understand." He cleared his throat again. "We'll set up a meeting to get the board's approval. I don't see a problem with this new way of doing things. Your operations in the first aid sector and security services are ranked the highest in all categories." The warden wobbled toward the exit. "I'll get my secretary to draft a new agreement and mail it to you. Where can you be reached again? I don't believe we have an address on file." He raised his brow.

The way the warden spoke seemed peculiar. His slurred speech reminded me of Aseret. For someone running a rigid prison, his tone was too calm, shadowed by sloppiness.

As if in a subconscious response to the hunched warden, my father straightened his back and spoke for the first time since entering the prison. "There's no need to mail. As agreed, Ms. Mitchell will come back in a week to sign everything and discuss the details of the deliveries."

"And where would you like us to deliver the blood?"

I grabbed the collar of his shirt and shoved him against the wall before he'd even blinked. His feet dangled above the floor. "Don't patronize me, warden! You know the arrangement has nothing to do with our location. Continue to ship them to our plant in Mexico," I grated through clenched teeth.

My father touched my arm, and I dropped the warden the floor. He pushed himself up against a chair, grunting.

My self-control was usually intact, but today, a ravaging force flowed through my veins, as if someone fiercer than me had entered my body to show this nitwit who he was dealing with. I enjoyed watching him squirm.

"Like I said, you'll discuss it next week," my father interjected, before I threw the warden against another wall. "The shipments can continue as always."

The secrecy of our location was necessary. No one could know about our rebuilt cabin in the Amazon. When people questioned where I lived, even unintentionally, I fumed. The warden's questions today seemed premeditated, and I didn't like it.

"Yes, of course. It was nice to finally meet you, Mrs. Mitchell." The warden almost pressed his hand against my lower back to rush me out, but I turned just in time. To my surprise, he'd regained his composure quickly after being attacked by a vampire. I studied him. He seemed the same as the first time I'd met him: too quick, too subtle.

"Pleasure." I shook his hand, forcing a businesslike smile.

The warden stepped back; a strange creature for a human, he acted as if nothing had happened. My aggression hadn't startled him enough. He controlled his emotions in an almost unnatural way. I hadn't met a human who wouldn't fear a vampire when they first met. Was this odd? Or was this a new way of life in a changing world I was no longer accustomed to?

When I opened the door of the viewing room, the curtain covering the execution area fluttered. A lifeless body rested on a bed with side extensions that made it vaguely resemble a crucifix. Its flesh was as pale as the metal it lay on. The vampire still licked bloody residue from his lips, looking at the limp body as if he wanted to tear it apart in search of more blood.

He'll need to be retrained. Biting into a victim and drinking from a bottle were not the same for vampires. Thousands of years of imprinted feedings had to be erased through hypnosis. Vampires had to learn to drink blood, not suck it, and most had.

Few were left like this one, to finish their jobs to execute humans on death row.

I walked alongside my father through a dimly lit hall. The lights above flickered on and off as we passed.

"The anger you're holding inside can destroy you," my father murmured, placing his hand on my shoulder.

I stopped before reaching for the door handle at the end of the hall. "Is it that obvious?"

"To me, not to others. I feel your pain. I understand why you'd lose faith in those closest to you. We failed you."

"She tricked us all, Dad. How could you have known?" I tried to hide the rage boiling inside me, never admitting aloud the hurt I still felt from my family's betrayal.

"Yet your heart tells you we should have known."

I looked to my father for guidance. "Am I wrong to feel that way?"

"No, but keeping it inside is. It allows evil to connect with you. You never accepted our apologies."

"I did, and I do." I hugged him.

"Actions speak louder than words."

I shut my eyes, pictured him smile, and tightened my embrace. "I promise to fix it." The father I had denied and hated most of my life was the closest person I had to reconnect me with my life. I wouldn't disappoint him.

"Good." He gripped my shoulders and held me away from him to look at my face. The sun beamed through the peephole of a window in the door, warming the side of my arm in a criscrossed pattern from the wires on the inside of the glass. "Because I never want to lose you again."

"Nor I, you."

Never say never! The thought running through my head wasn't my own, but I had a good idea who it belonged to.

My father opened the steel door of the prison, and I squinted reflexively at the high sun. We rushed through a fenced-in pathway toward the parking lot, stopping a few feet in when the ten-foot chain-link fence shook behind us as it locked, sounding like someone had dropped fistfuls of dimes on a glass floor. Chills ran down my spine.

The spring's aroma of fresh buds and blossoms disappeared.

"Can you smell that?" I whispered to my father.

His arms tensed. "What?"

We sniffed the air, crouching and scanning the naked fields, barren except for the mesh of fresh sprouts.

"Seekers?" Doubt crept into his question.

I couldn't detect the stink of dirty socks and rotten eggs, the common scent of the seekers, so I took another whiff. "No, demons." I wiggled my nose. Sulphur and electricity fused around my nostrils.

The air swirled in front of us, mixing dust with pebbles. My hair blew over my face, obstructing my sight. I picked the strands out of my mouth, then covered it with the neckline of my shirt. Goosebumps spread over my arms. The hairs on my arms stood up, not from fear, but from the electricity that encapsulated us.

Two demons stepped out of the vortex. Smug grins stretched across their faces. A hint of purple glossed over their eyes. In the past four years, their sense of fashion had not changed, but the hooded cloaks smelled fresh; the material had been sewn within the last two days. An embroidered sphere decorated the upper left chest of each, where a heart was supposed to be. Either Aseret had rewarded old followers with custom clothing, or they had been just recruited.

I cocked my head to the left and smirked. *New recruits.*

The taller one eyed the settling dust. His gaze darted up to a stork's nest perched atop a broken pole, and he watched the birds nestle over their eggs. Then, he looked to the tops of the trees swaying on the edge of a nearby forest.

A mover.

The shorter one, standing just under four feet, hadn't moved since stepping out of the vortex. *A freezer. Great combination!* I held back the rolling of my eyes.

"He said this was going to be difficult," the first one complained, his steps calculated as he closed in.

I bared my fangs and flexed my knees. So did my father.

"Who?" I clenched my jaw.

They looked at each other, though the freezer only moved his eyeballs in their sockets.

"You're not strong enough to defeat us. We've heard about your fight in the underworld. Had we been there, it would have all been over," the mover said.

"What's Aseret promising you?" I asked.

"What do you think? Power. Not like it will matter to you soon." He laughed.

"You're stupid to believe him." I laughed too, but they remained wary; keeping their focus on us, and only us, would be tricky.

"Where are the kids?" the second one asked.

I'd practiced deceiving demons and seekers every day. Today was just another test, and I hoped my heart would not give away my children's location. The speed of the blood flow through my body remained constant as I regulated the rhythm of my pulse. My focus held on the demons instead of the yellow Hummer with tinted windows parked among the other cars.

"After today, you won't even think about my children," I warned.

"You sure about that?" the freezer taunted, twirling his finger.

The gesture was familiar. I looked down at my feet. Blue light circled my Dockers and my father's shoes, holding our feet immobile. Ekim's eyes found mine.

The demons grinned.

"Ah, you've seen this magic before," the freezer said.

At this point, I knew William was watching the scene unfold, but he wouldn't come to help. He couldn't. Our priority was protecting the children.

"Where are they?" the demon asked again, his jaw clenching with impatience.

"You. Will. Never. See. Them," my father grunted.

"So you think. Once you're out of the way, we'll get them." The mover laughed. "Soon, your kind will be extinguished."

A car at the end of the parking lot shook as if it were affected by an unseen earthquake. The mover lifted his palm higher, and the car hovered above the asphalt, its metal vibrating and squeaking as the pressure built and pushed it upward. The demon swept his hand toward us, and the car zoomed through the air like a plane. I braced my glued feet, shoving my arms up to deflect the vehicle, but it stopped just short of hitting us.

"Kill them," the freezer ordered.

"I . . . I can't." The mover's gaze flew from the car to his hand. Frowning, he flexed his arms, but the car hung like a feather caught in an updraft. "I'll do it the old-fashioned way." The mover sped toward us but jolted to a stop halfway, as if he'd hit a low barrier. His upper body continued forward, his nose almost touching the asphalt before he sprang back upright. Blue light shone under his feet.

I smirked, and my father laughed. We knew the culprits helping us.

"But you can't . . ." The freezer's face sagged.

The air spun behind the demons, fluttering the backs of their cloaks. The entrance to the vortex enlarged until the force sucked the demons in. The car crashed to the ground beside my father, and the blue light disappeared from around our feet. I glanced at the smashed Miata as we hurried across the lot; its owner would not be happy.

William waited with the twins in our rented yellow Hummer. The paint shone bright against a lowering sky; the clouds ready to break and release the pressure. He pointed to the twins as I jumped in the back between the two booster seats. "They passed out as soon as the vortex closed."

The twins didn't need the seats, but knowing they were buckled properly soothed my worries and prevented possible confrontations with law enforcement. Even with our abilities, I made every effort to make them part of a normal human world, or as normal as we could allow.

"They do look drained." I brushed my hand over the twins' pudgy cheeks. They hadn't lost their baby fat. Now that they rested, their rosy complexions paled. "I'll have to thank Eric for showing them those powers."

William laughed. "Say it."

This time, I did roll my eyes.

"Come on. You know what I want to hear," William teased.

"I was wrong. There." I crossed my arms.

"You're cute when you know your mistakes."

Yes, I experienced a surge of apprehension when Eric and the siblings first told me they'd be training the kids as early as six months old. I wanted them to remain kids, to enjoy their childhood. But when a seeker tried to kidnap the twins on their first birthday while we were in Pinedale, I realized training them was a necessity. They had to know how to protect themselves. And they did a great job helping us, as well.

The first raindrops hit the windshield and I buckled my seatbelt.

"I don't like the warden," my father said suddenly, staring at the open logbook in his lap. He flipped its pages in haste, crossing out tallies with a red pen.

"You don't have to, but it's better this way." William leaned back to kiss me. The sweetness of his lips flowed through me like honey, soothing aches and regrets from the past.

"There's just something odd about the way he looks at you, Sarah," my father continued. "Like you're the next in line to go into that room."

I chuckled. "The vampire wouldn't be able to drain me."

"Don't joke about things like that." He lifted his gaze from the logbook. "I must say, you handled yourself well in there."

"What happened?" William asked.

"I shoved the warden."

William's eyebrow rose. "Good for you."

In truth, I didn't recognize my newfound rage, but I liked it and wanted it to be me. It had been a long time since I'd had a good fight with the seekers. Hostility and the intensity of a violent force revived me. When Xela stole my body, she also took the rage of a vampire, leaving only resentment toward my friends and family, though I never let them sense it. Perhaps they knew and tiptoed around my every wish, but that wasn't what I wanted. My only wish was to be me, the me I didn't think I'd ever regained, and that included ferocity.

Today, the demons reminded me of our battle against Aseret, when I discovered my strength four years ago. *Four years.* I sighed. Our only fight since then had been against one seeker and a few demons, all of whom were weakened and destroyed before I had a chance to sweat.

I didn't mind the quiet; it allowed us to concentrate on raising the twins. But the mover and freezer we'd encountered today showed magic I'd forgotten; it reminded me of the strength I missed.

Blood rushed through my veins as my gut warned me of a stirring in the underworld. I could smell it in the air, almost taste it on the tip of my tongue. Anxiety prickled up goosebumps along my arms, and I tightened the grip on my seatbelt to control the jitters.

It passed.

"You're sure the demons didn't see them?" My fingers twined into the auburn curls of each twin.

"Yes, they were discreet with their powers." William buckled his seatbelt.

"Good. Smart little cookies. We've been training them beyond what a three-year-old should be exposed to."

"Except they're not your typical three-year-olds." He turned the key in the ignition.

Silence.

William tried again.

"What's the matter?" I asked.

"Don't know."

"Did you have a problem before?" my father asked.

"No, this is an almost new vehicle. And the tank was filled when I took it."

The Hummer was William's favorite car. He owned one in the jungle and washed and polished it every day before tucking it under a tarp on one side of the cabin.

Ayer opened his eyes. "Let me try, Papa." He wiggled in his seat and twirled his finger. A red stream of light flowed from his fingertip to the ignition. The car purred to life.

I looked at William; his face reflected my questions. The twins' abilities had grown beyond what we understood. Like sponges, they absorbed the skills we taught them. Eric and the siblings took care of the demon training; our parents showed them how to hunt; we tried to instill whatever human aspects we could. Each new skill had to be demonstrated or explained before they tried it; that was the only way they could recognize it and connect it to their training. But this one was new. And, for the second day in a row, the stream was red. Not blue. Red; underworld's magic.

"Who showed you how to do this?" I asked.

Ayer shrugged.

"Was it Auntie Mira?"

He shook his head.

"Eric?"

"No. He told me not to say."

I twisted to face him. "Who, baby?" I asked, struggling to keep the urgency from my voice. "Who told you not to say?"

Crystal opened her eyes. "Lord Aseret, Mama. It was Lord Aseret."

CHAPTER 4

Lord Aseret.

Crystal's words still rang in my ears. The hours that passed
as we flew back home felt like days. The twins now slept in their
bedroom, guarded by Ekim and Atram, who wouldn't leave their
bedside. William, the siblings, Eric, and I sat in the sun room.
Mira sipped her coffee, staring at the top of Eric's head. He
leaned forward, elbows resting on his knees as he massaged his
scalp with his fingers. The evil-bender hadn't said anything in
over half an hour. Eric had tested the children's skills at the
emerald lake but wouldn't talk about it. We'd been debating how
to approach the children and how to protect them. Now the sun
had set, and our discussion had stalled. How in the world did

Aseret get to our children, and when? They'd never been left alone, and our cabin in the Amazon had been sealed off from the world by the orchids. No one knew about it. No one.

William poured me orange juice. Drops of condensation travelled toward the jug's rim as it filled my glass.

"Thank you."

He kissed the top of my head.

"The children are ready." Eric broke his silence as if woken by an alarm clock.

"They're three. They're not ready," I growled.

"Their mark can appear at any moment. The keepers had said the prophecy will be active as soon as the imprint is there."

"How do they know about Aseret?" I asked, looking from Xander to Mira, then Eric.

"He could be speaking to them through a vortex," Eric suggested. "The children seem to know more than they're willing to share. I can't make them tell me what they're hiding."

"It's not a vortex. You would have felt one." Xander got up and paced the room.

"What are you thinking?" Mira asked.

"I don't know, but the only time they'd be most vulnerable would be while sleeping." He focused on their room.

"You think he can get to them in their sleep?" Mira stood and moved to her brother's side.

"It's possible. How else?"

"Wait." Willow's hushed voice crossed the room before she rushed out of the lab. Treading across the marble floor she pushed her geeky glasses to the top of her head, lab coat floating behind her. "They mentioned a man in their dreams so casually, I thought nothing of it."

"When was this?" William asked.

"Two nights ago."

I gripped my mother-in-law's shoulders. "Willow, tell me exactly what they said." Then, realizing what I was doing, I released her. "I'm sorry. I didn't mean to be so harsh."

Willow rubbed her arm, and guilt for loss of control swept through me. She sat down alongside William. "It's fine, Sarah. We all love them. They said the warlock is not their concern. I didn't think anything of the conversation. They made me feel it wasn't important at the time." She covered her mouth.

It wasn't unusual for the children to trick one of us by controlling our emotions, but it was always done in a playful way. Up until now, they hadn't used their ability with purpose, or perhaps we just didn't know about it.

"But why would Aseret not be their concern?" I asked.

"Maybe they weren't talking about Aseret," Eric murmured under his nose.

"Then how do they know his name?" William said, taking his mother's hand in an effort to ease her worry.

Mira placed her cup on the table, then straightened and looked around. "Why don't you guys ask them?"

Everyone stared at her as if she'd fallen off the moon, but perhaps she was right. Why speculate? If the twins already knew about Aseret, why not ask them? I chewed my thumb as the thought brewed in my mind. With my eyes shut, I listened to their systematic breathing contemplating whether I should wake them up and keep them without sleep for as long as I could.

"He's getting to them." Willow's face and voice were tight. After she had been held captive in the dungeons, developing a serum to hide the children became her obsession.

"And I couldn't foresee it." I regretted my inability to predict the future. My and William's demonic energy had transferred to the children in the form of other abilities.

"Sarah, Mom, we won't let him near them. And I think they're better prepared than we expected anyway." William put his arm around his mother's shoulders. I loved his tenderness toward her and leaned in closer on his free side, sandwiching him between us.

"Prepared for what?" I asked.

"To bind Aseret." Eric stood and took over Xander's pacing from one end of the glass wall to the other. Xander took his spot. Beyond the window, the forest blackened, impermeable, except for the glow of a few light bugs. Looking at the flickering points outside, I shivered.

"I thought he was bound," I asked.

"Yes, to the underworld, but that does not prevent him from recruiting minions," Xander explained.

"The kids are meant to bind Aseret to the hereafter." Mira took Eric's spot on the ottoman. It seemed like the trio of siblings and evil bender were playing musical chairs, switching the routine between them.

"And you didn't tell me before because . . ." I coaxed.

"Because you don't need to concern yourself with the problems of the underworld. We do." Mira sat down at my side. "What they need from you is to be a mother they love more than life."

"Tell me about the hereafter," I insisted, zipping up my vest. "I want to understand."

"It's where your mother's soul is." Eric placed his hand on my shoulder as he sat on my other side, squishing in between me and William.

"If we bind Aseret too early to the hereafter, the lost souls will feel his wrath. We've been rushing to find all the bodies to reunite them with their souls for their last breath before Aseret is sent there," Mira added, pushing up her sleeves.

"The children will open a doorway for Aseret. He will be locked within it, unable to harm the souls," Eric said.

"How exactly do you bind a corporeal demon like Aseret to the hereafter?" I began to chew on my thumb.

"He'll have to be killed," Eric explained, turning my attention toward him, "but his death is not enough. We cannot let him die until the hereafter is in order."

"But he'll be locked up anyway," I said, trying to follow, tapping my fingers on my knee.

"It's a precaution. We cannot take the chance he's not locked up and only bound." Mira took another sip of her coffee.

"Otherwise he'll torment the hereafter," William added.

Mira nodded. "He'd use the energy of the remaining spirits to gain strength and possibly reincarnate."

"Of course it couldn't be simple, could it?" I chewed my thumb again. William reached over Eric and pulled my hand away from my mouth. The reddening blotch on my finger would remain for few seconds.

"It's not so easy to get rid of him. Killing him too early may not be the best strategy," Eric said.

"Great! And I suppose Aseret knows what the children are meant to do?"

They didn't have to answer. I could read the truth on their faces. The gut feeling I'd had earlier returned. The underworld stirred; the warlock was trying to get to my children. "How long have you known about this?"

"This morning. The keepers told me this morning," Eric whispered.

I pushed the empty ottoman away with my foot. It squeaked on the marble floor before hitting the glass wall of the lab.

Sarah, don't do anything stupid, Eric warned in my mind.

"I'm going to the tree house." I gripped the side of the coffee table so hard I left indents in its edge.

William sighed, probably because he'd have to replace the trim again.

"We'd better leave as well," Eric said. "Xander, we could use your help with the souls tonight."

Xander made his do-I-have-to face but didn't complain.

"Come on, sugar, maybe we can find more bodies." Eric slid his arm around Mira's waist.

"If you can keep your hands off each other," Xander mumbled under his breath. Their constant touching and kissing when they thought no one was watching didn't bother me and Xander had stopped asking them to get a room six months ago. I had assumed their open affection no longer bothered him, but I guess I was wrong.

My three watchers disappeared in a void of twirling light that closed with a purple lavender mist.

"I have work to do." Willow went back to the lab, murmuring to herself about the serums.

Atram and Ekim, my father, resumed their app development on their iPads by the twin's bedroom door.

William's gaze skidded toward the two vampires' impending work before he turned to me. "I'm coming with you." He scooted closer to my side and rubbed the dent in the table with his fingers.

"No, please stay with the kids," I said. "I won't be long."

He wrapped his arms around me. "You're not going to the tree house, are you?" His brows high, he leaned back to look at my face. I missed his loving eyes, longing for his lips to bless mine the way they used to, when we met.

"Am I that obvious?"

"I know you." He kissed my forehead. "I know who you are, better than Eric does."

William must have read Eric's face. My husband confirmed what I'd doubted inside: who I was. Did he know my true feelings of regret? Of course he knew; he was my other half. I couldn't hide much from him.

"Just promise me you'll be careful," he said as we stepped out onto the porch. The air was still, the way it always was before a storm. But I knew the weather over the clearing was supposed to remain pleasant for a while, and this calmness felt out of place. Perhaps wearing jeans wasn't the best choice tonight.

"I promise." I leaned my head on his chest. "You're the only one who keeps me grounded."

"You don't let me keep you grounded enough." His heart vibrated worry against my cheek.

"You do." I wrapped my arms around him.

"I miss you." He tightened our embrace.

"What do you miss?" I tilted my face up to see his.

"The you I never got back." William kissed the tip of my nose.

I pulled away. "What do you mean?"

William's face came closer to my ear until his breath warmed me. "Sarah, it's time you admit you're not you. Help me get you back."

My head tilted to the side, and I stared at him a moment. Today was the first time William mentioned I wasn't myself. I didn't think he noticed. Elatation sped up my pulse. I knew I couldn't bear to continue doubting who I was, and William seemed to agree. Accepting my life as a half-breed vampire couldn't happen unless *I* controlled all of my abilities, senses and emotions—not a witch who tried to steal my body.

"What if I don't know how to get me back?"

"Talking about it would be a start." Williams hands glided along my bare arms until he twined his fingers with mine. He let go of my hands, cocooning me in his tight embrace. "I'm always here for you, my love."

"Okay." I exhaled. "We'll talk as soon as I come back. Maybe I'll have some answers."

"And I'll have you back the way we were always meant to be."

The squeeze of William's fingers as his hands slid down my body to my hips awoke urges inside me.

"And which way is that?" I bit my lower lip.

"Me, you," he kissed my nose, then my cheeks, "no clothes."

"Sh, you'll wake them up." I giggled. "I . . . I need to—"

"See Xela again?"

I nodded.

"Everything all right?" He pushed his finger under my chin to lift it.

"No, it's not." I shook my head. "Let me figure this out, then I'll explain. I promise."

"I'll be waiting." He pressed his body to mine again. I longed for his touch. His mouth covered my lips, fingers weaved through my hair, and I had no choice but to respond. Kissing William was as euphoric as eating chocolate mousse topped with whipped cream and raspberries. Each kiss tasted like a new brand of cocoa. I was addicted to chocolate, my favorite delicacy—next to pancakes, of course. William's kisses remained vibrant and intoxicating.

I remembered to breathe when we pulled apart, and I ran my hands down his arms and wove my fingers back into his, recalling how my body responded at their touch. The electricity that flowed between us no longer hurt, but it hadn't disappeared.

"Stay," he whispered, teasing me with his sweet breath.

"Soon." I hushed him with a deeper kiss, composed my swaying body, and rushed out before I changed my mind.

William's low whimper sounded behind me and almost broke my resolve.

With restored hope, I jogged to the edge of the clearing, then ran at my fastest speed. I wouldn't have much time, perhaps five minutes, with the witch before Xander sensed me. The timing of Xela's voice in my head and the children's mention of the warlock wasn't a coincidence. This realization triggered the rage I'd missed earlier.

Was the witch responsible for Aseret's presence in my children's lives? Did she help him get to them? Was she warning us, or threatening us?

Distracted by my thoughts, I stopped in my tracks and closed my eyes to remember the way, feeling the trail of my warm breath on my face. Although I'd peeked on the trip home with Xander, nothing looked the same at night. Hearing the stream not far from where I stood, I decided to rely on my instinct and follow the water along the canyon.

The walls of rock rose sky high, extending beyond the canopy, while white water rushed below, rumbling and spitting foam like cotton balls made for a giant as it forced its way through the chasm. I moved upstream until the river narrowed and divided, the water calming to a gentler flow. *Which way?*

Above, on the edge of the cliff, moisture shimmered in a white glow in the moonlight. I inhaled the clinging water, remembering a jump over the brink that made my insides weightless; the height seemed to match Xander's leap. With the moon as my guide, I turned toward the cliff where the stream narrowed, knelt, and tasted the water. *That's it!* The water had left an imprint on my tongue, as all liquids did, its mark in every drop flowing downstream. *This way.*

I sped forward until I heard a laugh, then screaming, arguing, and another laugh. *Xela! And . . . who?* My run turned into a sprint. Branches slashed at my arms, but my only concern remained with the intensified bellowing. Xela's cackling led me to the front of the cave.

Around me, sudden silence lurked as if it had a mission of its own. The bats overhead broke through the quiet with high-pitched hunting cries.

I stared at the rock as if it were the entrance to a secret Egyptian tomb. I braced my feet and pushed the rock aside before descending the ten steps to the lower cavern.

The wooden door at the bottom opened by itself.

She knows I'm here. I stepped forward.

Xander's scent still lingered in the cave from this morning, reminding me of our encounter yesterday and raising goosebumps on my skin.

Xela sat in the chair, her silence ominous. I ignored her, crossing to lift a log from beside the hearth and throw it into the fire pit, fueling its flames. Then I turned to stare at the witch.

She lifted her eyes, then her head toward me. The witch held my gaze, her eyes closing for a moment before scanning my body from the bottom up.

"She's here." Xela's voice lacked the sarcasm so familiar to me. Her tone was eerily calm, even tired.

I looked around to see if she spoke to someone else, but her gaze pierced mine.

"What does Aseret want with the children?" I added bravado to my voice without preamble.

"To lure them, then kill them." Each word out of Xela's mouth seemed to exhaust her.

"Why?" I took a step closer, straining to hear her frail voice.

"They're the only ones who have the strength to bind him forever. They're the reason he wanted the prophecy stopped, though it wasn't." She smiled.

"Didn't you want it stopped?"

"Not me. Miranda did."

Who? "Are you playing with me, witch?" I growled, striding over to stand in front of her and leaning forward until I was only inches from her face. My fingers found her throat, ready to tighten their grip. The rage I'd missed had returned, as if summoned into my body.

"No. I'm telling you the truth." She blinked lazily, her eyelids closing once every few seconds. Xela seemed odd today— too composed and straining to speak. Her eyes struggled to stay open.

"You're a lying, deceiving witch. You're helping Aseret to get to my children." I squeezed my fingers into her neck. "I . . ." The tip of my nose almost touched hers. " . . . want you dead." A rush of power flew through my arms when I threatened her, and I remembered who I was: a fierce vampire and devoted human mother.

She tried to writhe out of my grip, but soon stopped struggling. "I'm the only one who can help you defeat Aseret," she said, her voice nearly a squeak through a tight throat.

I dropped my hands to my sides. "And you think I could ever trust you? You stole my body! You wanted to destroy me and my family."

"It wasn't me, Sarah."

I studied her eyes and saw that her hatred had disappeared.

"I've been hearing you in my head," I said. "You're taunting me."

"Not me. Miranda."

"Who is Miranda?"

"She's here, but we've been able to silence her."

"You're conniving again." I swooshed around but saw no one else in the cave.

"I cannot keep this body for long. I'm too weak. She's powerful. Help me."

"You will not trick me again." The bravado disappeared from my voice as shivers climbed up my spine.

A cool breeze swept across my body, pushing me back. For a moment, it felt as if all the air I had in my lungs had been sucked out. When I inhaled again, filling my lungs to their full depth, a ghostly figure stepped in front of me, as if it were stepping out of me. My mother. I hadn't seen her ghost in four years, since the time she guided me to reclaim my body from Xela.

"Mom?" The lump in my throat formed instantly.

"I don't have much time, sweetheart. There's a witch chasing me. Her name is Miranda. She's threatening that Aseret will kidnap the children."

"He won't get his hands on them," I growled.

"You cannot protect them without her." She placed her translucent hand on Xela's shoulder. "He's grown too strong for the keepers."

"How do you know?" I tried to touch my mom but failed. Her ghost vibrated.

"Because the real Xela knows his secret. You have to trust her."

"She's lying, Mom. She's a black witch. And what is she doing among you?" I pointed to teh witch.

"Not the Xela you know, darling, not this one."

"Help." Xela's voice had weakened even more.

My mother's ghost swirled, disappearing like vapor being absorbed into the witch.

Xela's frail body stiffened. "Your mother and aunt are helping to keep Miranda's spirit away," she whispered. "They cannot do it much longer. She's been attached to this body for decades. And she's powerful—very powerful." She shivered as she uttered the warning.

"You're saying I never had Xela's soul—your soul—in me?"

"No, it was Miranda. Her magic is strong. She changed my body as well." Xela's voice was different from the one I'd heard in my head—not crackly, but genuine, with true emotion flowing through it.

"How do you know?" I asked.

"I've known his secrets for decades. My magic is one of the few that can help you." She took a slow breath; her energy seemed to drain with each exhalation. "I lived in a lair similar to this one until events over twenty years ago cast my soul adrift."

"Your soul?" I repeated, trying to concentrate.

"Aseret entrusted Miranda to punish me for not turning Xander to serve the underworld."

Xela's cheeks flushed.

I covered my mouth to hide a smile. Life radiated from Xela's body when she mentioned my best friend's name. "You're his soul mate."

The passion of true soul mates reminded me of William. The lust I'd felt for Xander yesterday was Xela's. I sensed the same desire in her now and couldn't mistake it for anything else. Xela had tried to get to Xander through me, connecting her lost soul with my body.

My limbs tingled. "He's keeping you here because he thinks he can change you back."

She nodded.

"Can he?" Curiosity pulled me closer to the witch.

"I don't know. He knows I'm lost in this body. He doesn't know about Miranda but suspects it's someone else. I can see him here, trying to get through, but I cannot speak. She won't let me." The contours of Xela's face tensed, then softened. She swiveled her shoulders forward, then back, as if she were getting used to possessing her own body again.

"Then how come I can hear you?" I crouched in front of her, keeping our gazes leveled.

"It takes much of our essence to keep Miranda astray. We cannot do it again. Today is the only day for the switch."

The wind howled outside before entering the cave. My hair fluttered around my face when the breeze hit my back.

"What switch?" I stood and stepped back until my shoulders hit the wall of the cave.

Suddenly, I smelled pancakes in the air and could almost taste the warm syrup flowing off their edges. Only one person made my favorite food smell mouthwatering.

Two ghostly figures now stood beside Xela's body, partially embedded in her silhouette as if emerging from her arms. My mother was back, along with my Aunt Helen.

I gave my head a sharp shake to make sure I wasn't dreaming, then focused on my spine, where the sensation of chills would normally arise, but there were none.

"We're helping her, but we cannot for long," my aunt said.

"You're helping Xela," I repeated.

"You must too, darling," my mother whispered.

"If you don't trust me, trust them." Xela pointed to a corner and twirled her finger.

I turned toward the brush. The black roses unnaturally blooming in the cave turned crimson in the middle and out walked Crystal and Ayer.

"How in the world . . ."

"Hi, Mama," Crystal said, and my children smiled.

I ran to them and squeezed each until they wiggled out of my embrace. "What are you doing here?" I asked before facing Xela again. "How dare you involve them!" I growled and felt my fangs against my bottom lip.

"But, Sarah, they are involved."

"Mama, you can trust her," Ayer said.

How could I? Yet I trusted my children. They knew their destiny better than me. *But they're only three.* "Why are you here?" I looked into their round eyes that shined like polished buttons.

"Don't worry, Mama, you will be back." Crystal cupped my cheek with her palm. Her warmth soothed my anxiety. It wasn't unusual for her to speak in riddles we couldn't understand, and I understood this gesture perfectly. She wanted to ease my worries and knew her touch would do it.

"We'll watch over you. Don't be afraid. Ever," Ayer said.

And my son would help with the fear. "I'm only afraid for you." I smiled.

"Mama, you'll be stwonger as a spiwit when we need your help. We can draw on youw full essence. Xela needs your body to help us too, and you'll be able to work together," Crystal added. Although she spoke through a lisp, my daughter sounded like an adult.

"We will?" I widened my eyes.

The children perked up. "Yes, you can help us. Learn what it's like to be a ghost."

Somehow, what my children said didn't seem daunting. They made it feel like a natural step. "All right. If you say so," I agreed.

"Yay!" They jumped up and down.

Now the "switch" made sense. My children needed me to give my body to Xela and let my soul flow into hers. I had to do it for my children. They understood our destinies better than I did, and I had to trust them. My stomach grumbled as the nausea of my memories in a witch's body returned. I pressed my hand just below my ribcage. "I can't do this," I whispered.

"You have to." My mother nodded her encouragement.

"Will I have my body back?"

"We cannot promise," my mother's sober tone echoed throughout the lair. "Only if we can find Miranda's and reunite her soul to die with her own body. The risk is great for you. If we cannot find the witch's body, you will be stuck in a ghost's form, alongside her soul."

"She doesn't scare me. Not anymore. And I think I can do it. I can help. For the children."

"It won't be pleasant, Sarah," my aunt warned.

"They'll know I'm gone. William will know." But I wondered if he would. After all, he hadn't the last time.

"No one will know if we trick them. Anything can alert Aseret to strike earlier. Take this." My aunt handed me a ruby ring. I could almost feel her fingers brushing mine. "It's a fake. It doesn't have powers. You'll know what to do with it."

The ruby shone in my palm. It looked identical to the one I wore. I held it up, examined it closely, and couldn't tell the difference.

"Crystal, honey, you keep this hidden." I removed my real ruby from my finger. "It will be our secret, okay?"

"Yes, Mama." She tucked the ring into the pocket of her slacks.

"Do you know what I'm about to do?"

The kids nodded, both saying, "We know, Mama."

"I love you so much." I hugged them hard, as if I were saying goodbye, and dared not think I would never hug them again. *This is temporary. Everything will be all right.*

As I pressed their deceivingly frail bodies to mine, I snuggled my nose between them and tried to memorize their smell. The mix of my vanilla and aloe tinged with William's woody musk blended with their honey-lemon scent. I wondered when I would feel their touch again. Then I kissed each one over and over, only hoping it wouldn't be long before I saw their pudgy pink cheeks again.

I straightened, wiping my eyes with my sleeve. "Send the kids back first."

They squeezed my legs. "We love you, Mama."

My spine froze with the thought that this might be the last time I saw them. I shook it off. "Go home before Daddy finds you gone. I don't even want to know how you snuck out."

They nodded, backing up until they stood within the crimson-hearted roses. Then they were gone, and the red shade in the blossoms faded to black again.

I squared my shoulders and, with my chin held high, said, "Let's do it."

CHAPTER 5

Expecting the switch didn't mask the pain. Unlike the first time, when Xela—or Miranda—stole my body, I didn't sleep. My soul detached from my limbs as if torn from the flesh, and for a moment, I wished I'd been asleep this time too. The air in the cave wrapped around the white light I became and flowed through me, stinging as if it were salt poured on a fresh wound.

From above, I looked at the empty corpse lying on the dirt floor at Xela's feet. My dead body. Motionless, empty, without a glow, skin almost gray. Even the colors of the orchid tattooed on my left wrist seemed bleached.

It takes time to get used to, my mother's voice soothed in my head.

My ghost drifted ever so slowly over the three feet that separated me from Xela's slumped form, passing her soul on the way. I didn't see what the witch Xander had fallen in love with looked like. Similarly composed of light, her soul wasn't like the one I imagined. Perhaps because I'd expected Miranda's: the black soul of a wicked witch. Xela's appeared more like mine than I'd have liked—clear and bright. For the first time, I'd felt like we had something in common.

"You'll learn to control it," my mother cooed again.

Before I touched Xela's host to be transferred into the spirit realm, I wondered if I'd ever leave through the door of the cave. It would be a while before I could walk again.

The leaves outside rustled as someone pushed through them. *Xander.*

Xela's spirit vibrated. She looked back at me; uncertainty circled her aura. I supposed she doubted if she could control herself around him. She'd been gone from this world for decades, trying to find a way back to her love through me. Now she'd see him, touch him . . . deceive him.

We couldn't turn back, though, not now.

I entered the body I once possessed, using it as an entranceway to the hereafter of lingering souls. Inside, the ghost world seemed identical to the world I'd lived in except I saw my mom the same way I'd see anyone else and my old body, which was being taken over by Xela, appeared ghostly. It was like I entered a new dimension through Xela.

"Mom!" I ran to throw my arms around her slender figure. "How is this possible?" My arms squeezed around her, feeling the flesh as if it were real.

"I don't know." My mother laughed.

"But I'm not a ghost." I examined my arms and my body, nipping the skin at my waist but unable to feel the pinches.

"You are; but as spirits, we feel just as if we were in flesh."

Xander's clambering footsteps echoed down the stairs. Xela had already entered my body and stood, waiting for him. *She did it!*

"Come, Sarah, you need to leave this body before Miranda returns," my mother urged. "We need to hide you."

"Where is she?" I asked.

"Chasing us in all the wrong places." My aunt winked. "She cannot know you're a ghost."

My mom pulled my hand, and suddenly, we stood beside Xela's limp body, slouched in the chair.

"Xander will see us."

"No, we can choose to appear for humans; now we're not visible. Sh."

Xander pushed the door open. "I told you to stay away, didn't I?" he growled, placing food on a stool by Miranda's body as he glared at mine. He looked ephemeral, like a ghost.

"Stay still," my mother whispered when I shook my head again, reflexively trying to clear my vision.

"Did you hear that?" Xander looked right at us.

Xela distracted his acute senses with, "I needed answers, but the witch seems to be asleep." She crossed her arms, imitating my mannerisms.

Unexpectedly, Miranda lifted her head, her cunning eyes examining Xela in my body.

I gasped.

"Don't worry, she won't suspect this," my mother whispered. "She can't see you while she's in human form."

"You pinky swore, Sarah," Xander's disappointment pinched my soul.

"I'm sorry. But like you said, it's complicated, right?"

"Right." Xander's shoulders drooped as the fury on his face washed away. He glided toward Xela as if pulled by an invisible force. "We shouldn't be here," he whispered, his breath flowing through the cool air toward her.

Xela closed my eyes. "I know."

I felt her struggle inside. She had mustered all the will she could find to resist him. The tension was like that of a volcano, inactive for thousands of years, ready to erupt; the suppressed passion heated the cave. Xela's hands clenched into white-knuckled fists.

"Then why do I want to stay here with you?" Xander asked.

"I . . . I want that too, Xander."

I tightened my lips at the sultry way she'd said Xander's name.

He noticed the change. "I miss you." Xander moved closer, closing his eyes. The fire flared in the pit, flickering oranges and reds. Their breathing deepened.

A cackle vibrated through the cave. Xander's hands flew away from Xela's hips—my hips.

"Ah, look at the lovebirds," Miranda mocked, licking her lips.

"The next time I see you, witch, you will be dead," Xela threatened as sincerely as a promise. Whirling toward the door, she pushed past Xander and rushed out of the cave. He followed.

The minute I saw them leave, I wanted to listen to their conversation; as if something was granting my wish, my ghost was pulled through the cave toward the forest, passing through rock and soil to the outdoors until the breeze swayed my spirit—or perhaps I moved it to the rhythm of the swaying branches; I wasn't sure. It was close to midnight, the moon shrouded behind the clouds. I remained within viewing distance of the couple.

"You're connected to your body," my mother whispered. "When you think about where it is, you'll be pulled to see it. I need to leave, but when you're ready, just think about me and your ghost will be with me. The best time to do our job is when Xander is with Miranda. It's the only way we know her soul is occupied. Otherwise, stay clear of her."

"I don't even know where to start looking, Mom."

"You'll figure it out. It's a natural progression. I'll come to see you soon." She disappeared.

I found myself floating behind the trees, trying to hide, even though Xander couldn't see me.

"You know what happens when you're here." Xander came closer to Xela, brushing the back of his hand along the cheek he still thought was mine.

"That's why I came without you," Xela said.

"You weren't supposed to come at all." His eyes closed and his nose moved as if it were twitching. "You seem different." Xander's senses recognized Xela better than he did.

"I do?" Hope fluttered in Xela's voice.

Xander placed his hands on Xela's hips, pulling her in. I heard his pulse race.

Xela's lips quivered. Remembering how I'd wanted no one else except Xander a couple nights ago, I imagined the control she'd need to keep her distance. She bit her lower lip.

Don't. Don't screw this up.

Xela looked my way, as if she'd sensed my warning. "I shouldn't have come," she said, pushing away from Xander. "I won't do it again."

She strode toward the forest but stopped before entering the darkness of the foliage and looked back. Xander's body trembled, shaking off the lust. He looked from Xela toward the entrance to the cave, then back to Xela.

"I have to feed her," he said reluctantly. "I gather you know the way home?"

Xela didn't reply. She turned and escaped into the forest.

* * *

The night cooled more than usual, and I found it odd not to personally feel the change in temperature, only sense nature's reaction to the cooler air. Or perhaps it was the connection I had to my body, remembering the crisper air of midnight. It made me wish I could feel the air.

"I know you're hovering behind me," Xela said, hiking through the shrubs. She pushed the lower branches away, ripping some out with their roots. "You shouldn't be around me. Miranda will be curious to see the twins' progress. She'll be here when she's not with Xander or taunting your mother."

I chose to appear in my ghost form for Xela. "She's watching the twins?"

"Yes, she's planning their kidnapping."

"We have to stop her!"

"That's why we're doing this," Xela replied in a cool voice, keeping her eyes on the trail in front of her as she continued walking. "Sarah, I know it's difficult for you, but the best thing for you to do is learn how to be a ghost. Use your skills to find Miranda's body. I will care for your children."

Somehow, I believed her. I recognized her intentions toward my children as honorable, but it didn't prevent my feeling jealousy for her having my family and interacting with them, even though she hadn't done that yet.

"You're sacrificing a lot, Sarah. I know that. But it's the only way."

"It's hard for you to see him, isn't it?" I said.

"Imagine not being able to touch the only person you'd ever loved," she replied.

"I do." I thought about William and my children and recalled what it was like to watch Miranda in my body four years ago, touching William when I couldn't.

"For decades," she added, then picked up her pace.

"Oh . . ." It was like she knew exactly what I thought.

"It will take a few hours for me to remember all my human movements. And," she paused, "I'm not going to use your body."

"I didn't think about it that way." I avoided branches and trees, my human instincts intact. "Wait, what if William wants to . . ." My hand flew to cover my mouth.

"Don't worry. I'm still a woman. I know how to fake a headache."

"William will not fall for that."

"I'm still a witch, Sarah; I know how to deceive."

"*Are* you deceiving me?"

She looked my way. "What does your gut tell you?"

"No. I trust you." Speaking to Xela while seeing me—Xela in my body—felt strange. It was like looking at your own reflection in the mirror, but knowing it wasn't you. "How long will this last?"

"A few days. Your mother will call you when she's ready. I'll plot with the children."

"You're going to involve them?"

"Sarah, they were involved before they were born." She stopped on the brink of a canyon. "Believe me, they're fiercer than you think. They can handle themselves well. I've seen them in action."

I didn't want to know how or when. Being a ghost was enough to deal with.

Xela leapt over the edge, bouncing from one branch to another until her feet touched the ground. She crouched, scanning the forest, then ran. The witch didn't look like she needed a reminder of how to use her human form, or a vampire's skills. My new cohort was as graceful as vampire as I was. Perhaps the deception would work.

I followed. "What am I supposed to do?"

"Find Miranda's body. You're a ghost now—make your invisibility useful." She stopped by an overgrown fern. "Miranda has a way of knowing everything. Don't let her touch you. She's like poison ivy."

"I'm a ghost." I flowed beside her as she resumed a slow trot.

"It doesn't mean she can't touch you. Now that I'm gone, she'll be looking for me. Stay clear of her," Xela warned.

"So I need to find her body without Miranda seeing me. But I don't know what she looks like."

"She looks the same as the body in the cave. That is Miranda." Xela stopped and pointed ahead; I saw the lights of the cottage shining through the trees. "We're almost there."

"I-I guess I should go now," I said, fighting my reluctance.

Xela looked at me. "Don't worry. We'll get rid of Aseret before he gets to the children."

"You're so sure."

"I just know stuff." She smirked. "I promise to help."

Part of me wished for Xela's confidence. Her behavior, her movements were swift and flawless. I remembered being that way in Pinedale; then, somewhere between my body being stolen, my marriage to William, and the children's birth, I'd lost myself. I'd forgotten who I was—or perhaps I no longer paid attention to who I was.

"Sarah, you don't give yourself enough credit," Xela said softly, as if she were reading my face, the way I used to do with others. "I wish I had what you have: a loving family, strength, devotion. Don't forget who you are. Not many would be brave enough to do what you've done today."

"Thank you." Her words lifted my chin higher. "I guess I'll see you around."

"Very funny." She rolled her eyes the way I would have.

I waited until Xela was closer to home before letting my ghost disappear. *Home,* I thought, missing it more than I wanted to admit, stalling, not ready to leave just yet.

Xela took her first step onto the patch of grass in the clearing, then halted.

Eric stood on the porch with his arms crossed on his chest.

I rushed to the edge of the clearing, wanting to see what he'd do.

"Do not move, or I will bend you, witch."

Xela stood motionless. "You cannot. There's no other body."

"What have you done?" he asked, then looked at me, detecting the ghostly body that would be invisible to others. *And you let her?* he asked me.

Of course Xela couldn't hear what he'd said. Our telepathic connection remained private.

You can see me? I asked.

Don't you remember I'm bound to you? he replied.

I smiled.

"Sarah agreed to it. It's the only way to destroy Aseret," Xela said.

"Liar! You tricked her." He rushed across the lawn, stopping inches away from Xela. Blue sparks flew between his fingers. Fleshy spikes extended on his neck, vibrating as electricity roamed his body in spasms.

"Just listen to me, Eric, then you can check with Sarah if you'd like. Her soul is safe. We've been able to seclude ourselves from Miranda."

"I know where Sarah's soul is, witch." Then he froze. "Miranda's out?"

Xela nodded.

"I didn't think it was possible."

"No one did. No one knew. She's as conniving as she ever was, and in cahoots with Aseret."

"If Miranda's out . . ." He scratched his head. "What if—"

"I can help you," she interrupted.

He scowled at her. "I don't have much choice now, do I?" The flow of electricity around Eric's palms ceased, and he lowered his shoulders. "You're a marked witch. Why are you doing this?"

"Someone changed me, even if it's not obvious on the outside." She rubbed her hand, where the sphere mark would have been on her old body. "You cannot tell anyone, Eric, not even Mira."

He narrowed his eyes. "Why?"

"I'm not ready to face him."

You're all right with this, Sarah? he asked.

Yes, it's the only way, according to my mother.

That's what she's been scheming. Aloud, he asked, "So you won't let Xander know you're back?"

Xela shook her head. "William would be destroyed. I can't have him interfere and try to follow Sarah's ghost around. He'll be told when the time is right for him to step in to help us. Xander will be trickier. He'll be drawn to me."

"How did you do it? Are there marks on Xela's body?"

"No." She lifted her head in pride. "Miranda's powerful, but so am I. I do not need blood to switch bodies."

His stance relaxed despite him crossing his arms. "What's your plan?"

"I'll need your help. Miranda's had my soul imprisoned for decades, but now that I'm not there, she'll look for me."

"I'll distract her," Eric said. "I won't have trouble pinpointing her soul anymore."

Xela shook her head. "You cannot. She cannot know you know. Just distract her without her knowing."

Up went one of Eric's eyebrows. "You're asking a lot."

"I know but perhaps this way, I'll earn Xander's trust back."

The front door of the cabin opened. William stepped out on the porch. "Sarah? I was getting worried. Why aren't you coming in?"

"I just needed to speak with Eric about the children," Xela lied. "Are they sleeping?"

"Yes, sound asleep." William stared at Xela as if it was the first time he'd seen me.

Xela swept onto the porch using my vampire speed; from William's side, she turned to Eric. "Trust me, Eric, I know what I'm doing. The kids' training has already helped them, but come back tomorrow. I think we've missed some tricks they should know." She finished with a wink toward my watcher.

"I'll be watching them even when I'm not here," he said, his tone veiling a warning.

William, I'm sure, took it as generosity.

You and I need to chat, Eric said to me. *I gather you know how to find me?*

Yes.

Eric frowned, then swirled into nothingness through a vortex.

"So, how was your trip?" William wrapped his arms around Xela.

She shook her head. "He came earlier than I thought he would."

"You have to stop taunting Xander. Let his business with Xela be his own."

"You could say I had an out-of-body experience while talking to the witch," Xela replied.

He took Xela's hand and cradled it between his. William smiled at the fake ruby. To him, the ring confirmed that its wearer was me. His gaze flew back up at Xela, then at the ring. The distance between his eyes narrowed. A hint of doubt zoomed across his face. Then he exhaled.

If he only knew. I wished he could feel in his heart what had happened.

"Not the same kind of out-of-body experience you had already, I hope?"

He knows!

Xela laughed. "Like I would let that happen again."

"I know you wouldn't." He hugged her. "No soul-switching, as promised."

"As promised," she whispered, leaning her head against his chest.

William didn't know and I felt more invisible than I was already.

"I need to let Xander deal with the witch on his own," she said.

"Finally, you listen." William sounded relieved and kissed the top of her head.

I imagined the heat buildup between their embraced bodies and a tingle of regret crossed my mind.

"I don't think I have a choice."

"Good. I'm glad you're back. Perhaps we can start where we left off?" His voice dropped.

She pulled back, looking into William's eyes. I could feel Xela's nerves. If I felt them, would William? This was the part I feared. William would still want my body, the way he always had. Would she give him what he needed? Would she use my body to make love to my husband the way I did?

"I think you need to remind me a little," she replied, her tone teasing as she pressed her body to William's again.

That's when I understood what I'd given up. I'd given up the right to use my body, and Xela, after all, was still a witch. I wasn't sure fidelity was at the top of her list, even if she'd promised.

"You seem different," he stroked her hand and the ruby with his thumb.

"Because you haven't had me in a while." She bit her lower lip.

"Two days is a while?"

"It is right now."

"Then let me remind you of what you've missed." William picked Xela up and threw her over his shoulder. She laughed with my laugh.

The heart I remembered from my chest tightened and I knew what came next. Unwilling to watch, I turned my head aside and thought of my children. My ghost was pulled into their bedroom. Their sleeping faces were as peaceful as an angel's, their cheeks dimly illuminated by the yellow glow of the moon-shaped nightlight. I wanted to inhale their honey and lemon scent and to kiss their cheeks but failed.

Their eyes opened. "Hi, Mama," they said in unison.

I leaned back in surprise. "You can see me?"

They nodded.

I tried to hug them and couldn't. Again I straightened. "I need you to stay close to your daddy and Uncle Eric. Can you do that for me?"

"We'll try, Mama, but we won't be here long," Crystal said.

"What do you mean?"

"We need to be big like you," Ayer said.

I laughed. "Take your time growing up."

"We'll grow up fast," Crystal said solemnly.

"I know, I know," I answered. "You're already growing up too fast."

William and Xela's giggles from *my* bedroom echoed through the house. *Couldn't they be quieter?*

"I need to leave, but can you ask your daddy to bring you water for the night?" I asked the twins.

Smirking, the twins nodded.

"Don't worry, she won't harm Daddy. We'll make sure." Crystal winked.

"Thank you. I love you. I need to go."

"We love you, Mama."

Ayer called out for William. I smiled as I floated away through time and space to see my watcher.

CHAPTER 6

Eric didn't reply to my calls. I ended up in my tree house, spending the night hovering above the wooden floor. It wasn't as if I could show myself to Mira or Xander, my two best friends; they'd freak. Or perhaps not. The siblings had seen their share of odd creatures, including ghosts. They wouldn't be afraid, but they would be upset. And how could I explain to Xander who was in my body? That was the last thing Xela wanted.

The black witch seemed more honorable to me than cruel. She knew Xander would be hurt; after all, he'd been trying to reach her for decades. Now Xela was here, and she couldn't reveal herself to her love. All that, just to help me, and my family. Would I ever be able to repay her?

Besides, the siblings had kept a secret from me for a long time. I didn't know they were shapeshifters for over twenty years. But then, I didn't share my secret of being a half-breed vampire, either. Now I'd love to show them myself as a ghost, but it was for their well-being that I must remain hidden. Otherwise, Aseret could attack too early.

Floating in the center of the tree house, I crossed my arms under my head, tilting it back the way I would if I were in the flesh. The great thing about the Amazon was the lack of light pollution. The stars were bright, and comets zoomed across the night sky, leaving lingering tails. I drifted higher, and the patches of sky enlarged. Once in a while, a bat flew overhead, following the sound of a cricket.

The rustling of branches below startled me. My ghost floated just above the canopy, sticking my head between the leaves to see who it was. I remembered the way my pulse would have rushed with anticipation as soon as the first swoosh of the branches sounded, even if I knew who'd come to the tree house.

William lay on the floor in the exact spot I'd occupied earlier. He stared at the sky the same way I had, and he smiled when a falling star flew by. I braved entering the tree house, keeping my invisible form. William turned his head toward the corner where I stood, and I froze until he went back to staring at the sky. Drifting lower, I admired the youthful face of a man I fell in love with.

"Why do you seem to be here when you're not?" he whispered.

I leaned close to his side, bringing my face to just above his. He looked at me—or so I imagined for he was looking at the night sky. My mouth hovered above his, and I touched his lips. It felt as if I'd kissed fog.

He closed his eyes, and the pulse on his jugular increased. "Come back to me safely," he said when I pulled away.

Did he know I wasn't in my body? Xela was in the house in my host body. Why would William ask me to come back?

I'll be back soon. I promise.

"I'm not sure I can deceive you," he thought aloud.

What? I felt my ghost vibrate and strained to keep myself invisible. All the trust I held in my husband floated away. *Deceive me?*

"To keep a secret so big . . . how can they ask me to do this?" His eyes flew open, startling me.

What are you keeping from me, William?

"But it's for the best. Otherwise, we'll never be safe. I have to protect you." He closed his eyes. "I love you so much. Come back to me, Sarah."

William, I'm here. My ghost quivered and I forced myself to not show my spirit to my husband. *Protect me from what?*

What secrets had he withheld from me? Part of me felt like I intruded on his privacy, but I wanted to know how my husband had deceived me. I'd trusted him with my body and soul and refused to believe he misled me willingly.

I wished for simpler times: when I was back home, when the only secret I kept was being a half-breed vampire.

When I thought about Pinedale, my ghost was pulled away through the forests and the mountains toward my home. I reached for William, but the need to return to my roots yanked me north, and he disappeared.

* * *

Ghost living: a world as tangible as the one I'd been used to, yet I missed being corporeal. For a vampire who could run and not be seen, being a ghost had its similarities. My soul just floated through things instead of running around them. Time and space had no meaning.

Dawn neared when I arrived in front of my house. The two-story Georgian home, now abandoned, stood as I'd left it four years ago, although overgrown shrubs and vines now shrouded its facade. The siblings had referred to it as a haunted house that no one in town dared enter. My visits were less frequent; only long enough to take care of the business I'd left, and ensure the police chief didn't order a search party or file a missing persons report.

The white gate framed my ghost like a piece of art. The rising sun prompted me to move indoors. I drifted toward the front door and floated through it, right into the gloom cast grey shadows by the shut drapes. As the sun rose higher, dust motes sailed through the narrow streams of light between the hanging fabrics, and I promised myself to clean this place once I had my body back.

An upward draft yanked my spirit toward the attic. The dust motes hung in the air floating to the current of the wind that whizzed through the broken window. Boxes toppled and the room no longer resembled lined up rows and columns. After we'd moved to the Amazon, Mrs. G and the siblings used the attic to store some of their belongings. An empty mice nest of shredded fabrics and papers lay in the corner. I hovered by the dusted mirror but my ghost wasn't reflected.

The grandfather clock downstairs struck seven: the time I'd normally leave for work. My ghost was pulled three blocks south to my flower shop, where I'd spend days and nights working on serums that would turn me back into a human. I chuckled inwardly at that goal; it seemed so silly now.

Kirsten would be here at any minute. She managed the greenhouse, renovated after the seekers destroyed my store. Her skills in caring for the plants showed in the bookkeeping; the extra income went to help a veterinary clinic—Mira's and Xander's business.

I waited across the street from the store. Would I ever see my reflection in the glass window again?

Rustling newspaper pages interrupted the chirping of a blue jay nearby. A man seated on a bench flipped through the pages, grunting at each headline. A top hat rested on his head, slightly off center. The black coat nearly touched the ground and fashionista shades did not match his older demeanor. I floated closer, intrigued by the familiarity of his groan, and hovered in front of him. The man lowered his paper and took off his sunglasses to look through me, across the street to my store. Another familiar snort sounded deeper from his throat.

What's the warden doing here? He had to be up to mischief.

"I will get it from you," he muttered as he stood to leave. The hump in his back seemed smaller than I remembered. His wobbling smoothed as the distance between us grew.

Get what? From whom? Was he still looking for my address? I wanted to follow but saw Kirstin arrive at the store. She'd sent me letters often, and my worries over her personal life had escalated in the past year.

You are on my to-do list, warden. My ghost crossed the street. *When I sign the papers, I'll deal with you, too.*

A cab ran through me, but with my focus on the store, I didn't react. I passed through the glass window into green oblivion. The flower shop, now turned into a greenhouse with an extension in the back, had been my oasis before I met William, before I lived in the Amazon. Kirsten set her purse under the counter and checked the phone for messages, then turned on the lights while talking to the plants as if they were human. She headed to the back of the greenhouse, misting the leaves on either side from a water bottle she carried. I imagined the plants opening their invisible eyes to greet her as I sensed their stems stretching upward.

She is perfect for this store. I followed her along the green path, instinctively ducking under the lower branches.

She sat in a chair in the back, waiting for coffee to brew. The glass-walled room reminded me of the solarium in the cabin. When renovating the store into a greenhouse, I ensured the serenity of the room where I'd spent so much time had been kept. I wanted Kirsten to have similar the peace to the one I enjoyed in Amazon.

Snow jumped onto Kirsten's lap. She stroked the cat's head before spooning some food into his bowl. Smiling, I noticed the white fur stuck to her black tights, and I drifted to the side of the chair. The cat lifted his head, hissing.

"What's the matter, Snow?" Kirsten asked.

The cat hissed again, arching its back at me, white fur spiking.

Does he see me? I bent to look at him, and Snow jumped back into the potted shrubs. Leaves trembled as he found a spot to curl into.

"What are you afraid of, silly cat?" Kirsten asked. "Come here, kitty. Chi-chi-chi."

The front door opened. "Kirstin, where's my coffee?" a male voice called.

My ghost rushed to the front. *Chris?* The face of a heartthrob I remembered from high school stared through me. He wasn't as good-looking now as back then. Two pimples the size of thumbs stuck out on each side of his neck, and he had the beer belly of a long-time drinker. His hair greased—not styled with gel, but unwashed. Yesterday's sweat had left stains under the arms of his shirt. Was this the dweeb Kirstin was dating? How could I ever have thought he was a hunk? Yuck!

"Hi, honey." Kirstin rushed out, carrying a cup full of coffee. "Here it is." She handed him the mug.

"Did you start late? It hasn't cooled." He pointed at the steam rising from the mug.

Jerk!

"I'm sorry. I had to feed Snow and—"

"Baby, you know what happens when I get upset."

What happens?

Kirstin's hands trembled. "I know. I'm sorry. It's my fault."

Like hell it is! Kirsten! Stand up for yourself!

"What are you going to do about it?" Chris looked from the mug to her, then back to the coffee.

She started cooling the cup with her breath, blowing the steam out of the way without spilling the liquid within. "I was thinking," she said between inhalations, "that perhaps we shouldn't see each other anymore." She blurted the last words. It sounded as if she'd rehearsed the sentence a dozen times, and she finally got it out.

That a girl!

Kirsten continued to cool the cup resting in his hands, eyes on Chris, squirming before he even spoke.

"Aw, baby. You know I didn't mean it. Besides, who else would take you in?" He sipped the coffee. "Shit! It's hot!"

Because it was just brewed, you nitwit!

"I think I may be getting a place of my own." Kirsten's voice was hushed, and she shifted her body back.

"You can't live on your own."

I made a mental note to give Kirstin a raise, enough so she'd never have to hear from this dipstick again.

"No one would take an ugly duckling like you. You need a man like me to support you." He grabbed her arm.

Ugly ducking? Kirstin had the most natural face I'd seen, not the typical Barbie, but well taken care of, reflecting intelligence and thoughtfulness. She jogged every night, and I'd seen more than one man lusting over her. *Who are you to say she's ugly, Frankenstein!*

"Ouch, you're hurting me." She tried to pull away, wincing as he squeezed harder.

"You try to leave me, and you'll see what hurt means." He leaned toward her and I imagined his coffee breath on her face.

"Please let go," she whispered as her eyes filled with tears.

I rushed to find Snow. *Come on, stupid cat. Help a ghost out!*

The bushes had densed since the last time I'd been here, but finally a twitching tail came into view. *Ah-ha!* I showed my ghostly eyes to the cat. Snow leapt out of the bushes, tore into the front, and jumped right onto Chris's back.

"What the hell!" Chris spun around, trying to dislodge Snow, but I let the fur ball see me again, and the cat dug his nails into Chris's shoulders.

Kirsten watched the scene unfold with an expression that clearly revealed her mixed emotions—should she help, cry, or jump for joy that the bastard of a boyfriend was getting what he deserved?

Snow must have had a run-in with Chris before, because the satisfaction in the cats eyes as he retreated to the back of the greenhouse was priceless.

"Look at this!" Chris pointed to his torn shirt. "You will pay for your cat's claws." He stormed out of the store.

No, she won't! I followed the dirtbag outside and along the sidewalk as he rushed away, bumping into an older lady and continuing onward without apologizing. Chris kicked an empty beer can toward an alley. The aluminum missed a boy who had just crossed the street by an inch.

He laughed. "I'll show her," he muttered. "I'll pour some salt into those stupid plants, see how well they grow then."

I'd had enough. Chris turned into a quiet side road and when he was out of anyone's sight, I showed my ghost to him.

He staggered back. "What—"

"You will not call, stalk, touch, or torment Kirsten again," I warned, making my face as scary as I could, drawing on my vampire side to show my fangs. "And you will never step into that store again!"

"Who... who... a-are you?" he stammered.

"You know the line 'I am your worst nightmare'? That'd be too tame to describe me. Boo!" I pushed my face forward, almost bumping my ghostly forehead against his.

Screaming like a little girl, Chris ran and didn't look back. For the first time since assuming my ghostly form, I felt good about it.

I hurried back to the store and found Kirsten humming under her breath as she wiped the coffee off the floor. The cat approached and rubbed against her arm. "Thanks, Snow." She scratched behind the cat's ear. He purred.

Wanting to touch her to let her know she wasn't alone, I placed my on her shoulder. Perhaps she'd sense me. Kirsten turned toward the window and looked through me. I listened to her heartbeat. *Calm. She'll be all right. Now, one more person to take care of.*

As I drifted away from Kirsten, she placed Snow on the front counter and began checking the day's orders.

Care to join me at The Grill? I heard in my head while floating back toward my house.

Eric?

Were you expecting someone else?

I'm coming! My ghost whippedaround and flew across town. Not wanting to travel by the streets, I let Eric's presence carry me through buildings, trees, and people, so quickly everything blurred. In seconds, I was sitting at the table with my evil-bender at The Grill, the town's main restaurant.

"What are you doing here? Did you see the kids? Are they all right?" I asked as my gaze travelled around the empty restaurant. The breakfast crowd had left, and I'd just flown through Mike, the owner, who was preparing for lunch with his staff in the back.

Eric sat at a table set for two. He pulled out a piece of bacon from his sandwich and stuffed it into his mouth.

"Everything is fine at the cabin. You need to calm down, though. You're vibrating too much." He spoke low enough not to draw attention from the kitchen.

"Okay." I tried to breathe slowly to ease my excitement, the way I did when in the flesh. Even though I did not need to inhale, the exercise helped. "Why are you here?" I finally asked in a composed voice.

"I had some business to take care of."

"Watcher business?"

"Bender business. Just keeping my eye on the evil that lurks." Eric widened his eyes, then laughed, but part of me knew he wasn't joking. He was hiding something, and he wouldn't share the secret with me.

"You don't feel odd eating by yourself?"

"Years of practice." He winked as he took another bite of his BLT. "And you're here." A piece of lettuce fell out of his mouth. Eric packed it back into his chipmunk cheeks as he chewed.

"I miss that," I said.

"Eating?"

"Eating, touching, feeling."

"You still feel, just differently." Eric cleared his mouth in one enormous swallow and wiped his lips with a napkin. It seemed he didn't bother to swallow in smaller bites. "Now, tell me—" he sipped on his water "—why would you do something so stupid?" He pointed to my ghostly form.

"Did you talk to my mom?" I leaned in.

"Yeah, yeah. She explained." Eric sat back in his chair.

"And you still think I'm stupid."

"Brave." He placed his hands on the table, tapping his fingers.

My eyebrows rose. "What?"

"You're brave. I don't know many humans who'd sacrifice their life the way you seem to do, way too often. It complicates things for me."

"How?" I cocked my head to the side. The clattering of dishes in the kitchen echoed through the restaurant, but I kept my focus on my evil-bender.

"It's—"

"Please don't say complicated." I rolled my eyes.

"It makes my job a bit more difficult, but that's the way it usually is with watchers. Your sacrifice means I'll have to make one as well. I'm bound to you."

"I don't really grasp the binding thing yet, but you do that anyway, all the time. Especially for me." With hesitation I placed my see-through hands on top of his.

"It's my job, Sarah, it's who I am. I'm not as virtuous as you think."

"Watching me is more than a job for you, Eric. You know it. I don't deserve to have a watcher, and you've always protected me. You've given me everything others have failed to give." I moved my fingers as if I were embracing his hands between my own.

"What's that?"

"Love, respect, trust."

"Because I'm a watcher."

"Because you're you."

He dropped his shoulders. "You know, we may not be able to get your body back."

I quelled anxiety. "I can't think about that."

"Good. Think positive. Save your essence." His gaze flew toward the window. "Meet me at the hill tomorrow at sunrise. I'll try to be alone, but if I'm not, don't show yourself."

"Mira?" I asked, pulling back my hands.

"Sugar just likes my sugar in the morning." The lustful smirk on his face made me think of William who had the same one last night, before I gave my body away.

"You're all alike." I melodramatically dropped my head into my hands.

"Hey, I'd rather be a lover than a fighter, but that hasn't worked out too well for me until recently." The evil bender stood, squaring his shoulders in a business-like manner. "I'll see you there?"

I nodded.

Eric left money on the table and went to the bathroom. *Don't wait for me to come out,* he said in my mind.

A moment later, I heard the wind blow behind the closed door. The trailings of a purple mist escaped through underneath the door, and I imagined it smelled of lilac and lavender.

Great, alone until tomorrow and it's only noon. I eyed the clock over the bar. The cat's tail swung off each second. What seemed worse for me was that, as a ghost, I had no sense of time, nor did it matter. If I closed my eyes, hours could pass in a second. If they remained open, the seconds could become hours.

Soon after Eric left, Pinedale whirled in front of my eyes, and I found my ghost floating away from my home town, all on its own. My senses recognized the direction; I was being undeniably pulled toward Huntsville—my spirit wanted me to go to the prison. I concentrated on the warden until I was zooming through the intervening cities and trees, mountains, and valleys, faster by the second. If the warden returned to the prison, he wouldn't make it back for another three hours—that is, if he'd left Pinedale right away. Travelling as a ghost was similar to flying through time in a vortex, minus the nausea.

In the city, raindrops the size of beans splattered on impact. Though I didn't get wet, the storm made the prison look spookier than usual. In the tower, the warden's office was dark. I drifted higher toward his window; the shut drapes blackened the window, and the lights in the room beyond were also off. *Good.* But before I had a chance to enter and search the office, I glimpsed someone wobbling toward the main entrance so quickly that his mud-covered shoes splashed through puddles, splaying water to the sides. The cuffs of his pants had been soaked from dragging through the water that streamed along the walkway.

I hovered lower. *Can't be.*

The oversized steel door of the prison entrance opened before the warden touched the handle. He walked toward the main door, and lamps on each side of the path lit before he passed them, then dimmed to their usual brightness.

Who are you?

Instead of going to his office, the warden strolled through the hall that connected the execution quarters to the guards' desk, mumbling under his breath, leaving a trail of rain water on the concrete floor. I followed above him, trying to eavesdrop, but he seemed to be mumbling in a different language. Every so often I'd catch a word—"brother," "betray,"—but as the storm got louder, it became difficult to hear and understand the muttered words.

My ghost vibrated, wanting to leave on its own. *Why was I pulled here then?*

Thunder sounded outside, but I preferred to face the storm which seemed safer than this facility. The prison held murderers, rapists, and terrorists. It was the harshest in the country, and as much as I despised being inside, the prisoners did not seem as harsh as this man.

The warden stopped. He looked toward the end of the hall, his gaze skimming the ceiling, then, eyes still upward, he turned and examined the corridor behind me, then the other end of the hall. "Who's here?" he said calmly, searching with his gaze for something I couldn't see.

I checked to see if anyone else had entered, but no one had, neither corporeal nor ghost.

"Those vampires are trouble. It's not wise to sign the papers with them," he grumbled. "Don't think it's wise."

What? Why?

Supporting his weight on a cane, he shuffled up the stairs to his office. I wanted to follow, but something told me not to. Today wasn't the right time to deal with the warden, especially as a ghost.

Not wanting to spend the approaching night at the prison or in the pouring rain, I thought about Mrs. G and the hill and allowed my ghost to float north. When the storms passed, I stretched my arms out, drifting through the forest and the glowing sunset. I imagined the last heat of the day encasing me as I arrived in Yellowstone National Park.

CHAPTER 7

I waited outside the hill through the night, watching nocturnal creatures as if they were still my prey. Most mammals were oblivious to my presence and continued their routine, with the exception of a mountain cat. He stared at the spot where I sat, sniffing, then turned on its hind legs and darted into the darkness. Time blended; I couldn't gauge whether an hour had passed, or a minute. If it weren't for the nearing day, I wouldn't know when nighttime turned into daytime.

Eric left Mrs. G's house just before sunrise, when the orange glow lightened the trees from the bottom. As a daily ritual, he followed Mira through the forest in a vortex, helping her search the perimeter for seekers. Mornings at Mrs. G's, afternoons in the Amazon—every day for the past four years, they'd secured our homes. I followed them for fifteen minutes before daring to come closer than the treetops.

I know you're here, Eric said in my mind.

How?

When are you going to understand the meaning of me being your evil-bender?

My evil-bender, I repeated. The voice of my ghost sounded dreamier than my normal voice.

I'm not yours that way. But if you want to think about it that way, fine. Sugar will be a little jealous . . .

Stop it! You men all think alike.

What do you expect? We're men! Thoughts are the only thing we get to keep to ourselves. Well, usually. You stole internal peace when you gave your body to the witch.

I got serious. *Eric, the warden from the prison is hiding something. I don't think—*

You stay away from him, he warned.

Why?

Don't you have other things to worry about?

Yes, I answered, *but when I have my body back, I'll need to confront him.*

Prioritize, Sarah, prioritize.

Have you told Mira about me? I asked.

No, and you'd better keep yourself hidden until I'm alone.

Mira stepped in front of Eric. "You're distracted."

I sighed, missing my witty friend.

"Just doing my job, sugar." He grinned.

"Which job?" Mira placed her hands on her hips and pouted. "You're hiding something from me."

See what I mean? Good luck keeping a secret from her. I laughed.

"Nothing can get by you, can it, sugar." Eric lifted her chin with his fingers and skimmed her lips with his.

"Nope. I've worked with you and the ghosts before. What's the big deal?" She peeked behind Eric, as if trying to see who he was talking to.

"This one's a bit difficult. She doesn't know what's good for her and makes stupid mistakes that could cost her life."

I do not! I screamed into his ear. Eric grimaced.

"Sounds like someone interesting," Mira scanned the forest.

Ha! I'm interesting.

"Someone who thinks she has nine lives."

Take it back or I'll show myself, I teased.

Stay back, Sarah, Eric warned.

Take it back, I whispered into his other ear, flowing my ghost through him.

Stop that! He wiggled his body like he could feel me.

You don't like it? I passed through Eric again.

"Eric, why are you wincing?" Mira asked.

You show yourself, and you're running the chance Xander will find out the truth. He knows Mira better than anyone, Eric warned.

Then you'll just have to keep your sugar busy so Xander doesn't suspect. I let my ghost appear.

"What the hell!" Mira jumped back.

"Ta-da!" I swept my arms to the side as if I'd just finished a dance rehearsal and twirled.

"I guess this would be a good time to explain that your best friend switched souls again." Eric pushed Mira's chin up to close her gaping mouth.

The sun rose higher. I missed its warmth and the earthy smell of the moss in this forest. The morning fog had almost disappeared, the crisp night air strangling each warm breath.

"Sarah? Why?" She tried poking her finger against my arm.

"I'll tell you on the way."

"Where exactly are we going?" Eric crossed his arms.

"You need to take me somewhere where I can safely see my mother." I flowed through him, just for fun.

"Stop that." He brushed me off as if I were dust.

"I like this Sarah." Mira laughed. "It's like you were born again!"

Eric didn't agree. Scowling, he twirled his finger to open a vortex. Waves of heat flew toward us, and I didn't have to feel them to know where we were going as the orange swirls pulled us to the underworld.

* * *

Eric was the first to step out of the vortex. "This is Xela's old lair."

We stood in a cave identical to the one Xander had forbidden me to visit. I recognized Mira's wiggling nose as her effort to find a pocket of fresh air she could stick it in; the air must be stale. A fire burned in the hearth on the side wall. The waves of heat floated languidly toward the root-webbed ceiling; even if I couldn't feel the warmth, my memory of the underworld's caves was clear. The intensity reminded me of Aseret's grand hall.

"Who's tending to this?" I asked, pointing to the hearth.

"No one needs to keep a fire going in the underworld." Eric explained.

"Right." I hovered over to the mantle with its collection of Xela's jars and pointed to a blob of green mush bobbing in what looked like water. "This one looks like snot."

"It probably is." Mira grimaced.

"Can you two be serious for a moment?" Eric motioned for us to come closer.

"How is this place safe?" I asked. "We're in the underworld."

"Miranda wouldn't think to look here."

"But Xela escaped. This is the first place she'll look." I tried to lean on the wooden table but fell through.

Mira contained a laugh. "Yup, you're definitely reborn."

"It's a habit."

"Leave it to me to confuse Miranda," Eric said. "I'll keep you invisible in this lair. When you need to see your mother, come here. She's expecting you to come to the lair and will be checking when you need her."

Eric held out his hand and out popped a blue sphere. The sparks sizzled, then calmed as he stared at the ball of blue fire, bending its shape with his mind. The sphere composed its sparks until it almost purred, then transformed into a holographic display of the underworld.

"What else have you got up those sleeves?" Mira asked.

"More than you know, sugar. More than you know." He pointed to the sphere. "The orange dots you see belong to dead bodies waiting to reunite with their spirits."

"Waiting? I thought that's what you did—reunite them," I said.

"For the past year, we've pretended they cannot reunite. Aseret thinks we've lost our touch." He turned the sphere, revealing more orange dots.

"Why?"

"We have a few hundred locations left, and that can be cleared up in a day or so. With the children's help, it should take a few hours." He leaned against the table with both arms.

"You can't expect them to do this!" My ghost vibrated.

"Do you trust me?" Eric asked.

My best friend was no longer smiling. Mira's expression became serious.

"I do," I said. "I'm sorry."

"No, I am. I shouldn't have spoken that way." He wiped the sweat off his forehead. Mira must have shifted her internal temperature as no beads appeared on her face.

"You have every right to." I shook my head.

"They're your children. I understand your concerns, but believe me, they can handle this." Eric paused. "The problem is Miranda's body."

A few loose pebbles fell from the earthen ceiling.

"Why?"

"Spirits come to me at free will to be reunited with their bodies. Someone like Miranda obviously wants her identity secret. I am the last person Miranda wanted to know about her." Again he paused. "Because I was the one to bind her, and I would do it again."

"My bender." Mira hung on his arm, beaming with pride.

"How do I help?" I asked.

"In the next twenty-four hours, find her body. Your mother will help you."

"And if I can't?"

"Let Miranda find you and then trick her into showing you where it is." Eric took Mira's hand. "We need to go. I'll leave the plans with you." He placed the blue holograph on the table. The light hovered inches above the surface. "The orange body markers will disappear as I finish. Our family is the only one who can see it."

Eric and Mira began to fade, their outlines blending into the background before disappearing through the vortex.

It felt like seconds passed, but perhaps it's been hours. Either way I'd feel the same.

"Sarah?" I heard my mom's voice before her ghost appeared.

"Mom." I hugged her like I never had before. Holding my mom as if she were real still seemed like a dream—one I'd had for decades, and now, I had her. I didn't know for how long, but she was with me.

"You know, Sarah, if everything goes well, I will no longer see you." She'd read my mind.

I nodded. "I know." Part of me wished I could remain a ghost, just to have her at my side. Now that I had children of my own, I knew how difficult it must have been for her not to see me grow up.

"But I will be watching over you." She found my gaze, holding onto my shoulders.

"Does Father know?"

"No." My mom shook her head.

"You need to show him," I said.

"It's not a priority right now, and I'm afraid I may not have time." Turning, my mom floated away, staring into the fire.

"But all these years, you could have shown yourself to him." I followed to stand right behind her.

"And hurt him?" Her ghost turned, and she took my face into her palms. "Sarah, I let him dream of me. That should be enough. Reminding him of what happened would torture your father."

"What about reuniting you with your body?" I asked.

"Eric already has it," she said. "I'm allowed to stay here for a while longer."

"So, how do we find Miranda's body?" I asked.

"One place I haven't searched is Aseret's dungeons. The mazes here shift." She pointed to a point near the center of the sphere, then looked up at me. "I've been told you know where the dungeons are."

"If you take me to the grand hall, I'll remember the way." Aseret had imprisoned me and my family in one of his magically protected cells. He'd allowed our escape so we would trust Xela—or at the time, Miranda—who posed as a witch named Alex, using Xela's body.

"Miranda's ghost has been spotted here." She touched the map as a maze shifted again. "I have a feeling that's where she's hiding."

"Let's go, then." I pulled on my mother's ghostly hand.

She halted before we flew through the wall. "Make yourself invisible, Sarah."

"Right." I shut my eyes. It was the only way I knew to become invisible.

Stifling a chuckle, my mother pulled me through the rock. We flew into the soil and earthen walls, then through empty corridors toward the center of the underworld, the grand hall.

At first, we passed a seeker or two in the passages; some were training, others frozen like statues with glowing orange eyes, waiting for their next order from Aseret. As we neared the hall, their numbers multiplied. I thought I'd seen many seekers, but their population here had grown. The closer we came to the hall, the more numerous and rowdy they became. Fights broke out, the zombie-like creatures screeching and yelping in their high-pitched tones while pouncing on one another, reaching with their twig-like fingers to slit the skin of an opponent with their nails. One swing, and a seeker died.

And if the nails weren't enough, they heated their palms, frying each other—an ability gifted from Aseret. They'd burn flesh on touch, scorching the skin or boiling the flesh beneath the blisters, then the sick smell of burning meat . . . The seeker's iron hold on my shoulders in the Amazon four years ago had similar result. My ghost shivered.

I often wondered why warlocks chose to turn to Aseret to become lifeless. Mira had explained that many had lost their incomes as medicine developed, and humanity no longer needed therapeutic help through herbs and chants. They dwelt for decades, lost in the underworld. Aseret promised immortality if they were to recruit others, and they did; without a return ticket from the underworld, they all became Aseret's subjects.

We floated into the turgid air of the grand hall. Heat waves rose to some point lost in the height of the granite ceiling. From it, a chandelier, its hundreds of candles all lit, was suspended over a roaring firepit. Along one wall, a river of molten lava flowed before turning to cross the floor beside the fire. The crater I'd almost fallen into with William still gaped. The seekers should have felt lucky they didn't need to tend to the fire, as it would have been impossible to reach it. I imagined the stench of rotten eggs and dirty socks that emanated and wanted to vomit. The acid taste imprinted on the inside of my mouth, or perhaps I imagined it.

The hall, although identical to what I remembered, seemed grander. New bridges ran over the crater and connected one end of the hall to the other. The crisscross of wooden planks smoldered at some spots from the bubbling lava beneath.

"I don't like this," I told my mother.

"Sh, I don't want him to sense us." She pointed to the throne at the top of a staircase covered with velvet carpeting that matched the drapes hanging over the entrance points.

Aseret slumped in his seat, the hood of the demon cloak covering his bald head. In his translucent palm, he balanced a sphere similar to the one Eric had left, except this one spat red and orange sparks instead of blue. His gaze wandered toward us, following our movement across the hall. The warlock narrowed his brows, and the sphere rolled to one side, almost falling from its position hovering above his palm. He focused on the sphere again, keeping one eye on the seekers' training.

I led the way toward the end of the hall, where we passed through the drapes concealing a circular staircase. We hovered down the steps, my shoulder stuck into the wall as we squeezed through. The unsavory sensation of the dungeon's dim and dank atmosphere was just as I remembered.

"That's odd."

"What?" my mother asked.

"Where are the prisoners?" The corridor of countless openings held no prisoners. I recalled the cell openings covered with magical spells floating like fog, preventing escape. My gaze focused on the third cell, where I'd been imprisoned. The side walls had been destroyed by our escape. Aseret's minions hadn't fixed them yet.

"I've never been here before." My mother's gaze warily scanned every corner of every cell. "You know how you get a gut feeling as a human?"

"Yeah?" I checked the square compartments from left to right as we drifted along the corridor.

"Well, I'd always had that feeling to not come here. I think we should leave."

"No one's here, Mom. We'll leave as soon as we check for Miranda's body."

I pulled her along with the breeze that seemed to be guiding me. We checked each cell, just in case, but found them all empty. Not even a trace of a prisoner. No bones. No ashes. No dust.

"Your gut means to tell you this is the place to be." I smirked. A wave of excitement flew through me. The anticipation of danger would have pumped my blood faster if I had a body; instead, only waves and vibrations floated along my ghost's silhouette.

"Stop that," my mother cautioned. "You're showing your ghostly form."

I looked at my translucent arms, then focused.

We reached the end of the tunnel. A stone wall, identical to all the walls in the caverns, marked a dead end.

"Now can we leave?" my mother asked, looking anxiously behind us.

"Can you feel the breeze?"

She nodded. "I thought I had some help floating."

"We've been drifting toward the end. Care to see what's on the other side of the wall?" I grinned like a little kid, hoping my mom wouldn't argue.

My mother's apprehensive expression turned into a smirk of anticipation. We were more alike now than ever before, and she looked as if she was getting her spark back—one she'd forgotten.

I took her hand and forced my spirit through the wall. Part of me hoped we'd end up embedded in the rock, but I knew we wouldn't. Whatever lay beyond the stone wall had to be a big secret, and it wouldn't be soil.

The moment we decided to go ahead, the breeze pulled us in like a vacuum. My body whooshed through the stone barrier into a barren room. The air was filled with the stale scent of black roses, a scent that conjured a faint memory from the past.

"I can't see anything." I tightened my grip on my mother's hand.

"Hold on a minute." She let go, and I waited, suddenly feeling alone, until the sound of a match being lit preceded a flare of oval light on the other side of the room.

"I found it in the cupboard." She shook the box of matches.

"How did you do that?" I asked. "You're a ghost."

She smiled. "Years of practice." Her translucent features shimmered in the glow as it faded, then flickered out.

My mother hit another match against the box. She held its flame as she carried it across the room, shielding it with the other hand. Shadows of objects she passed—a jar, a chair, a broom, a table—danced on the walls until she reached a candle. The match went out before she touched the wick. She lit a third match and held it close to the wick until the flame transferred. Soon the squared room was illuminated by the light of over twenty candles of different sizes.

None of the four walls had a door or any entrance. The jarred ingredients, hanging herbs, and bundled feathers bore an eerie resemblance to those in Xela's cave, but it was colder here.

"How does she get in here?" my mother asked.

"She's a ghost, Mom."

"She wasn't always a ghost."

The room breathed gloom and despair, hatred and pain. I walked over to the centered table to examine a leather-bound book with the symbol of the sphere embossed on its front. *Spells.*

A familiar blade rested beside the book. Miranda, when I'd thought she was the good witch Alex, had used a dagger to carve stones in one of the cells to open the wall for our escape. "There must be a hidden entrance through the rock," I said.

"I won't ask how you know this, but there are no bodies here. We should leave."

I looked at her ghost. "Mom, you're shaking."

"We need to leave. Now!"

But it was too late. A loud cackle vibrated the walls as Miranda entered her lair. Dust fell of the earthen ceiling. She walked instead of hovering and stalked around the perimeter of the room, eyes on us. Miranda was poised to pounce, as if we were her prey. Walking was unnatural for a spirit and took more energy, but Miranda didn't look like she lacked any strength. Tangled hair, saliva hanging on her lower lip, crusty nails, sunken, shadowed eyes burning with hate, this witch was identical to the witch I'd seen in Xander's cave and thought was Xela. Except this time, I knew where Xela was.

Remembering Miranda's host body when she'd switched our souls and the rage that burst through me when I'd awakened in the woods, my ghostly form shook.

Miranda threw her head back and cackled, and I realized, both my mother and I were now visible.

I remained still, promising myself that this time, she would end up dead, in both realms.

Rocks scraped, one against another, as the wall behind us slid to the side. I whirled, but it felt like it took hours before I faced Aseret's expressionless eyes. A scar on the right side of his neck, just beneath the cloak's hood, matched the one on the left. He stood, hands tucked into the opposite sleeves of his cloak, and regarded me for a moment. Then he smirked. "I thought I'd felt your prresence, up above, but I didn't think you werre dead. Hmm, to whom should I pay my ressspects?" Before I could respond, he added, "Neverr mind. We could have worked together, but your soul will give me more than you ever could."

"Is that why she's a ghost? So you can use her?" I pointed to the witch, who continued to circle around us, watching us with cunning eyes. "Clever of you. Hide her body so she's trapped to serve you," I taunted.

"Stupid girl!" Miranda hissed. "There is no body! Why do you think I had to steal Xela's?"

My mother cautiously pulled at hoop in my jeans. We backed away, my mom keeping herself protectively in front of me. I wondered how much we should actually fear; after all, we were already ghosts. But Mom's face showed we had plenty to worry about.

"You're lying," I said. "He's using you." This was my chance to get more information from the wicked witch. I wouldn't give up, even if my instinct told me to run.

"My body burned centuries ago," Miranda retorted. "Hannah should have told you. She's the one who sent me down the fire pit. I'd been stuck in the hereafter until Aseret freed me through Xela."

Was she telling me the truth? If so, how could we ever return our bodies to their rightful souls?

She laughed, almost choking on her spit. "*You* are stuck here. And I'll ensure Aseret makes good use of your essence."

"You will not touch me." I remembered Xela's warning and wished my voice didn't shake.

"How is William doing? Last time I saw him, he was doing very, very well," she mocked. "He must be mourning your death. Poor boy. Perhaps I should find *your* body and make him feel all better again. I'm sure I can make him feel way better than you could."

"He'd know it's not me," I said.

"Ah yes, the petty ruby ring. I can work around that." She smirked, closing in.

"Run! Now!" My mother pushed my ghost toward the back wall. Miranda reached for me, but my mother blocked her. Somehow, her ghost had enough energy to stop the witch. The last thing I saw was Aseret's shocked expression fading into its usual emotionless mask. My mother's painful cry echoed in my ear as I thought about my home and let my spirit be carried to the Amazon.

CHAPTER 8

As much as I wanted to turn back to help my mother, I couldn't. We'd both be doomed. My mother had saved me. I'd killed her as an infant, and now her spirit would suffer endless tortures because of me. My invisible insides twisted with guit.

I will be the one to save her, I promised. *I have to be.*

Feeling hopeless, I slumped on the top of the climbing wall in the Amazonian cabin. I peered down at Xela in the kitchen, stirring dinner, the ruby glinting on her right finger. Though I knew it was a fake, it seemed to glow. *Hmm . . . could the ring trick Miranda again?*

With Xander's help, Crystal and Ayer pieced together a jigsaw puzzle spread out on the floor in the hallway. Lying on their stomachs, feet swinging lazily in the air, all three looked like kids. William leaned over the dining room table, drafting a map with my father and   Atram. They were sketching the vampire territories and marking those in need of training and hypnosis.

I wasn't surprised to see Willow in the lab, continuing her work with the serums behind the glass wall. Her bravery and dedication in bringing peace and her devotion to her family reminded me of William. Though she had no supernatural skills, she blended into this world as if she was meant to be here. She never feared for herself, only for others. In her own human way, she possessed supernatural powers she wasn't aware of.

Xela kept her distance from Xander though her eyes smiled and I knew her thoughts were with him. William, preoccupied, couldn't read her face the way I did. She swung her hips as she stirred the goulash. The witch looked like she had lost herself in her own world when no one was paying attention. I imagined the aroma of sweet onions and peppers wafting through the house, mixing with the scents of the forest.

Xander looked up. "Do you smell roses?" His gaze flew toward Xela. He frowned, focusing his energy on the witch.

Mira perked up and inhaled. "Nope." She shook her head, letting her eyes fall to the book on her lap—too quickly.

Stay calm, Mira. Don't blow it.

"You're lying. Why would you lie about smelling roses?" Xander sat up, looking from Mira to Xela.

"I . . . have a stuffed nose." Mira kept her eyes fixed on her book.

He's gonna know! I warned, but she couldn't hear me.

Xander's gaze remained on Xela and her hand circling over the pot as she happily sprinkled parsley and garlic into the mixture. Had happiness released the witch's floral aroma? Xela put her head into the steam, inhaled, then added another ingredient.

Even I began to smell her soul's potent rosy essence! *How am I smelling this?*

My attention darted to the children.

Don't worry, Mama, we're on it. My son's voice in my head startled me.

Ayer's body slumped on the floor, his head resting on his arm as he pretended to sleep. His soul rushed out of the house. I'd never seen his soul leave his body, but it seemed natural for my son to be in this state.

Be careful! I called after him.

Before I could ask Crystal what he was up to, her brother returned to his body and continued to fake sleep. Crystal nodded in her brother's direction, then answered, "I picked flowers in the forest." The exchange had taken seconds. No one noticed.

"When did you go to the forest?" William asked.

"Training with Uncle Eric." She shrugged, then tapped Ayer's shoulder to wake him up. They returned to their puzzle.

Thank you. I smiled.

The children winked. In their faces was a maturity I hadn't seen before. Their bodies were still those of three-year-olds, but the twins were wiser than many adults.

You're welcome, they said together.

Did Uncle Eric teach you to speak to me in your mind?

Yes, Mama. We can hear you, too. Crystal smiled my way.

William looked from our daughter to where I sat, then back to her again. "What's so captivating?" he asked her.

"I'm drawing a picture of Mama," she said.

"May I see?" He braced his hands against the table to stand, but she stopped him by freezing his feet with blue light.

"Not weady yet." She smiled.

"All right, I promise not to look until you're done."

Crystal took the light off William's feet.

Xander had risen and now strolled toward Xela. "Where did you get this recipe?" He inhaled as he approached the pot.

William's gaze followed them.

He'll recognize her.

But my husband's gaze went back to his iPad, and he murmured about referencing the vampire locations he'd marked with my father. He'd been obsessed with the device for several weeks, creating what he called a supernatural app.

"From Mrs. G." Xela stuffed a spoonful into his mouth. Sauce dripped on his chin, and she wiped it away with her thumb, then pulled her hand away as if she'd been burned.

You are playing with fire, Xela.

As if she'd heard me, she took a step back and wiped her hand on her apron.

Xander dipped a piece of bread in the goulash, then popped it into his mouth. "I don't remember hers tasting this—"

Xela began to stir with haste, keeping her gaze on the bubbling pot.

"Better not say it's not good," Mira warned.

"It is good. It's just . . . different."

Xela stopped stirring abruptly, as if a memory had slammed into her. "I added a few more spices," she said, her lie easy for me to read on my face.

Unfortunately, so could William. He'd observed the exchange between Xela and Xander, and his temper flared. "Xander, step away from my wife," he growled.

All eyes focused on the couple by the stove. The electricity between them sizzled. I'd heard Willow's test tube smash to the floor in the lab and she peeked from behind the glass wall into the kitchen. No one moved.

My best friend took a step back, wary. He shivered as if trying to shake off overpowering thoughts. "I didn't do anything." His hands flew up in defense.

William bared his fangs, the way he did whenever Xander crossed the line of our friendship. He understood Xander and I had a connection no one could explain, but William had his limits as well. On more than one occasion, I had cleaned up the house after their rampage of testosterone. After a while, I made them clean up their own mess. Today, I found their tiff both amusing and frustrating. I understood William's pain and appreciated his trust, his understanding, and his forgiveness.

"It's not what you did," William said. "It's how you looked at her."

"Like how?" Xander said in confusion, obviously unaware of how he'd acted around Xela, whom to most people in the house was still me.

"He didn't do anything, William." Mira rushed to his side and pushed his shoulder to make him sit down. Her biceps flexed. My husband sat reluctantly. She pointed to her brother. "You. Outside. Now."

I left Mira to lecture about Xander crossing the line and stayed to see Xela handle William's jealousy.

"Willow, will you watch the children, please?" Xela wiped her hands on her jeans, the way I would have.

"Of course." Willow emptied the broken glass into the trash.

"You guys better stop wandering too much." Xela winked to the children. "Come with me." She took William's hand.

Confused, he obliged. I'd hush him with kisses and puppy eyes, but perhaps Xela didn't want William's affection. Maybe she'd keep her promise.

I followed Xela and William as she led him to our tree house. They climbed up the kapok tree toward the blooming canopy as I floated alongside the trunk, passing our orchids. The pollen was denser near the top, covering the branches in yellow dust that drifted from one limb to another with the push of a light breeze. The sun made for a perfect spring day.

Xela sat cross-legged across from William. She took his hands in hers and squeezed them. "You didn't recognize me."

What is she doing?

"I'm sorry," he repeated, the same way he had for the past four years.

"I know, but I need you to stop being sorry and be the William I met in my dreams."

How does she know about my dreams?

"I'm trying, but seeing you with Xander makes things awkward."

"*I'm* sorry. That part is my fault, and I mean it."

Is she talking about herself, or me? Was Xela trying to fix my life?

William rubbed his thumb on the fake ruby Xela wore. The doubt in his expression concerned me. He looked from the ring to her face, then back to the ring again, but he didn't say anything.

"I know I've asked you before, but you must trust what I'm doing. I can handle Xander."

"I'm afraid I can't. You're different around him. The way you look at him . . . I wish you'd stop going to the cave."

"All right. I'll stop." She paused. "I can't promise you things aren't going to be difficult for a few more days, but I can promise I'll do everything I can to make things right."

"You know something I don't." He narrowed his brows.

"I do."

"And you can't tell me."

"Not yet. You have to trust what's here." She pressed her palm to William's chest, atop his heart.

"If I trust what's in here," he placed his hand on top of hers, then took it away and pressed his palm on her heart, "then it tells me you're different."

I gasped.

"Then listen to your heart," Xela whispered. "I'm going to visit Mrs. G now. The children need you—"

"They need you, too."

Xela shook her head. "No, I've done everything in my power to prepare them, sacrificing things I shouldn't have." Her gaze flew my way. "They need the William I fell in love with to help them. You will face a great challenge soon. Show the children your fearlessness. It's the only way they'll succeed. They look up to you." She closed her eyes. "And you need to do it by tomorrow."

"You speak in riddles, as if you were a—"

"Sh, trust it." She tapped her chest, kissed him on the cheek, and left.

I remained in the tree house, hovering where she'd sat. The sky was clear, but the branches hadn't been trimmed in two weeks, making the sun difficult to see.

William lay down on the floor, head cradled in the arms crossed under his head. He took a deep breath, then exhaled. "If things are all okay, then why do I feel your presence more when you're gone?" he asked.

I smiled. *Trust your feelings. Trust your heart.*

I drifted away, thinking about a witch whom I no longer thought of as a black witch.

* * *

I followed Xela through the woods, the way she'd travel to Mrs. G's. With my eyes closed, I let my spirit be carried through time and space again. I caught up to her a few miles short of the hill. How in the world did she get here so fast? It'd take me two days, unless I used a vortex with Eric.

Xela leaned against a spruce while staring at the Grand Teton Mountains between the branches.

"These woods are important to you, aren't they?" I showed my ghost to the witch.

Startled, she jumped away from the tree. Then familiarity covered her face. "I met him here." Xela closed her eyes, smiling.

"He sat on the ledge, up there." She pointed to the mountains in an exhale. "And I wanted him to come down to be with me. I wanted him unlike anything. I used magic to sway him, though he said I didn't need to." She twirled her hand in a circle, the way I'd seen Mrs. G do when she summoned powers, but nothing happened. Xela examined her hand.

"You miss your magic." I hovered closer to the witch.

"The last time I used it was to send Xander away from me. I still regret that day." Xela put pressure against a branch and let it go. Pine needles sprinkled down to the forest floor.

"Xander never mentioned it." I drifted in front of her.

She crouched picking up the stray needles, and then let them fall. "Why would he? He thought I betrayed him."

"But you didn't. Don't you want to tell him?"

She sighed. "Yes, when the time is right."

"Thank you for what you did up there." I wanted to touch her arm but remembered I couldn't.

"My magic has been used against you. It's the least I could do."

"You're not a black witch. Your heart is pure." I followed her cautious steps. It seemed like Xela was enjoying a life she'd been denied.

"I don't have a choice of who I am, and I can assure you, my heart is not pure," she said.

Xela could argue, but I knew the truth: a good witch had been marked with the sphere as a curse. It wasn't right and didn't feel right. I wished I could do something to help. Was there a way to bend the evil away from a black witch?

"Xander fell in love with you here."

"Yes." She smiled. The innocence of our conversation was similar to one teenage best friends would have. "The moment I saw him . . . I'd give up my magic for him—if I could." Xela's words flowed from her, simmering with love as fresh as if she'd experienced the euphoria of meeting Xander yesterday. Her fingertips stroked the spruce boughs and sent a few more needles to the forest floor. "And I should have given it up. I should have given him everything."

"You didn't have a choice, though, did you?"

"No. I thought our marks would keep us apart . . ."

"You sacrificed your life for him."

Xela whipped her body around to face me. "How do you know?"

"I can see it in you. I know my face." I pointed to her. "I understand what you're feeling."

"He didn't know," she snapped. "I told him, and he didn't remember. He chose to forget I'd never hurt him. Not by choice."

"Men are like that sometimes. You think they know you, and they don't." I held Xela's gaze.

"I guess you do understand. It must have been difficult, what she did to you. More so when no one believed you."

She found a boulder to sit on as I hovered closer her side.

"The same way no one believed you," I said.

"We have more in common than I thought." She scanned my ghost's silhouette with her gaze, and for a moment, I thought she was lost in her memories of the past again.

"We do." I laughed. "We love men who don't recognize who we are."

Xela joined in with a chuckle.

In a different lifetime, I could have been friends with Xela, very good friends. I was sure if Mira met her, knew her the way I did, she'd like her too. To think we were once enemies . . . or I'd thought we were.

"So, you think we can fix this?" I looked through my transparent hands. "Because there's a problem. Miranda told me her body's been burned. She and Aseret captured my mother's spirit yesterday. I haven't had a chance to speak with Eric yet."

"I assume she didn't touch you?"

"No, my mother threw herself in front of me to save me. Why?"

"She'll be looking for you." She picked an over-blooming dandelion and blew a strong breath, then watched the little seed parachutes fly away until they disappeared. "Or she'll use your mother as bait."

"What will she do to her?"

"Use her essence for energy until it disappears."

"I need to leave," I said urgently.

"Not yet. The right time will come quickly." She caught a stray parachute in mid-air, then opened her palm and let it float away. "You'll see your mother very soon." Her actions reminded me of Mrs. G's: mysterious and nature-bound.

"Miranda doesn't know you're in my body. She thinks I'm dead."

"That helps, but Miranda's smart. She'll suspect I'm helping."

"So, we can still fix this?" I pointed to my spirit chest.

"I don't know. I need Hannah's help, and I'm not sure she'll help me." Xela bit her lip.

"Why? She loved me."

"Yes, when you were you. She'll detect magic on me. I've been in this realm long enough, and she's a strong witch." She bit the top of my thumb.

Some things never change.

The crunching of the forest's undergorwth drew my attention. "Sh, can you hear that?" My ghost vibrated.

Xela's vampire ears, my ears, perked up. She sniffed the air, then her eyes widened. "Hide," she whispered.

As soon as I took my invisible form, Xander appeared from behind a spruce. I hovered and watched him approach Xela as if he'd been stalking prey. "What are you doing here?" he asked her, keeping his distance.

Lie!

"I . . . I was just hunting."

"Here? In this exact spot?"

"Is it forbidden?" She rolled her eyes the way I would have.

Perfect. She's good! I felt like a proud mother.

"It's not. Couldn't you find a spot closer to home?" He approached with caution, careful of where he placed his feet, warily examining Xela from head to toe. I thought he'd taken a few extra whiffs to smell her, too.

"I was on my way to the hill," she said.

"Why?"

"I have questions for your ma."

Mrs. G! I yelled, but I knew she couldn't hear me.

Xander froze. Still thirty or so feet away, Xela took a step toward him. "Stay there!" He pointed at her.

"How did you get here so fast?" she asked.

"I had help . . . from a gem, you could say." He smirked.

"Xander, what's the matter with you?" Her tone was accusing, the way I would have sounded, but I sensed a vibration in her voice.

My friend placed his hand in his pocket and pulled it out, fisted. When he opened it, a white gem the size of a golf ball rested on his palm. The sun shone through it, reflecting a prism of colors.

Gasping, Xela covered her mouth.

"You recognize this, don't you?" Xander stood with his feet apart. His fingers twitched in the palm where the gem rested. I'd never seen him as focused as now, and for a moment, I thought his gaze would burn a hole in Xela. Whatever he had planned, there was no way Xander would leave without executing it.

What is it? I asked, unaware of a transfer between them.

"Don't," she whispered.

"Why?"

"Don't," she repeated, taking a step back.

Is it a weapon? The wind blew, making my spirit waver as the gust passed through me. The elements made it difficult to concentrate on the real world.

Xander took his time wrapping his fingers around the gem. I thought I saw Xela's chest rise as she tried to control the beating of her heart, my heart. As his palm closed, a smile flickered over his face; hope and apprehension roamed his cheeks. He squeezed the diamond and vanished—then reappeared in front of Xela.

"I knew it," he whispered, straining to contain the longing in his eyes. His muscles struggled to control their twitching.

"Xander—"

The hope changed to fury. He grabbed the back of her head and gripped her hair. "Where. Is. Sarah," he said through clenched teeth. The Xander I knew from Pinedale, my watcher, my protector, had taken over.

Xela did not fight. "She's fine."

"Liar!"

"Xander, stop. It's me," she pleaded through a tight throat.

Come on, Xander, trust her! I urged. At least one of us ought to be happy.

"You betrayed me."

"No." She shook her head in his grip. Tears streaked Xela's face, my face. "It wasn't me, Xander."

Xander's hatred faded. He pulled her head forward, pressing his lips against hers. She couldn't breathe. I couldn't breathe. His eyes were shut. His tense cheeks softened; the grip on Xela's head, my head, loosened. Their bodies melted together.

"Oh my God, it is you! My black witch." Xander held her head in his hands, staring at her face, my face, for a moment before picking her up and spinning in a circle, his head pressed to her chest. "How?"

"It's complicated." She laughed.

"The stone worked." Astonished, he observed the gem in his hand.

"I told you it would always bring you to me."

"And it has." He pressed his lips to hers again, then set Xela back down on the forest floor. "Wait, where is Sarah then?"

"She's here. With us. Don't freak out, Xander," she cautioned.

"Sarah?" His gaze skimmed the forest.

I floated behind him and became visible. "Boo!"

"Shit!" He jumped and whirled, then took a step back, looking from me . . . to me. His mouth hung open. "How?"

Xela dismissed his question with, "Why did you come here?"

"Let's just say I had a hunch." He smirked. "The minute I tasted that goulash, I knew it had to be you."

"So it was my food that stole your heart." Xela's body swooshed closer to Xander.

"I remember it differently." He grinned, eyeing her like he wanted to rip the clothes off her body.

"Too much information, guys," I interjected. "I can't plug my ears."

Xander looked back to me. "Are you really a ghost?" He pushed his hand through me.

"Are you blind?" I tried to wiggle out of his reach.

"Part of me wants to strangle you for being so stupid." He moved to the rock and sat down. "The other part wants to thank you, because I don't think I'd have her here without your meddling. You two have some explaining to do." He wiggled his finger between Xela and me.

Now my best friends and my evil bender knew my secret and William still didn't. I thought back to my previous conversation with Xela and my promise to keep our secret, but it didn't wash away the betrayal I felt inside.

"You can't tell William." she said to Xander.

His gaze flew to his witch.

"You just need to trust me on this one, Xander." Although I'd heard my own voice, when Xela spoke to him, it sounded like it came from a different individual instead of me.

"Is it weird seeing double?" I asked him.

"Hell, yeah! If you're here," he pointed to Xela, then to me, "and you're here, then who's in the cave?"

"Miranda." Xela replied.

A stronger gust of wind swept the forest floor. Needles lifted, pinning into Xela's hair.

"Miranda?" He shrugged, pulling Xela onto his lap. "Doesn't tell me much."

"She's the one who took my soul, the morning you were marked," Xela said. "I need to get to your mom to borrow her book."

Xander bellowed with laughter. "Good luck convincing her to work with you."

"She would with me, right?" I asked, hovering closer to the reunited couple.

"The problem, Sarah, is that she'll see right through me," Xela explained.

"You mean through me," I corrected.

"No, I mean she'll know I'm in your body the minute she sees me. You can't fool a witch twice."

"So what do we do?" I asked.

"Don't worry, I know how to handle Ma." Xander smirked, lifting Xela off his lap and gently setting her down. "Let's go."

CHAPTER 9

I hovered with Xander and Xela, who stood in front of the grassy mound dotted with shrubs that effectively concealed the siblings' home in the middle of the forest. Neither one dared to open the door, which looked like a deceivingly natural part of the hillside. The hill's interior was much larger than it appeared on the outside as well, thanks to Mrs. G's supernatural powers. Even when smoke rose from the top of the hill as Mrs. G, Xander and Mira's mom, brewed in her cauldron, no one would see it.

"Stand behind me." Xander stepped in front of Xela. "You, hide," he said to me before taking a deep breath.

"Mrs. G won't hurt me." I stepped closer.

"Yes, but we don't want her to have a heart attack. Disappear," he ordered.

"Fine, but I don't think you know your mother well," I grumbled as I assumed my invisible form.

Before Xander pressed his hand against the trunk to open the secret door, the outline of a doorframe materialized in the hill, pushing grass and earth forward, then aside. The ground shook.

Mrs. G stepped out through the oval doorway, her left hand on her hip. The water mark on her wrist shone through several dangling bracelets. I'd never seen it this bright. She'd braided her hair across the top of her forehead, the twines dark against her pale skin. Her right hand clutched a dagger with a red gem embedded in the pommel, and silver thread wrapped up the grip. Miranda owned a similar blade when she stole my body; she'd used it to cut her chest to free her soul.

"Blood, witch." Mrs. G eyed Xela from toes to head through her glasses. "You will not come in, otherwise."

"You know?" Xander asked.

"Shouldn't I? Fool me once, shame on me; fool me twice— not possible," she said calmly, her sweet voice at odds with her unyielding stance.

I wanted to stand in front of Xander to tell him, "I told you so," but he wouldn't hear me so I remained hovering behind them. Mrs. G's gaze skidded over Xander's shoulder for a moment, and I thought she saw me.

Xela held out her hand. Mrs. G slit her palm, leaving a red line behind the point of the blade. Then she cut her own palm open. They pressed their hands together, mingling their blood.

"The promise of peace is sealed," Xela said in answer to Xander's questioning eyes. She pulled her hand away from Mrs. G's and watched the slit heal into the thin white line of a scar. "That's the coolest thing I've seen," she hushed toward Xander.

"But the blood is not yours," he whispered to Xela, narrowing his brow.

"It doens't matter. Come on in," Mrs. G answered before Xela could.

I followed my friends inside. Mrs. G's floor-length skirt danced with her steps to the tune of a song she hummed under her breath. She placed the dagger on a table beside her magic book and moved the cup of herbal tea that had rested beside it to the mantle. The embers in the hearth spat and hissed when the mixture bubbling above them overflowed.

The fresh pepper and rosemary aroma I remembered from the siblings' home probably filled the room, but I couldn't smell anything; I tried. For the second time in two days, I missed being corporeal. I floated through the room, avoiding the cloths, herbs, and dried flowers that hung from the protruding roots above as if they'd bounce off my head. It just seemed wrong to float through everything in my way.

"Nice lair, Hannah," Xela commented, pulling her fingers along the tops of the chairs, drawing the tip of her toe along the earthen floor close the hearth.

"I prefer to think of it as home," Mrs. G replied, her tone mildly rebuking.

Xela looked at her. "It's been a long time since I've been here."

"You've been here?" Xander asked.

"Decades ago." Xela touched a bundle of herbs dangling from the ceiling. "Not much has changed."

"No need to." Mrs. G sat down on the wooden stool in front of the fireplace, resting her elbows on her knees while nudging the embers into flames with a poker. "I hear Miranda has fooled us both. Is that why you're here?"

"I hoped we could work together again. Help me right what's been wronged."

"Last time did not turn out as planned, did it?" Xander's mom lowered the spectacles on her nose.

"Yes, you got blamed for our share of magic, but I had no choice." Xela's arms remained rigid at her sides, and her jaw tightened.

"You never do, do you?"

Xela's eyes fell to the floor. Shame covered her face. "It was a different time and a different me. Before I met Xander." Xela took his hand and squeezed it. "He changed me."

I imagined she understood sacrifice better than most people.

"I see." Mrs. G inspected the couple, and I wondered if it looked odd to her that Xander held my hand, but it didn't seem to bother her at all. "And I gather you have a plan?"

"I do." Xela looked toward the leather book on the table, embossed with a water mark symbol set between three gems: red, white, and blue. An aura wrapped the cover like a shield, casting a glamour that made the book seem insignificant, but if magic gems had taught me anything, I knew Mrs. G's spell book must be powerful.

Mrs. G didn't move for a minute, typical of her habit of drawing out her actions. Then she pushed up her other sleeve, eyes on the tome of spells. "I guess it's time the book returned to its original form." She sighed, turned, and threw another log into the fire. The flames rose, dancing higher, as if they too understood what Mrs. G and Xela were talking about.

"It is time." Xela moved to the wicker chair suspended from the ceiling's roots by a weaving of ropes and settled in it, the stiffness gone from her body. "Someone will need to find the other books, so the spells can transfer freely between those worthy."

"Yes, someone will." Mrs. G's face seemed to suggest she knew the perfect culprit for the job, but she changed her expression too quickly for me to deduce who it was. In that single moment, I felt her gaze rest on my ghost.

"You afraid to show yourself, Sarah?" Mrs. G looked right through me.

My ghost floated to the side before I showed myself, remembering Xander's warning about a heart attack, although I doubted it was possible to scare Mrs. G with anything. Somehow, this powerful witch knew things before anyone else did. As far as I knew, no one has ever surprised her. "Not afraid, but someone told me to hide."

Xander shrugged as I gave him a pointed I-told-you-so look.

"And how do you like being a ghost?" Her tone was still casual, but I detected an undercurrent of fear I hadn't heard before.

"Takes some getting used to. I don't know exactly what I'm supposed to do," I replied.

"She does." Mrs. G pointed to Xela. "Don't quarrel with me now, Xander. There's no time for that." She raised her hand. "And don't say you weren't going to, either."

Xander slouched again, retreating to a corner couch. He knew better than to argue a witch's prediction.

Xela laughed. "Gosh, it's so good to see a witch at her best."

"You're a pretty good witch as well." Mrs. G relaxed and pushed the spectacles on her nose to their usual position.

"I haven't practiced in decades. That's why I need your help."

"I take it there's a reason you're in Sarah's body?" Mrs. G asked.

Xela nodded. "It's the only way to trick Miranda, make sure she stays where she's sent this time." She paused for a beat. "We need three witches."

"Don't really know a third witch who could handle the task."

Mrs. G and Xela communicated in a secret language I could neither hear nor understand. It was as if they could read each other's thoughts, and plan without planning. Perhaps they communicated the same way I did with Eric and the twins.

"She'll be after Sarah's essence, thinking she's dead," Xela said. "She's seen her ghost and imprisoned her mother's. She and Aseret have plans to kidnap the children. "

"I think I know someone strong with a witch's blood." Mrs. G focused on the cut on her hand before adding, "We should assume Miranda knows where you are, Xela. If she has Sarah's mother, they could extract the information from her."

I cringed, imagining Aseret and the witch Miranda using Egyptian utensils on my mother's ghost, the way the ancient embalmers removed the brain through the nose, though a witch's tool would probably involve magic lights probing through my mother's soul.

"Information, Sarah, information," Mrs. G answered before I got a chance to ask.

"You're right. I guess I've been out of touch too long," Xela agreed. "She'll expect us to plan her demise."

Xander stared at his mother and Xela, turning his head from one to the other as they spoke. I think he was still stunned they weren't ripping each other's throat out.

"And the twins are ready?" Mrs. G asked.

"Yes, but I need to refresh the spells, if I may." Xela looked at the magic book.

"It will take you weeks to read that thing," Xander pointed out.

Curiosity pulled me toward the table where I'd seen Mrs. G, even Eric, flip through the pages many times. The thickness of the book never translated itself, for me at least, to the amount of information it held. *I* wouldn't know what to do, but then, I wasn't a witch. The book was eerily similar to the one I'd seen in Miranda's lair in the underworld.

Mrs. G strolled over to the table. Xela followed, eyes sparkling. Side by side, the witches concentrated, breathing in and out at the same time.

"Ma, I know I trust her, but you . . . I thought black witches were your worst enemies," Xander interrupted.

"They are, but not this black witch. I've already seen her future. If she knows what's good for her," she eyed Xander, "she'll do the right thing."

Mrs. G and Xela held each other's gaze, drew a deep breath, then exhaling, each put her left hand on the book of spells. They closed their eyes, chanting a spell that unified into a hum as the foreign words flowed in streams of light toward the spelled papers. The leather binding glowed, transferring another beam of light toward their chests, that continued for another three of their deep breaths. The witches' bodies rocked back and forth, heads swaying in circles on their necks. The chant rhymed every thirteen syllables, reminding me of a poem. Though I didn't understand it, I sensed the mantra was meant to unify.

When the humming stopped, the room was silent; even the fire didn't make a sound nor the simmering liquid above it. Then, the leaves outside rustled, and sound returned to the hill.

"Ah . . ." Xela exhaled. "That's better." She lifted her hand, eyes sparkling with her newfound knowledge. The hairs on her arms stood straight out as her body—my body—adjusted to the magic it had absorbed.

"You're sure you can contain it, after so many years?" Mrs. G said as she motioned Xela back to the wicker chair.

Xela took Xander's arm, leaning on him instead. "I feel as if it never left me." She twirled her finger, and an arrangement of red roses in bloom hugged the rim of the magic book. Their heady aroma flowed toward everyone's noses in the form of pink mist. "Thank you."

Mrs. G nodded. She suppressed a smile, but her eyes and the vibrant pulse under her skin belied her composed face. "You have everything you need?"

"I do."

"You hurt my son again, and you will deal with me, Xela." Mrs. G's spectacles slid lower on her nose.

"I will never hurt him again. I promise."

"Ma, I can take care of myself," Xander protested.

"I know you can, but this time, I'd like to protect you as well. I've seen you without Xela." Mrs. G sat back down by the fireplace. "And you're much better with her at your side."

"Thank you, Ma." Xander bent to embrace his mother. He reminded me of a little kid who'd just received a new toy. I understood that Mrs. G's acceptance validated Xander's past choices and justified the pain he'd suffered. Now, his heart thumped as if reborn.

"I gather you have a plan to return Sarah's body to her," Mrs. G said, throwing a fistful of herbs into the concoction above the fire. The simmering eased, and the liquid devoured the new ingredient, then began to boil again.

"Yes, but the plan is not foolproof." Xela stepped closer to peek into the mixture.

I leaned in, waiting for the steam to spill over and reveal the prediction Mrs. G sought.

"No plan is, is it?" Mrs. G laughed.

Their conversation didn't seem funny to me. *I* wanted my body returned. And whatever Xela's plan was, it'd better work, especially since Miranda had no host body to go back to. My ghost vibrated. The way they spoke in riddles baffled and frustrated me, and instead of chills climbing up my spine, waves of energy passed through my spirit like an unseen nuclear toxin.

"What do I do?" Xander asked.

"What you always do: be a shapeshifter. Your part of the prophecy is done. It's time for us witches to step in. *You* need to follow your instinct now." Xela touched his chest.

He took a deep breath, as if all his questions had been cleared.

"Allow me to read before you leave." Although Mrs. G phrased it as a request, I knew no one would refuse.

"Of course." Xela bowed her head. I'd never thought of Mrs. G's readings as an honor.

Xela plucked a hair from her head—my head—and gave it to Mrs. G, who let it fall into the pot of liquid. Xander eagerly scooted to the hearth. Mrs. G squatted and threw a fistful of dirt into the steaming cauldron. The pot's bubbles surged, hungry for more. Mrs. G reached above the mantle. Xela passed her a jar containing dried ingredients that looked like frog legs. The next jar held moth's wings. Mrs. G crumbled the pieces in her palms above the cauldron, letting the dust fall into the mixture, then adding a pinch of ash from a can.

Leaning forward, the witches blew the rising steam over the rim. Mrs. G held her hand above the pot and squeezed her palm, breaking open the freshly slit palm. Drops of blood joined the now furiously boiling brew. More steam escaped, then the mixture calmed.

"Hmm . . . " Mrs. G hummed.

"What is it?" I floated closer to see the surface of the cauldron. The liquid swished back and forth in waves. The concoction didn't reveal anything to me, other than being a broth. Xela stepped forward as well.

"Your journey home is safe, but . . ."

"What's the matter, Ma?" Xander edged in behind Xela. "What do you see?"

"The children are there, but I cannot see them."

"Why not?" Xela examined the pot.

"William . . . he's gone as well."

"Gone where?" I asked.

"He will not return home for a while." She looked at me. "The children are there, but they're not," she repeated.

Xela locked her gaze with Mrs. G. "They're only there in their body, not in spirit."

"Where are they?" I asked, knowing they could leave their bodies anytime, whether to visit the keepers, or Eric. The twins usually told me of their whereabouts ahead of time, but I guessed that would be difficult now. My ghost vibrated. "Where would William go?"

"They've embraced their destiny." Xela turned toward me. "They're ready."

"What does it mean?" My gaze flew from Mrs. G to Xela and then back again, waiting for an answer.

"It means we have to hurry," Xela replied.

Mrs. G frowned up at me. "Your fate is still unknown. Aseret and Miranda will not be the ones to decide it."

"I will decide my fate." I lifted my chin, but my ghostly form trembled. "Something is wrong." My voice shook.

Xela's and Mrs. G's eyes darted to the door. Xander growled, then shifted from one animal to another within seconds before settling on his own form. His face took on a green cast.

A tremor shook the hill as something banged against the earth covering Mrs. G's home. The wind howled as if a tornado had touched down on top of us. A loud cackle vibrated around the walls. Dirt crumbled to the floor.

"Impossible." Mrs. G tilted her head back. "She cannot enter here."

Yet she did. Miranda's laughing ghost floated above our heads, near the ceiling.

Mrs. G remained calm. Her eyes turned black, as if the eyeballs were filled with tar. Xela took Mrs. G's hand, and her eyes filled with blackness as well.

Miranda focused on me, mouthing words I couldn't understand, but the words didn't matter. Bright light crushed into my spirit. I'd been cursed.

Xander pushed the front door open. He screamed at me. Though I couldn't hear him over the howling and Miranda's laughter, I obeyed his frantic gestures and rushed through the doorway and into the forest without looking back. The greens of passing branches and underbrush blended into a blur as I thought about our cabin in the Amazon and departed.

* * *

The front door was ajar, and I flew through the hall into the solarium. The blinds were shut, shading the cabin, though light filtered between a few broken slats. The children sat cross-legged on the floor beside Eric, all three juggling blue spheres of light in their palms. The darkness helped their concentration when they worked with the globes of cold fire.

They're here. I heaved and exhaled an invisible breath, more out of habit than practical relief.

Of course they're here. What's the matter? Eric shut his palm, extinguishing the sphere hovering above it.

Everybody else out? I asked.

Yes, orchid harvest.

I showed my ghost and knelt beside the kids. "You're all right?"

"Yes, Mama," Crystal said as she and Ayer balanced the spheres in their hands.

"I'd been told you're not here."

They laughed. Crystal blew on the spheres, shattering them into dust motes, and placed her palm on my ghostly shoulder. I could almost sense her touch on my ghostly skin. Warmth flowed from her hand to me, calming my trembling. "Don't believe everything you hear and see, Mama." The lisp had vanished from Crystal's voice. She spoke like a young teen.

"Mama, you need not worry about us. For us, the realms are connected. We travel between them at will." Ayer smiled.

My concern faded, as if he'd placed his own magic spell upon me.

"You've been cursed," he said, closing his eyes.

I nodded and lowered my ghosts form closer to the ground.

"Who?" The spikes around Eric's neck extended. They vibrated like they were the tongues of a cobra tasting the air.

"Miranda. She also has my mother, knows about Xela, and entered Mrs. G's home." I tried to squeeze as much as I could into one breath.

"The witch is intruding." He stood.

"Of course she is! She's a witch! Didn't you expect that?"

Eric's hands flew up into the air. "Sarah, even witches have to abide by some rules."

Crystal and Ayer seemed oblivious to our discussion, staring into each other's eyes like they were having their own conversation.

"Since when?" I threw my hands up. "Every time we deal with the sphere-marked ones, they don't follow any rules."

Eric lowered his head. "Did you follow the rules when you decided to give up your body?"

"I had no choice." I didn't look at my children, who were responsible for my decision. Did they know something Eric didn't? If there was anyone I'd ever trusted, my children were at the top of the list.

Eric's head swung toward the door. "They're coming back. You should—"

My spirit disappeared before Eric finished, my ghostly form slouching in a chair. The cushioned seating felt oddly comfortable and my silhouette didn't fall through as it usually would.

William stepped through the door, a woven basket strapped across his back. I imagined the aroma flowing from the fresh orchids, a sweet blend that used to intoxicate me when I inhaled. The worry for my husband faded when I saw him. There was nothing more I wanted than to rush into his arms and confess the mess we were in.

Mrs. G's prediction resonated in my mind: *William's gone too*. Yet he was here, in the flesh.

The children ran to him, shouting, "Hello, Father!" They flattened themselves against his legs, as if they sensed he'd be leaving.

"Father?" He looked down at them. "Your mother's right. You guys are growing up too quickly." My husband tousled their hair before placing his harvest on the marble floor. The basket's straps left red marks imprinted on his shoulders on either side of his tank top. William unlocked the glass door to the lab as Ekim and Atram carried their harvests into the room.

Crystal picked an orchid from her father's basket, its yellow petals shining in her hand. "This one's potent." She handed the flower to Willow.

"I may need to hire you, darling." My mother-in-law kissed Crystal's forehead.

Crystal smiled. "After we get rid of Aseret."

"It's all right," Eric said, calming the alarm on my family's faces. "Their training is progressing well. It won't be long before it's time."

"Time?" William asked.

"Nothing to worry about yet, my friend, but yes, it will happen soon."

The children sat down and resumed their balancing lesson. No one ever asked why Crystal and Ayer decided to train in their leisure time, for we knew they controlled their own destiny.

William's eyes wandered to the chair where I sat. "Is Sarah here?" he asked.

"No, she's still at Mrs. G's," Eric answered.

William's gaze fell. He put his hands in his pockets, fiddling. No one else but I would detect the hidden frown. William knew something the others didn't. His eyes glossed over, and head low, he bit his lip.

"I can go check on her if you'd like," Eric offered.

"No, I'm sure she's fine." William looked in my direction again, though he couldn't see me. "Xander's probably with her." He pulled a bandana from around his neck and used it to wipe the sweat off his forehead.

At that moment, Xela and Xander rushed through the front door, laughing.

Xander held Xela's hand, their fingers intertwined, lost in a conversation about magic she'd like to use on his body. They stared at each other, oblivious to anyone around them—love-struck.

I rose from the chair. *What the hell?*

Someone growled a threat.

CHAPTER 10

Xela's gaze flew to William, who braced his body against the doorframe. She released Xander's hand as if she'd been burned. My husband's face flushed for less than a second. She took the matching bandanna off her head—my bandanna.

I remembered the earlier growl and struggled to figure out where it had come from. I'd never heard William release such a fierce sound, though it did come from his direction. Now, his casual posture added to the mystery.

"Hi!" Xela smiled with my smile. It faded as her gaze fell to his hand. I hadn't noticed when William took the ring out of his pocket.

No! It's a trick! I tried to show myself to warn her, but something prevented my ghost's transformation, as if someone blocked me.

"What's this?" William displayed my ruby on his forefinger.

I looked at the fake one on Xela's hand.

"Where did you get that?" she asked, taking an involuntary step back.

"Crystal's jewel box fell off the night table. Put it on." He took a step closer.

"No." She shook her head.

"Why not?"

"Because it's a fake. I have my ring on. I know who I am."

"I'm not sure I do." He narrowed his brows, looking from Xander to Xela. "If it's a fake, then you have nothing to worry about, do you?"

"Look, William . . ."

"I've had enough of this! Who the hell are you? Where is my wife?" He dashed across the room until he was tightening his fingers around Xela's throat.

He knew! He'd finally figured out it wasn't me.

She pushed him off.

Xander moved in front of his witch, face tinted green. "Do not touch her again." His forehead furrowed, and his upper lip quivered.

Willow peeked from within the lab. "Let them settle this," she whispered to Ekim and Atram.

"Why in the world do you people keep choking me?" Xela backed up, rubbing her throat.

"Where. Is. Sarah!" William bared his fangs, taking a calculated step forward with each word.

"Sarah?" Warily scanning the cabin, Xela paced backward, until her back pressed against the wall. She held her palms flat against the wall, like she was ready to run.

Our fathers and Willow braved to emerge out of the lab, obviously drawn by the commotion. Xander began shifting, first into a wolf, then a vampire, then a bear and last, a combination of all mammals.

William didn't hesitate. "You don't scare me, shifter."

Xander continued the shifting until he settled on a vampire's form—a worthy opponent for William.

"Sarah?" Xela called out again, her voice shaking. "They're going to kill each other."

I wasn't sure I should show. Would William be mad? Of course he would, but at least he'd know the truth. Didn't I owe him that much?

I should have never kept this from William. I thought she said I couldn't show myself to him, I said to Eric.

The children continued their training, lost in their spheres as if nothing had happened. I noticed a grin on Ayer's face and knew his share of power played a role in the commotion.

Your choice. Eric smiled grimly. *But Xander is strong and a lot has happened since Xela told you to stay put.*

Believe me, I know. But you underestimate my husband's fierce nature.

A blue light appeared under Xander's feet. His gaze flew to Eric. "Take it off!" he growled.

"Don't look at me, I didn't do it." Eric put his hands up, grinning.

William smirked at our kids and proceeded toward Xela.

"You touch her and I will kill you!" Xander warned.

William passed just beyond his reach. My father and Atram's shoulder's tensed.

The same light appeared under Willow, Ekim, and Atram when they tried to interfere.

"She's fine, William. Sarah's fine. She knows about this," Xela said. I was as fast as William, but Xela didn't know him the way I did. He'd read her face, know where she'd want to go before she took a step. Though she had my abilities, she didn't know how to use them, the same way I hadn't before I met William.

"What exactly does she know about?"

Three steps and William's grip would find its way back to Xela's throat. I had no choice; I had to help her even though it meant he'd know I'd betrayed his trust and given up my soul without telling him. It wouldn't matter that I'd had no choice when it happened.

Our plan to exclude William so he could help the children and not be distracted was ruined. It was a wrong plan in the first place. The more I thought about it, the more it bothered me that I hadn't been honest with him. Miranda fooled us all when she stole my body, and I couldn't hold a grudge any longer. All I wanted was to be with William, always. And now, we lived our lives further apart than I could have ever imagined.

I couldn't leave Xela, either. Between William's strength and with her unfamiliarity with my supernatural abilities, she had no chance.

"Sarah. Now would be a good time—"

William grabbed her throat and squeezed. If I let him, he'd kill her. He'd kill the body we needed to get me back into.

Come on! Fight him off! I yelled.

Xander growled and howled, reaching toward William, his hands swiping empty air. My family, frozen in the blue light, stared helplessly.

Somehow, my father didn't panic; he kept looking from me to Xela, though I was sure he couldn't see me.

She tried using my vampire strength to shake William off, but his determination won out. He would not let go. I knew he wasn't killing me; so did he. Xela's pale skin turned gray. Her pupils disappeared as her eyes rolled back.

Let her go, William, you have to let her go! I tried again, but he couldn't hear me. *Shit! Eric? What do I do?*

I can't get involved in this one, he said. *I need to leave. Your mother is in distress.* With that he disappeared into a vortex.

Xela's hands flopped limply to her sides.

I finally showed my ghost. "William, stop!"

He eased his grip. Xela coughed and dropped to crouch on the floor. "It's true," he whispered.

"What in the world . . . ?" Willow plopped into the wicker chair as the blue glow disappeared from under her, Ekim, and Atram.

"Sarah?" My father stared at my ghost, perplexed.

"Yes, it's me." I shrugged, looking at William, who stood frozen.

"How? Why?" My father collapsed to the floor and braced himself up on his arms.

The blue light faded from under Xander's feet as well; he ran to help Xela up.

"It was the only way to get rid of Aseret," I explained.

"By giving up your body without telling me?"

"I had no choice. I made a mistake. I'm sorry."

"We always have a choice, Sarah." The sadness I saw in his eyes devastated my spirit. I wanted to cry, but my ghost wasn't capable of shedding tears.

By this time, Crystal and Ayer had taken up their nap positions at the end of the wicker sofa in the sun room, drained. Their eyes closed, and the twins fell asleep.

William composed himself and shook off the confusion as if he were trying to get rid of a nightmare. Pain covered his face. My heart broke when I read William's expression, recognizing his sorrow in the curves of his cheeks and his hollow eyes. That was what I must have looked like when I lived back in Pinedale, before I accepted myself, before I knew my true purpose; when I was waiting for William to come for me, and he did. He saved me from a life of loneliness and misery. He taught me how to love and fight for those I cared about.

How come I couldn't see it before? William had fought for me since the day we'd met, trying to reach me at a depth only he knew, but I'd been too selfish, trying to deal with my problems, instead of *our* problems. All he'd asked for was honesty, and I'd failed him. I betrayed our trust and the promise that we could work together instead of separately. We were much better as two equals, rather than two halves.

"Watch the children," he said to his parents and my father.

"William, wait!" I cried as he stormed out.

My father and Atram sat down by the twins. I read my father's frustration on his face. I'd lied not only to William, but my entire family.

"Sarah, what's going on?" he asked.

"Are you disappointed?" My ghostly figure trembled.

My father rose and stepped forward. "Surprised, yes. Disappointed, no." He shook his head. "I do wish I could hug you."

"I'm sorry I didn't tell you, but I had no time and can't explain now. You need to guard the children. I have to get

William." The door still swung open after my husband had pushed it.

"Honey, give him some time. Please." Willow's eyes begged me to stay.

I pointed to the witch in my body. "Xela will get you caught up. You can trust her."

"Trust Xela?" My father's head swung from me to the witch. "No time to tell us you switched bodies? Whose body do you have?"

"I . . . I don't have a body."

"What?" My father pointed to me. "What maddness has driven you to do this? I can't lose you. Not again." The sorrow in his voice pained me.

"I need to find William." I floated toward Willow, but my ghost began to drop closer to the floor, as if weighted. "Willow, I should have told you."

"No." She shook her head. "You're a smart woman, and you did what you needed to do. Don't doubt your choices."

"But I deceived you."

"You protected us. It's time you begin thinking about yourself first. Go, find your husband."

I concentrated on the outside trying to pinpoint where my husband had gone.

"Hold on, Sarah." My father tried to grab my wrist but failed. "Where are you going? He may be far away by now."

"I'll find him. Please, guard them." I nodded toward my children.

"Find yourself as well." He eyed me from top to bottom. Yes, my father knew how to find humor in grave times. "The anger you hold onto will destroy you if you don't," he warned.

"I will fix it. I promise."

He leaned forward to give my cheek a peck, and I thought I'd felt the cool warmth of his lips.

I tried to leave through the wall and instead bumped into it. Stunned, I used the front door to let my ghost exit.

"Going somewhere?"

On the other side of the clearing, the warden leaned against the trunk of the fallen tree. With his black hooded cloak covering his head, the grumpy man reminded me of a demon. The hump in his back was gone, but the tick in his left eye was as disturbing as when I'd first met him. Gold embroidery on his garment reflected the sunlight that slipped under the late afternoon clouds hanging above the treetops. The cover on his head fell to his nose, concealing his eyes under a shadow.

I tried to make my ghost disappear as I moved toward the left end of the clearing.

The demon tracked my movements. "Not so easy to hide when you cannot disappear." He laughed.

I recognized the cackling, but not as the warden's. It belonged to someone I dreaded seeing and wondered how he'd found us. Was it him?

"Having trouble in this shape?" he asked as if he'd known I couldn't disappear or float through tangible objects. "The witch still has her touch, even without a body." He yelped wildly, slurping saliva between the words and laughter.

Miranda. She cursed me to stay visible in the moment I chose to be so.

"Why are you here?" I asked as I considered how to overcome my predicament. My ghost couldn't disappear nor float through objects. He'd follow me if I ran, but running wasn't my priority; my unguarded family was.

"You got rid of my top two trainers, sending their souls to be refurbished, but you cannot get rid of me."

The freezer and the mover from the prison's parking lot.

"That's right. I know what happened, and your little ones will pay for it." Now, the laugh reminded me of the warden's, but it's yelping belonged to someone else.

"You will not touch my children." The threat vibrated in my vocal chords.

"Ah, but I already have." He cackled from the back of his throat.

The sound sent chills down my back, something I found odd as a ghost without a body. The familiarity of this demon was striking nerves in my spirit. The warden's odd personality transformed each time he spoke.

I floated to the side of the clearing, just beyond where Ayer had blown up the tree, drawing the demon's gaze away from the cabin. He followed with a step to the side. The way he carried his weight didn't remind me of the warden's wobble, but of someone floating above the ground.

"Liar!" I shouted, then thought, *Eric! I need you!*

"Ah, silly Sarah. It's difficult to recognize me in this body, isn't it?" my foe hissed in a slow drawl, pausing between each word as if to draw breath. "Yesss, I can see why. Silly Sarah. Silly half-breed."

If I could, I'd have had a difficult time swallowing the lump that had formed in my tight throat. *Aseret,* I thought. *In the warden's body.* My ghost trembled.

"That'sss right. I'm sssomeone you should fear. Your mother's esssence is quite potent. Yours shall be, too."

I took another step to the side, but the warlock mirrored my move.

"Ah-ah-ah, not thisss time," he said in mocking disapproval.

If I could get him to follow me, at least I'd take him away from the children and my family; I was certain they'd been listening intently to our conversation.

"You stole the warden's body," I accused, hoping Eric would show up soon. I knew Xander wouldn't leave the children, so unless my evil-bender heard me, I was on my own. Mira was probably helping Eric. And what had happened to William? He must have left before Aseret showed up—I hoped.

"No losss compared to what you've lossst." He smirked at my ghostly figure. "You should have joined me when you had a chance."

"To hell with you."

"Ah, and soon it shall be with you, too."

"How did you find me?" I asked to buy time.

"You've gotten sssloppy, sssilly creature. GPSss tracking is younger than our kind, but much more effective than traced magic."

I remembered the electronic thank you card Willow found in last week's mail package. *He tracked a shipment from one of the plants.*

"That'sss right. Not as bright as you thought you were. It won't be long before you have no thoughtsss at all."

The wind swayed the tops of the trees. I wondered why Aseret hid within the warden's body. He hadn't attacked or used magic to strike at me. Did he still fear me that much? Why? Would he have been careless enough to leave his body in the underworld? Was his body stuck there?

I pointed at my translucent chest. "You cannot use this body."

"No, but it won't stop me from getting the children, will it?" He stepped closer to the cabin.

"Ha!" I mocked, straining to not seem protective.

The warlock took another stride toward my home, but I remained in the same spot. What could I, as a ghost, do anyway?

Aseret resumed his original spot across from me. I moved away from the cabin again. He mimicked my motion. "I will get both you and your children."

"If you're such a powerful warlock, then why don't you listen for their heartbeats? They're not here." I smirked.

Aseret's gaze flew to the house, then back to me. He gritted his jaw in frustration.

It worked, I gloated. Either he didn't have his powers and couldn't sense the kids, so he believed me, or he didn't hear their heartbeats because my children had left this realm.

"Hmm." He cocked his head to the right and levitated toward me. The wind whistled between crevices and nooks in the forest, picking up stray blades of grass as it crossed the clearing; William had cut it yesterday.

William. Where are you? I prayed he was safe but feared Aseret had him. The warlock hadn't mentioned my husband.

As Aseret approached, I wondered whether he would strike me with a hot stream of fire. His palms twitched, but I held my ground, though my translucent legs wanted to run.

"You can't get me." I laughed, squeezing confidence into a voice that had betrayed me earlier.

"That'sss what you think. You will not get away, sssillly creature." He threw his head back and laughed, and the hood slid off his bald pate. When he lowered his head again, Aseret's eyes glowed orange, so bright that their sheen seemed to pierce my retinas, and I felt my soul being pulled toward him. He reached out, his palm stretched forward, dragging my spirit inexorably forward. I tried to remain still but the energy jerked me across the lawn, closer to the warlock.

"You sure you want me to get close?" I warned, feigning bravery I didn't feel, hoping Aseret would believe the bluff.

The pull eased, and he wiggled his nose, then smirked and yanked again, yelping laughter. "You are powerless!"

The wind picked up in the clearing, filling the air with a lilac-scented purple mist. Hope sparked in my invisible heart as a swirling vortex opened to my left, lifting the stray grass clippings into a miniature whirlwind. The demon's face fell.

"She may be, but I'm not," Eric declared as he stepped from the vortex and moved up beside me. He braced his feet and thrust his hands out, palms facing forward.

Took you long enough, I complained in my mind.

Sorry, things are getting out of hand. The fleshy spikes on Eric's neck fanned out above his turtleneck. The dark hollows under his eyes and the sweat stains on his clothes meant an underworld creature had kept him busy.

Really? I hadn't noticed.

I'll explain later, Eric replied. *Let's send him back to the underworld first.*

"You're meddling in my businesss, evil-bender," Aseret hissed, planting his feet solid on the ground. His hands twitched. The warlocks eagerness to hurl electricity our way stretched across his face, but he couldn't harness any power.

"You keep forgetting *you* are my business, demon!"

"You can't fix what'sss been done."

"That's what you think." The spikes vibrated on Eric's neck.

Aseret's face grew taut, then distorted, fighting an unseen force I knew came from my friend's body as he began bending the warlock. "You will not ruin me this time."

"We'll see about that." Eric jerked his head sideways, letting the spikes extend. I hadn't seen them protruding this far in all the years I'd known him. The color faded from his face, and his eyes went blank as he dropped into a trance. At the edge of the jungle, an orange-rimmed portal opened, within waited the underworld.

Eric forced his palms forward, streaming cold fire into the center of the warden's chest. The warden's body shook and convulsed as Aseret's soul strained to remain inside it. Then the body thumped to the grass as Aseret's soul fled its host to uncoil as a ghostly figure beside it. Even in this form, the warlock's wrinkly, scarred face sent waves of fear through me.

Aseret rushed at me, grabbed my hollow torso, and hauled my form with him toward the opened vortex. Heat pulsed in waves from the portal and somehow I could feel it waft through my soul. Eric struggled to separate us, new power circling his body in blue and purple streams, sparkling outward like fireworks. My evil-bender strained to save me, yet when I read his face, I knew my destiny wasn't to be rescued. Aseret's grip tightened as we neared the outer rim of the vortex.

Eric's face was nearly white, drained from the bending, and he dropped to his knees, apologizing with his eyes. The pull into the underworld intensified. Underworld's heat and the stench of spoiled eggs wrapped my soul, sucking me in. A cackling laugh vibrated against my eardrums, as Aseret dragged me back to hell.

CHAPTER 11

My ghostly insides twisted—or perhaps the memory of the spin had tangled them. The nausea stopped when the vortex closed. The scent of honey and lemon flew through me and I looked for my children, but they weren't here.

My spirit uncoiled in the underworld. The instinct to run passed when I couldn't sense anyone else near me. My ghost whirled around, inhaling air I didn't need. Then I crouched, my invisible heart pounding, as I scanned the dim room and the tunnel beyond for Aseret's ghost. The hum of hot air and lava that flowed under the rock filtered through the corridor I found myself in. The rock wall beside me glistened with moisture; I reached out to touch it, surprised I could. The humidity in this oven-like heat was like magic; all moisture should have evaporated. My palm, instead of falling through the rock, flattened against it. Miranda's curse held; I couldn't pass through. I shut my eyes, straining to be invisible, but that didn't work either. Floating forward, I ventured further into the passageway, then pressed my back against its wall, wary of who I might encounter.

The path seemed clear for the moment. I drifted down it, turning every few feet to ensure no one followed me. Sounds drifted from the maze of corridors, and I perked my ears, intent on hearing everything and identifying what creatures or features might be making the noises. The splashing of a geyser above echoed through the hot air of the maze. I took a whiff and tasted the tart acidity of sulphur on my tongue.

How is this possible? I thought, swishing the insides of my mouth with saliva and spitting to clear the unpleasant taste. Then I stared at the spittle as it was absorbed into the dust on the floor. *Should a ghost smell or produce spit?*

Even my floating wasn't as high as it could be. I tried to rise higher to avoid being seen from the other end of the hall, but I couldn't. Instead, I drifted closer to the rocky floor until I had to walk. "Damn you, Miranda," I muttered, "just when I began to feel comfortable as a ghost, you had to curse me."

My hand slid across the rock wall until my fingers touched a wooden surface—a door. By this time, I was no longer transparent. I stopped, wishing I could stick my head through to see what was on the other side. A light shone through a keyhole. Crouching, I placed my eye to the small opening. The lit room beyond looked familiar. The smell of burning wood from the roaring fireplace on the side wall floated into my nostrils. In one corner, black roses bloomed. *Xela's lair.*

A shadow passed in front of the door, sending me scuttling into the far wall. "Crap," I groaned, then paused in confusion after I bounced off the wall. I did not feel like a ghost as I pushed away from the wall and brushed dirt off my jeans.

"Hello?" a voice called from the other side of the door.

I gasped. "William?"

The door opened a crack, squeaking on its hinges. William peeked through the slit, then swung it ajar. "Sarah? What are you doing here?" He pulled me inside and shut and locked the door quietly, drawing the chain hung midway along its groove. His tousled hair looked clumpier than usual. Before I could comment, he threw his arms around me as if he hadn't seen me in days.

"Me?" I blurted. "What are *you* doing here?"

"Oh my God, you're real! You're back!" William lifted me and pressed my body against his chest, the way he had when we met. Somehow, he was able to touch me as if I were in the flesh. "You have a body."

"No," I denied. "I don't have my body."

"What are you talking about?" He squeezed my arm, then pressed his lips to mine. "I will never let you go again. I thought I'd lost you forever."

"No, you haven't, but I'm still a ghost, William. A cursed ghost." I took his hands. "I promise I will make things right. I should have told you the truth. I'm so sorry." My promise was more like a vow, and it would not be broken.

"Cursed? Why would you do such a stupid thing and not tell me?"

"I know. I should have." I hung my head, unable to bear the disappointment in his eyes.

"Come here." He pulled me in, held me tight. "I know you didn't have a choice. I'm sorry I blamed you. I know some secrets aren't meant to be shared."

I looked up at him. "You have a secret too."

He closed his eyes. "Yes."

"And you cannot tell me."

"No."

He was right. Some secrets had to remain intact.

"Are you mad?" he asked.

"That would be a little hypocritical of me, wouldn't it?"

"Yes." He kissed my forehead. "But when all this is over, no more secrets. No more Aseret, or anyone else, for that matter. Agreed?"

"Agreed." I sighed. "It's so good to be here with you."

"In the underworld?"

"Oddly, it feels right."

"Which means we should be here. Look." He pointed to the blue sphere sitting on the table. "Eric's been able to transfer my mappings to his magic sphere."

"Is that what you've been working on with your father?"

"And yours. There's more. We can track vampires in need of training, prowling demons, underworld shifts. We've developed an app on the iPad to use Eric's sphere markings as my virtual map." William's eyes sparkled with an excitement similar to what he displayed when he talked about the serums and the orchids. His love for all beings and his desire to improve the world fired his soul. William's own troubles didn't matter when it came to helping others. I loved that about him. The trouble we found ourselves in always seemed secondary, or perhaps less urgent, because we knew we'd free ourselves . . . eventually.

"How did you get here?" I asked.

"The children sent me. As soon as I stepped on the porch, I found myself here."

"What do you mean they sent you here?"

"Through a vortex. They told me you'd come, and they stepped back into the roses." William pointed to the corner. "I think there may be a hidden entrance behind them, but they advised me to stay here. Crystal and Ayer sounded like adults."

"They always do."

"This time it was different. They cautioned me to stay here. With you."

The black roses released a pungent aroma as if in agreement.

"You think there's an exit?" he asked.

I shook my head. "No. At least, not one we can use. This is Xela's lair." I scanned the room, so eerily similar to the cave where I'd given up my soul.

"I won't ask how you know that, but there's something I need to tell you."

My gaze found William again.

"I know I've said how sorry I am for not realizing Xela stole your body."

"Miranda," I interrupted.

"Who?"

"It's a long story. Xela never stole my body. Miranda did, to try to stop the prophecy. She also punished Xela for not turning Xander to the underworld."

"So I almost killed Xela, not Miranda." My husband seemed confused.

"Yes." It would have taken him one twist to snap Xela's neck. "What stopped you?"

"It was still your body; I couldn't." He held my eyes. "Sarah, I promise once this is over, we will no longer have to fear anyone. You won't need to give up your body again."

"All right. So . . . Aseret dragged me into the underworld." I bit my lip.

"Then where is he?"

I scratched my head. "I thought he was kidnapping me, but he didn't come through the vortex with me. I think the children separated us."

"It's working," William whispered.

"What's working?" I asked "William, what did you do?"

"Mama?" Crystal's voice murmured from within the roses on the back wall.

We turned toward the bushes as our children walked through the black blossoms, the lair filling with the scent of honey and lemon.

Crystal stood at least five and a half feet tall, slightly taller than me. My daughter's freckled face resembled mine when I was a teen, not too long ago. Ayer matched her height. My son's eyes shone with the courage I'd fallen in love with when I met William. Our children no longer looked three years old, because they were no longer three.

Their unnatural growth spurt didn't stop me from covering their faces with kisses. "How did this happen? I didn't want you to grow up so fast."

"It's our time," Ayer replied in a deeper voice than I expected.

"Time to do what?"

"Bind Aseret to the hereafter."

"I feel like I've missed most of your life," I moaned.

"You haven't. We can shift later." Ayer looked at William. "Everything is going well?" He and his father exchanged a look I couldn't understand.

William nodded. "Your mother is right," he said, including me again. "We'll miss your childish laughs and cuddles."

"Oh, we still laugh a lot." Ayer winked at his sister, then turned to me. "The scare you pulled on Chris in Pinedale was pretty good."

"You saw that?" My hand went to my mouth.

"We keep tabs on those we need to, even ghosts." Crystal strolled over to the fireplace and blew hard on the flame; instead of extinguishing it, it flared as if renewed.

"He peed his pants." Ayer burst into laughter.

"Really?" I squeaked. I doubted Chris would ever see Kirsten again, and she'd be more than pleased if he didn't call.

"Who did?" William asked, looking between us.

"Someone who deserved to be taught a lesson," I explained.

"You've been a busy ghost, haven't you?" William wrapped his arm around my waist.

"I don't want to be little again," Crystal insisted.

"You be who you want and need to be, and we'll always love you." I took her face between my palms. "Just give a little warning before we need to change diapers again," I joked.

"Never that young." Ayer rolled his eyes. I guess there was a bit of me in him after all.

"Mama, when did this happen to your ghost?" Crystal closed her eyes.

The twins stood side by side as William walked around them, examining their new bodies.

"Miranda." Ayer locked his gaze with his sister's as if reading her thoughts.

"She's scheming."

"This will make things a little more difficult."

"Why? What will?" I asked.

"You're still a ghost, but in human flesh. We cannot put you back in your body unless you're a pure ghost." Ayer stroked his hand across my bare arm, like he was checking the extent of my curse.

"You need to get your pure ghost back," Crystal added.

"I hope you can tell me how to do that." I widened my eyes.

"Miranda cursed you, so she can undue her spell. You need to find her. Miranda's touch will lift her magic. It's her weakness."

Hearing that, I almost preferred to remain a ghost. "You're asking the impossible. She won't do anything at will."

"If anyone can do it, you can," they said in uncanny unison.

"I wish we could help you, but some things just need to run their course naturally." Ayer ran his fingers through his hair, the same gesture William had.

"And remember, even when things make it seem like life is not worth living, it is. You'll need to be strong." Crystal squeezed my hand.

"I'm a ghost. How strong can I be?"

"Not physical strength, Mama." My daughter embraced me.

"I'm still worried about you two," I said. "Miranda seems more conniving than Aseret. What if she curses you?"

"Like she could," Ayer mocked.

"We're powerful, but we still have a weakness like anyone else," I warned, not liking his arrogance, and suspected he'd picked up some of Xander's traits, unfortunately.

"They can use your loved ones against you," said William.

Ayer's face fell. He'd also learned love for family from my best friend.

"Don't worry, Gran is safe," Crystal said. "So are Ekim and Atram."

"Why wouldn't they be?" I asked.

"We found demons at the cabin—the same ones who tried to kill you at the parking lot."

"*What?*"

"Apparently Aseret wasn't the only one with knowledge of the location of our home."

"I will kill Aseret myself if he comes near my family again," William growled, shoving his fist into the wall by the fireplace. Earth shook and crumbled to the floor. The vibration from the punch sent a shock wave through the cave. Jars fell off the mantle and green goo spilled on the floor.

"Save your strength, Father." The twins gave him a knowing look.

The rage in William's eyes was the same as when I'd met him. William would be the one to end it all. Not the twins, not anyone else.

"Our training will finish by the morning. Then we'll be ready to bind Aseret." Ayer placed his hand on his father's shoulder.

Crystal's eyes turned up in their sockets, just as Mrs. G's did, but hers remained white, not black. "You have until tomorrow to get your true ghost back. You need to be able to float by tomorrow."

The children reminded me of Mira and Xander. Our twins had the same ability, the same traits. It eased my worries, knowing they could protect themselves.

"You may only leave through the rosebushes. Wait an hour and don't use the door." Ayer looked sternly at William, as if he'd known the door had already been opened.

"Please be careful." I hugged the children.

"No need to worry, Mama. We can handle ourselves. You . . ." Crystal closed her eyes, "You will need to unite as one to overcome Miranda. You will need to work together." Then telepathically: *As two equals.*

I was certain William heard it too. The love I'd missed in his face and eyes returned. Perhaps it had never left, and I'd chosen to see it as gone.

Crystal and Ayer backed through the bushes and disappeared. We stared at the black flowers.

"Wow," I murmured.

William's hand touched mine. "We have an hour before we can leave." His eyes beamed with hunger and lust.

"And what are we supposed to do here?" I bit my lower lip.

"Well, if you weren't a ghost, I'd know how to spend time with you." He stroked my arm. "Can you feel that?" William's heart was pounding.

I nodded.

"You can feel my touch," he repeated, as if he couldn't believe it himself.

"Miranda's curse, remember."

"It's not a curse. Miranda gave us a gift without knowing it." He took me in his arms. Desire radiated from his body. "Would it be wrong if I kissed a ghost?"

"It would be wrong if you didn't want to kiss your wife's ghost." I tangled my fingers into William's hair. How much I'd missed feeling simple touches, smelling his woody musk, and tasting his kisses!

"You had chocolate?" I asked when we parted.

"Coco." He grinned. "Whoever lived here liked coco." William covered my lips with his again.

William pressed harder against me. His longing spread through his body quicker than his blood flow. My thoughts no longer wandered beyond the cocoon of heat circling us. My vest dropped to the floor. He teased my neck and my shoulder, sliding the straps off my tank top to rest on my arms. His fingertips left a hot trail on my ghostly skin. The flames in the fireplace rose in response.

Shifting into a vampire, William lowered me to the bear skin rug and pinned me there. My shoulder blades sunk into the plush fur as he played with me as if I were a rag doll. Each taste of his lips provoked a hunger inside me that had been denied for too long. The saltiness of his flesh against my tongue was more delicious with each taste. His palms found my thighs. I didn't remember when he'd pulled off my jeans. I wanted to remain pressed against his flesh and to be lost in the moment that brought us together as one. If there was a benefit to Miranda's curse, this was it.

* * *

"It's been an hour." William propped himself up on his elbow as the yearning faded from his satisfied face. For the past fifteen minutes, we'd been silent, staring at the root-laced ceiling. No way in hell did I feel like a ghost.

For the first time since our night in New York City, I felt that I had my William back. Perhaps he'd never left, while I let the underworld consume me. The connection I'd denied had returned—no, William has always been at my side, only my perception had changed.

I dressed, trying to concentrate on the buttons of my vest, but I couldn't take my eyes off my husband. The light from the fire shimmered behind him.

He took my left hand, smoothing his thumb over the orchid tattooed there. I admired his tattoo, remembering how the flower had connected us.

"When did you know?" I asked.

"About . . . ?"

"About me, Xela?"

"I suspected since the first time Xela came into the house in your body."

"And you didn't say anything?"

"I figured you had a reason to keep it from me and wanted to be sure. Then Xela took me to the tree house. I read her face, but I don't think she knew her cheeks betrayed her. Her heartbeat sounded off—I know the rhythm of your heart. I'd never forget it." He placed his palm atop my left breast, though no sound escaped my heart right now.

"Because it beats the same way yours does." I touched his chest.

"Always." William's lips brushed mine. The kiss sent electric waves through my ghost as if it were really solid flesh. "I still wasn't certain, and I didn't want to confront you about something that has drawn a wedge between us in the past."

"I was asked not to tell you." I lowered my eyes.

"I don't blame you, Sarah. I never did, but I was angry at what you sacrificed."

"And I held my mistakes against you."

"It's not your fault. You are the strongest, most giving woman I've ever met. You'd give anything to save someone else, to improve their life. You sacrifice your own happiness and body to do so." He lifted my chin.

The fire dimmed, and the roses opened their blossoms to their widest, as if reminding us it was time to leave.

"Do you have a plan?" I asked.

William narrowed his brows. "I have no clue how to find the witch."

My loving husband gave me the courage I would need to get through the grand hall to Miranda's lair. I wasn't sure how we'd do it, but with William, I could do anything. "I know where to find her, but getting there is the problem."

He read my face. "Seekers?"

"Lots of seekers."

"Do you have your abilities?"

I pushed my feet, zooming across the room and back. It felt good knowing I wasn't completely useless.

"William, there are thousands of them." When I floated through the grand hall with my mother, the seekers gathered like a colony of ants. "I can't float or pass through walls. I'm not sure what they can do to a ghost that's solidified. And you . . ."

My voice shook, the heat of their searing palms was still fresh in my mind.

"I don't think we have much choice. I need you to promise me that, no matter what happens, you'll keep going," he said solemnly.

"Don't talk like that."

"Promise me. I need to know you won't give up. For our children and for humanity."

My face felt drained of blood. "Does this have something to do with your secret?"

"Promise?" he pleaded.

"I do."

Was I foolish to believe William could fight Aseret's army? The thought of the grand hall froze my spine. Its burned bridges and the lava underneath . . . even a ghost couldn't escape the bubbling flow of magma.

William took my hand as we stepped into the blossoming bushes. The aroma of the black roses soon left an acidic film on my tongue. I took another whiff while passing the last stem, and the stench of dirty socks and rotten eggs abused my nostrils. Since I expected we'd exit into an adjoining hall in the underworld, the smell didn't surprise me.

Instead, we stood in the middle of the hell I'd been thinking about on a swinging bridge roped to rotting posts, over a river of molten rock and lava, near the central fire pit of the grand hall.

CHAPTER 12

We didn't move. The throne was empty, but Aseret's absence didn't ease my anxiety. Throughout the hall, seekers and demons worked on their assigned tasks, clearly oblivious to our presence. Some trained; others repaired the damaged structures used to connect the two ends of the grand hall. A bridge adjacent to ours, broken midway along its span and dangling from thread-thin ropes, hung too low to cross.

Magma, its level higher than I remembered, bubbled and spat deadly blobs of lava upward. Its orange glow illuminated the hall, softening the light from the hundreds of candles on the chandelier above. The seekers' sulphuric stench flowed through the hall in waves of sweat, drowning all other scents. How could anyone stand breathing the acidic air? It'd take a minute or so before our scent reached the seekers' terrier-sharp noses, through their own toxic stench.

William pulled something out of his pocket. "Put it on. If it works, you should be a ghost again. Go," he whispered, sliding my ruby ring onto my finger.

My hands disappeared. The ring retained its power to show the true form of its wearer. It was the same ring we'd used to trick Miranda in the past, to show her real form when she stole my body.

"What about you? We need to get to the dungeons," I whispered.

Though William controlled his breathing and kept it shallow, beads of sweat rolled down his temples. It wouldn't take long for the seekers to recognize his smell.

"I'll follow soon. I just have to deal with them." He nodded toward the end of the bridge, where seekers concentrated on adding ropes to the existing supports to strengthen the structure.

Even if William ran at his fastest speed, he wouldn't make it to the dungeons. "I won't leave you. You cannot do this by yourself," I insisted.

"I can't fight them if I have to protect you, too. Now go."

"I don't need protection. I will *not* leave you. Stay still." With caution, I moved forward on the bridge, hoping my invisible feet wouldn't make it sway. I couldn't float; the ring seemed powerless to confer all of my ghostly abilities. The seekers at the end of the bridge were absorbed in tying one knot after another. My soundless footsteps carried my ghost as I approached. The demon eyes remained on the ropes; I squeezed past them, then tiptoed away, freezing when a seeker lifted its head and sniffed the air.

My eyes fell on a rock at my feet; moving slowly, carefully, I picked it up and threw it toward one of the doorways into the maze, well away from the direction I intended to go. The rock tumbled down the stairs. The grand hall fell silent except for the echo of a stone that bounced off the wall. All eyes concentrated on the doorway. The seekers left the bridge and moved toward the entrance to investigate the mysterious sound.

William sprang forward. The talented noses of Aseret's army inhaled in unison, their chests expanding at the same time. I felt as if all the air had been sucked out of the room with a giant's straw. The seeker's gazes darted to William, who'd reached the rock footing securing the bridge. Some of the seekers rushed to block all of the doorways, while others launched themselves at William.

I had no doubt he'd handle the first few, but more would attack in their wake. Those were already charging forward behind the leaders, screeching and releasing high-pitched yelps when comrades plummeted into the fissures bisecting the floor.

"If you don't remember me, you will now," I heard him growl as he shoved them into the lava-filled cracks. William's ferocity and power were a combination few could overcome, but even my husband couldn't fight thousands.

This is a suicide mission.

The grinning demons hung back, waiting with their arms crossed for their chance to attack. They'd probably let the seekers tire William before they used their powers. From beyond the doorway, I watched his defensive moves against their scorching paws and claws that sliced his arms and torso. I cringed at each cut, even though I knew they'd heal quickly. William threw one seeker after another into the lava below, their ashes floating like black feathers in an updraft only moments later. But he was nearing the brink of the crevice, getting closer to the edge.

Another dozen seekers approached William. He looked behind him, a yard remained, and he shoved a seeker at his side into the two behind it. All three dropped and tumbled, screeching and yelping, into the fissure. William had taken another step back.

Straining to keep my nerves intact, I picked up a rock and threw it toward the same entrance as before, but only a few of the seekers inspected where the sound came from.

William's scent for these creatures was like that of a bleeding seal in a bay full of sharks. I took a step forward to help him, drawing several pairs of glowing eyes my way.

Sarah, stay there, Eric warned.

I whirled around but didn't see my evil-bender. *You need to help him.*

I know. You go where you're supposed to, he ordered.

Before I turned to go to Miranda's lair, I saw William wobbling on the brink of the fissure. A seeker pushed one of its fellows into William. Arms waving in an attempt to keep his balance, William lost the battle with gravity. He toppled into the crevice. The hiss of singeing fibers and flesh preceded the smell of burnt flesh mingled with woody musk. Wisps of yellow mist rose toward the ceiling of the grand hall.

"Go!" Eric yelled.

Shock made me an automaton. I fled.

* * *

My feet led me down the circular staircase into the dungeon. Instead of following the tunnel to Miranda's lair, I skidded to the right, into the third cell, where Aseret had imprisoned me four years before. The fog-like spell that bound me at the doorway four years ago didn't confine me this time; I chose to stay in the murky room. My back pressed against the farthest wall, my legs pulled up to my chest, my arms wrapped around them. I removed my ring so I could sob and mourn my husband. My skin throbbed as shivers of grief rose from my toes to the tips of my fingers. My jaw shook, and I rested my chin against my knees, trying to stop its trembling. It didn't help.

I stroked my blue orchid tattoo. My moans returned, floods of tears sheeting down my cheeks. The vigorous shaking of my body made me gasp for air. The walls of the room felt as if they'd closed in to the size of a coffin. Part of me wanted to run up to the grand hall and give myself to the seekers, let them throw my ghostly flesh into the river of lava so I could join William in the afterlife.

Even when things seem like life is not worth living, it is. You'll need to be strong.

Honoring William's plea seemed impossible. Would I see his ghost beside me in a few minutes? I recalled Miranda's story and realized his spirit could never return to his body. He'd be lost in the hereafter. Could he even find me as a ghost?

Miranda. The pain shooting through my body turned toward the witch. The rage I'd forgotten returned. Adrenaline overpowered my veins. A growl came unbidden from the back of my throat. Inside, the anger brewed, steeped with guilt and the feeling that I'd failed to protect my family. Focused on revenge, I'd ensure the witch could never hurt my family again. The ire built to a frenzy under my skin, tingling. It moved into my organs, tightened around my arms and the back of my neck. The need for vindication fueled me further; it was exactly what I needed to ensure that Miranda died.

Body taut, I stood, fists clenched, and screamed until my lungs felt like they'd burst. The dungeon walls shook. Pebbles dribbled to the floor and rolled around my feet. I didn't care if anyone heard. In fact, I wanted to be heard.

Finally, I stopped, lips quivering, and slowly regained my composure. Bending, I ripped a strip from my pant leg, then pulled my ring from my pocket. I slipped it on my finger, then wrapped the strip of material around my palm, leaving my ring finger exposed, all before my ghostly form returned.

I headed toward Miranda's cell, silent fury fueling my determination. Leaning forward, I sped toward the wall at the end of the tunnel. Before I reached it, an entry opened and the witch's ghost stood in the entrance to her cave, hands on her hips. Her smirk faded when she saw me.

Game time.

"You're a ghost . . . who dared take off my spell? Was it Xela?"

I grinned.

"Hannah?" She floated closer. One more step and she'd touch me, but she cautiously drifted out of reach.

I shook my head, my arms crossed, and showed no fear. Miranda would think she had the upper hand.

"No one's strong enough to remove my spell. What are you hiding?" She glided around me with caution.

"You and I need to talk. Won't you invite me in?" I faked a sweet voice reminiscent of the old me.

Startled, Miranda moved aside, still careful not to get close as I entered her lair. "You know you're not getting out of here," she said.

"I don't care. My husband just died. The quicker I leave for the hereafter, the better. I need you to send me there."

The wall behind us slid and shut, rock grinding against rock. I hovered near the fireplace, for the first time understanding the reason underworld creatures tended to have one near. The heat energized me. It sizzled courage and dominance. Not many could face off against such a natural force, or control it.

My gaze found my mother's drained ghost tied to the wall with magic ropes of light. Her head hung between hunched shoulders, and her silhouette was beyond translucent; it was almost invisible. I wanted to rush over and remove her bonds, but I focused on appearing indifferent. Her eyelids fluttered open, and the burden of her pain was reflected in her hazel eyes. Shifting slightly so that my back was to Miranda, I let my expression show my mother my concern and that she needed to remain quiet.

The witch's book of magic rested on the table in the middle of the room, its pages opened to a spell. Detailed drawings of knots and ropes woven between ancient words filled the paper.

When I turned to face Miranda, the witch still seemed confused. "Hmm . . . " She put her finger to her lips. "William dead?" She narrowed her ghostly brows. "I shall welcome him soon. What about the twins? Where are they?"

"I haven't seen them in days." I lowered my head, feigning despair. "It's like they abandoned me too."

"You're lying?" Her accusation came in the form of a question.

Good; I needed her to be skeptical.

"Why? I've lost my husband. I've lost my children. I *want* to go to the hereafter. There's nothing left for me!" I raised my arms. "Nothing!"

"I told you, you're not leaving this place alive." Miranda rushed at me and grabbed my ghost's arm. "You will not leave this place until Aseret has his say. You will be the perfect bait. Ha! Stupid, silly half-breed," she hissed, her grin exposing crooked teeth. Even as a ghost, the witch held her persona.

"What are you doing?" The charade became easier with each minute that Miranda thought she controlled my actions.

"You think I'd let you leave and not use the energy of a half-breed vampire who's been touched by the keepers?" She wafted toward the table, gliding her hand along the dagger that rested beside the book of spells.

"They never touched me."

"Physically, no, but the magic is present in your essence. It runs in your family. You may not feel it, but we do. We always have. Not all has been transferred to the twins. Not all."

With caution, I slid my other hand behind my back and slipped the ring off my finger, knowing Miranda's touch had just done the opposite of what she wanted to accomplish. I hoped it would take just as long for me to change into a true ghost as it did for her original curse to work. Phasing into a ghost before she left would ruin my plan. And Miranda would leave; after all, my children were vulnerable and she'd want to brag to Aseret.

"Ha! I'm getting better at this," she gloated.

But it wasn't her magic that turned my ghost into flesh.

She moved toward the wall and shut the secret entrance. "Can't float through walls anymore, can you?" The witch grinned as she rushed toward the end of the cave.

Not yet, I thought, but I played along, trying to pass through, bumping into the wall, then the table.

Her form started to pass through the wall.

"Wait, where are you going? You can't leave me here." I pretended to panic.

She paused. "I can do what I want with you. And I want Aseret to see the power I'll gain. Your essence will be the most valuable yet, half-breed." Miranda's howl echoed through the lair as her ghost disappeared into the wall.

My invisible heart pounding, I rushed to my mother's side. "Are you all right?"

She slowly shook her head. Her weakened soul was almost transparent. "Sarah, you shouldn't be here. She'll drain your essence." I had to lean close to hear her faint voice.

"It's okay, Mom." The light ropes that held her soul left creases in her ephemeral being; if it were flesh, blood would be dripping from the wounds. I pointed to the glowing twines. "Do you know how to get these off?"

"It's a spell from the book. You need to read it."

I rushed to the table on which the magic book rested and peered at the open pages, but the letters unintelligible to me, meaningless markings and symbols. "I can't understand this. I'm not a witch."

"Channel Xela. She has your body. You're still connected to her."

I can't do this, I thought, feeling overwhelmed. The fire in the pit disagreed as it flared, the flames that never needed more wood to burn encouraging me with flickering oranges and reds. My focus on the foreign words intensified, and I thought about Xela and what she'd do. Aseret's accent as he spoke in an ancient tongue came to my mind. I imagined Xela chanting, like a witch. Waves of new energy rippled through me. The letters began unscrambling, and I heard Xela's voice in my head, except it was my voice. With Xela's magic linked through me, the words made sense.

"Asuma murani beco malima. Kera ma sukler miserio uff," I chanted, the spell escaping my mouth on streaming ribbons of light. The change flowed toward my mother's wrists and singed the ropes holding her arms and ankles. The connection of spell with magical knots erupted in sparkles of light before bands of sulphurous smoke curled upward.

Freed from her bonds, my mother dropped to her knees.

"Come on." I put my hands under her arms and lifted her. "We need to leave before Aseret comes back."

"I cannot become invisible. They'll see us. She took too much away from me."

"You don't need to. We're going straight up." I nodded toward the ceiling, both of my hands still supporting the light weight of her spirit.

"How? You can't pass through walls. She cursed you."

I shook my head. "No, the curse is off. Miranda unknowingly reversed her magic. Can you hold on for a moment?" Gently, I lowered her to sit on the floor, her head against the wall, and floated to the table holding Miranda's book of spells.

My plan was already working; I was able to pick up the book and stash it behind a cluster of roots on the ceiling. It fit perfectly in the nook. *Try to do magic now, witch.*

"Is William really gone?"

I froze, then nodded, struggling not to lose my composure. Assuming a brisk demeanor, I went over and helped her up.

"I'm so sorry, honey." My mother squeezed me, and my body switched to full ghost mode. The embrace rejuvenated me just enough to carry through my plans to destroy Aseret, the witch, and their seekers.

"Let's go." I took her hand, and we flew beyond the ceiling of the cave. As we passed through the solid rock, then compacted soil, I thought about Eric, Xander, and Mira, hoping to be taken to my watchers.

The time had come to give the witch exactly what she deserved. It was time to get my body back and bind Aseret and Miranda to the hell where they belonged. I needed vengeance, needed to right what had been wronged. After reading the spell, I understood Xela's and Mrs. G's task. I now trusted her as much as I'd trusted my watchers.

My grip on Mom's frail spirit tightened, and soon, we burst from the ground into a world of fresh greens lit by the rising sun, the morning glow waking the birds. I wished I could feel the warmth of the sun's rays on my face, remembering the streaks of light filtering through the canopy in the Amazon.

That memory pulled on my spirit, leading me through the deciduous forest of the Yellowstone National Park and onward. The trees soon turned into a jungle, their branches twined with webs of hanging vines. I imagined the sweet smells of the Amazon that I missed, the intoxicating orchids and the floating pollen carried by hot winds, the way the fresh grass tickled my toes when I ran through the clearing to our cabin.

Home would appear in a few seconds. I wasn't sure what day it was, or how long I'd been in the underworld. Has the news about William reached my family? My hope was for them to hear what had happened from me: I owed them that. But now, I wasn't sure whether I wanted to go back to my human form.

Home would never be the same without William. I couldn't live without him.

The closer I came to the Amazon, the pull to return to my human form strengthened and became more vibrant, as if arguing against my desire to die. The pledge I'd made to William before he perished couldn't be broken. I wouldn't break another promise or let him down again.

I'd live for my children, even though my spirit would forever remain with my love, my other half. Once again, we were torn in two: no longer together, no longer equals.

CHAPTER 13

My mother never let go of my hand as I dragged her weakened soul through the jungle, even when we reached the edge of the clearing in the Amazon. My ghost flew into the house, past my father, past Atram and Willow, toward the sunroom, the wind of my swift passage tugging papers out of their hands.

I lowered my mother's ghost on the chair and knelt on the marble floor beside the sofa, where my children, now back in their young forms, rested peacefully. My only wish now was to stroke Crystal's cheek with the back of my hand. The expectation to see them as teens eased my heartache, hoping they'd understand their father's fate. How was I supposed to tell them about their father? I'd failed, and Crystal and Ayer would be devastated. Would they want their spirits to remain with William, abandoning their bodies in this world? Has my husband's death decided my children's fate to search for his lost soul?

My mother knelt beside me, her gaze darting from the children to my father engaged with his iPad.

I remembered Mrs. G's words: *"Their bodies are there, but not their spirits."* Sure enough, their chests weren't moving. I waited five seconds for one of them to release a breath, but no air escaped. Was this what happened when they left their bodies?

"Eric!" I called out, hoping my evil-bender would hear me. Silence. I tried to concentrate on the children's spirits, letting my soul pinpoint their location and closed my eyes. Again, nothing. Were they preparing to bind Aseret? My worst nightmare would be for them face the demon alone. I had to help them. And they needed to know the truth about their father.

"Willow! Dad! Atram!"

My family rushed into the sun room, but my soul was still in its invisible form.

"I thought I heard Sarah." My mother-in-law searched the room with her eyes.

"Me too. Hold on," Atram froze, eyes focused on the twins. My father placed his tablet on the table. Then Atram frowned.

"What's the matter?" Willow asked.

"I—I can't hear their heartbeats."

Ekim ran to the sofa and fixed his acute sense of hearing on the still twins. "Me neither," he confirmed.

Willow covered her mouth. Unknowingly, she knelt beside me.

I showed myself. "They're not dead."

No one jumped; in fact, Willow's concerned expression eased. But it wouldn't for long, not after I told my in-laws their son was gone. Dead. And I was to blame for it all.

"Sarah?" My father looked my way. "They're not breathing." He pressed his ear against Ayer's chest at the opposite end of the sofa.

"I know. Their souls are gone." I placed my hand on top of my daughter's but failed to feel her soothing touch.

"Gone where?" Willow gasped.

"I don't know. I think Eric does. I've seen them do this before. They travel to the other realms, then return."

"But they shouldn't remain out of their bodies too long. Aseret will sense them." My mother joined the conversation, taking a visible form. Concern shadowed her face as she stood. Her hovering ghost still looked hollow and drained.

Everyone gasped.

"Saraphine?" my father whispered.

She turned slowly. Surrounded by a family she'd been denied, my mother looked from one to the other, rotating in a circle until she came to face my father. "Ekim," she said. "I shouldn't have done this. I'm sorry." My mother began to vanish.

"No, please don't go," he begged. "You're with Sarah?"

Her ghost showed again as she nodded.

My father's shoulders relaxed, and he stepped toward her. "I've missed you so much," he whispered, trying to stroke her face with his palm. Her ghost vibrated at the touch she couldn't feel.

The silenced room felt like the center of the universe, and my children weren't the only ones without breath. The wind outside stopped whistling; the birds ceased their mid-day chirping. The seconds that passed timed like hours. It felt as if the entire forest around the cabin were concentrated on one couple: a vampire and a ghost.

My father took a step closer, lowering his head to my mother's. She remained still and closed her eyes as my father's lips hovered above hers, then brushed the shape of my mother's mouth, as if kissing fog without dispersing it. My father closed his eyes. Now I was certain no one breathed.

Could this moment last forever, be real and my mother be alive? I wished my parents could reunite as a couple. The love they shared cocooned around them like a blanket, the same way it had between me and William. They'd sacrifice their life for one another. But boundaries between life and death couldn't be broken. My parents would never be together.

A tear escaped my mother's eye, leaving a glistening trail on her face. A real tear, rolling on a cheek that should have been incorporeal. Another drop trickled from my father's eye; from a vampire who'd been dead for decades.

Certain that ghosts couldn't shed tears, nor vampires, I could only think that magic had found a way to connect two people who'd lost each other too early in their life. My mother leaned into my father, and the drops joined as their cheeks touched. Glowing, she seemed to regain all the essence stolen from her by Miranda—the essence of love. Their tear, combined as one, fell to the marble floor. The drop didn't splatter but rolled out the front door into the Amazon forest.

That's when I noticed Mrs. G standing in the doorway, her eyes black.

I didn't dare speak and interrupt the magic I was witnessing.

My mother opened her eyes and stepped back. "I've missed you too. Thank you for taking care of Sarah." She took my father's hand as if hers was real. Could she actually feel his touch? With Mrs. G in the doorway, I wouldn't doubt it.

"It doesn't look like I've done a good job." He shrugged. "I was gone most of her life."

"You did what you had to, and you've done a wonderful job. Look at her. She's strong, passionate. Although I wish she didn't sacrifice herself for others. Just like you."

"And you."

"She's a ghost." Xander stood beside Mrs. G.

"Not for long." Xela stepped from behind him. Her eyes, my eyes, were still rolling forward, recovering from a spell she'd recently cast.

"It was necessary at the time," my mom explained, "but not anymore. Miranda thinks we're both trapped in her lair. She's gone to Aseret to tell him. It's time to move forward with the plan." She looked at Xela.

"We're ready," the witch confirmed, squeezing Xander's hand. It was still odd to stare at myself as if I'd been looking in the mirror, holding my best friend's hand. Did Xander see me or Xela? The way he examined Xela in my body, I was sure he only envisioned his black witch.

Xela turned to me. "You have a gift beyond that of a half-breed vampire. I heard you read."

"The spell? I thought you read it through me."

"No." Xela shook her head. "You must have had a witch as an ancestor. You read that on your own. It wasn't me you channeled. It makes sense for the twins to have powers beyond your understanding."

"What about the children? Will they wake up?" Atram asked.

Before anyone could answer, wind gusted into the cabin, swirling the air into a vortex. Eric stepped from a portal lined in purple mist. "They're ready too," he said as if he'd been listening. "No need to worry about their bodies. They have a better grasp of what's happening than we think."

"Eric, what happened?" I rushed to his side. "Did you help him?"

Eric looked down at the floor. "I'm sorry. I couldn't get him to you. They were supposed to be there." He looked at the twins narrowing his brows in confusion.

"No," I whispered.

"Where's William?" Willow looked at me. "Did you find him?" She came to stand beside my ghost.

"Willow . . . I . . ." I drew a deep, unnecessary breath. "I tried to help him. There were thousands of seekers, and he almost got past . . ." My head hung low. "I'm sorry," I whispered. "He's gone. William is gone." The quavering voice sounded as if it someone else spoke. The vibrations of my soul intensified. It was time for my family to mourn my husband. Guilt would remain with me forever for failing them . . . for failing William.

"What do you mean gone?" she whispered, her voice husky. Her hands trembled.

"In the underworld. He fell. The lava." I forced the words out.

"No." She shook her head emphatically. "I would have felt it." Atram took his wife's arm, supporting her, but Willow remained calm. "I would have felt it," she repeated.

Part of me knew exactly what she meant, because I couldn't feel William's absence. I still felt him here, with me, but in the flesh.

"I had to get my ghost back," I said to my staring family. "It's complicated, but we had to make it to Miranda's lair so she could touch me again."

"And who told you so?" Eric asked.

"Crystal and Ayer."

Everyone turned to look at the sleeping twins.

"Do you know where they are?" I asked Eric.

He shook his head. "No, but they know to meet us in the hereafter at sundown."

"Is everyone coming?" I asked.

"Your family will stay here." Mrs. G paced across the marble floor, as comfortable as if she'd been in her home. The hem of her dancing skirt flowed around her feet.

"You'll come with us to the brink of the hereafter," Xela interjected, "and if all goes according to plan, you will have your body back tonight."

But I wasn't sure I wanted my body. William was gone. Wouldn't it be better to let me remain a ghost so I could spend my life with William in the hereafter? Where was his soul?

The promise I'd made to my husband to remain strong pounded in my head. And this was a promise I wanted to keep. He'd asked me to protect my family and continue on, no matter what. Certain I could do a better job in the flesh, I knew my destiny remained on Earth, not in the hereafter. Even when I gave up my body without the guarantee of ever having it back, I knew I belonged here. It wasn't my time—nor William's. Yet he was gone. I wished I had a chance to say goodbye. I just wanted to feel his embrace one more time.

Atram settled Willow on a chair and brought her water as she repeated, "I would have felt it."

I couldn't imagine William dead either. To me, it seemed more like he'd gone on a vacation. Perhaps it felt that way because I was a ghost, but my gut told me otherwise.

My children's bodies begun shaking in spasms, like they were having a seizure, and I darted to their side. Crystal's chest expanded with an inhalation that reanimated her body; Ayer followed. They sat up, though their eyes were still closed. Crystal's arms twitched, then extended. Her hair grew until it was long enough to touch her bottom, rich auburn with blonde highlights. Her lips and her chest filled out as she shifted into her teens. She rolled her shoulder blades backward, releasing the tension in her neck.

The cracking of bones drew our eyes to Ayer, who tilted his head to the right, adjusting his spine, then to the left. The sound resonated like thunder in the silent room. Ayer's legs lengthened and the curves of his face sharpened. The skin on his biceps stretched until I thought it would rip.

The twins shook like they were shedding the years of life they missed. They opened their eyes, drawing their gazes from one family member to another. We stared back.

Crystal and Ayer's expressions shifted from blank to comfortable, and it seemed they were remembering their home. They examined the room and the family in sight as if they'd just come home after a stay at a boarding school. Their eyes assessed the height of the vaulted ceiling and the length of each wall. Crystal peeked out the window and squinted when the sun struck her eyes.

"Sorry, it takes a few minutes of getting used to." Ayer made small circles with his feet as they stretched out of his kid-size sneakers. The shirt he wore lay in ripped pieces on the floor. His slacks rose to his calves at the bottom, while the top band hung just below his hip bones. Ayer flexed one arm, then the other. He lowered his head and examined his muscles, watching his pecks dance in alternate pumps. "Cool."

Crystal rolled her eyes and stretched her arms. "Ahh. That's better." Her usually oversized t-shirt would split at the seams, any minute now. The stitches under her arms were already strained like over-wound guitar strings.

"It gets easier, the more you shift," Xander said matter-of-factly as he stepped forward and handed Ayer a bag.

My son pulled out new clothes from the bag Xander'd brought.

"They're like you? Shifters? How did you know?" I pointed to the sack.

"Ma did a reading," Mira explained as Xela handed a tote to Crystal.

"Not exactly shifters," Eric added. "They're crafters."

The twins were busy examining their new clothes. I smiled, recognizing their excitement over gifts. Though in their teens, they were still children; they always would be, to me.

Crystal held a black tank top against her bosom. "Nice. I like it." She looked at the identical top Xela wore. It was too tight for my liking and made my fist-sized breasts look like they were going to pop out.

Xela's apologetic eyes flew to me, as if she knew my reaction. "We didn't have much time."

The twins spun like Superman, so fast that their tanned skin blurred with the clothing, and when they stopped, they were in the new clothes.

My gaze flew to Eric. "Crafters?"

Eric pointed to Ayer. "Warlock, and a witch." He wrapped his arm around Crystal. "Along with shifters, demonic powers, and human DNA. Hence the need for constant sleep. Their energy has been drained until now. These—" he pointed to their left wrists "—connect them to the keepers' energy. They will no longer be drained."

Everyone focused on the marks shimmering on the twins' wrists. On the top, a blue sphere glowed with cold ice; on the underside of the wrist, a red sphere spat flares of fire; jagged lightning bolts connected both. The glow faded as the spheres cooled and became tattoos.

"What kind of mark is this?" Willow asked.

"The crafter's mark." Mrs. G stepped forward. She touched the children's right hands. "Neither one is stronger, neither one weaker. Both depend on each other, able to understand all— warlocks, witches, demons, vampires, and humans." Her eyes rolled back in their sockets again. "They are the only two to ever be crafted; they will bring peace and balance. As one breathes, so does the other. As one crafts, so does the other. As one dies, so does the other. They are two equals."

"Dies?" I repeated in a whisper.

Mrs. G turned to me. "Everyone dies, Sarah. You have— twice—already. It's a natural progression in life . . . For most."

"For most?" I asked.

She smirked. "You think the supernatural hasn't helped me sustain my beauty for one hundred and forty-eight years?"

I'd never paid attention to Mrs. G's age, but she was right. She hadn't changed a bit since the day I'd met her. But—

"What kind of life is it, to be the only ones of their kind?"

"They're not. They're crafters, but they identify with all three species. Whether they choose a future with a human, a vampire, or other warlocks, it doesn't make a difference. Not to them."

"Mama, don't worry. You were different too." Crystal came to my side.

I smiled at her. "Yes, I was, wasn't I?"

"Amazing." My father touched Ayer's arm. "Like a rock."

"More like a diamond." Ayer flexed his arm. This time, I was certain he shared some of Xander's characteristics.

"Hardest rock on Earth." Atram touched the other side.

"Stop showing off. We've got a few hours to prepare. Where is Father?" Crystal asked, searching the room with her gaze.

I drew a deep breath to brace myself for what I had to do. "Sit down, sweetheart. I need to tell you something." I motioned my daughter over to the staircase down to the basement. We sat on the top step together.

Ayer's attention shifted from his biceps to us, and he joined us.

"There was an accident. We went to the underworld, like you said. I got my ghost back, but before then William—your father—fell into a crevice and—"

The wind blew a heavy gust outside, seeming to disagree.

Crystal placed her hand on my shoulder as if I were flesh. Her touch soothed my soul. "Things happen for a reason." She took a deep breath and closed her eyes. "He's not gone, Mama. He needed to fool the seekers."

"What?" I blurted.

"You haven't seen him in the underworld?" Willow asked.

"No." Ayer shook his head.

"Good. That's a good sign. I would have felt it," she repeated, letting the corners of her mouth curve upward.

It would be easier for me to gauge William's whereabouts if I had a beating heart. My ghost confused me. "If he's not gone, then where is he?" I asked.

Ayer took Crystal's hand. The children's marks began to glow, rippling their colors before twirling around their wrists as the two spheres switched their location; now the red sphere was on top and the blue one, underneath.

A new vortex opened in front of them, and William stepped out, without a single burn on him.

I gasped, then shrieked, "You're alive!" and ran to embrace my husband but fell through him.

"And I see you got your ghostly form back," he said as he watched me turn back to him.

"I saw you fall." I didn't mean for my voice to accuse my husband.

"I'm so sorry. I didn't want to hurt you. My faked death was necessary. One day I'll explain. Just be glad I'm here." He kissed my forehead, and I imagined the warmth of his lips. I saw him exchange a meaningful look with the twins, like they'd planned for his fall to happen.

"Now that we're all here, we have a few minutes to finalize the binding." Eric nodded to the children, and I felt left out. It was as if they spoke to one another to each other on a different wavelength from what I could hear.

"Already? What if Aseret hurts you? What if Miranda tricks you?" I heard the quaver in my voice and wished I had my body to feel the chills up my spine; trembling would at least relieve some tension.

"No worries, Mama. We'll be fine. We can handle Miranda. With Mrs. G and Xela at our side, Miranda is the least of our worries." Crystal touched my shoulder again. Her invisible warmth soothed my tension.

"If you say so. When do we go? I need to help you."

"And who's going to help *you*?" Eric crossed his arms, nodding to the twins. I couldn't hear what they said telepathically, but I recognized Eric's expression as another exchange took place. His left cheek twitched the same way it did when he spoke to me, and no one else heard.

"I wish I could hug you." I tried to embrace my children. Somehow, the hug felt more real than I thought it would. Before they disappeared into a yellowish mist, I blew them a kiss. They left behind their scent of lemon and honey. *At least I can still smell.*

Soon you'll be able feel, touch, and walk. Eric wiggled his fingers the way he did when preparing to bend.

"Good. What do I do?" I asked.

"You stay with us, my friend." Mira put her hand around my shoulder, except it fell through. She flushed. "Guess I'm too used to seeing you as a ghost."

Xander stepped up on my other side.

Eric moved out in front. "Let's get your body back." He twirled his finger, and the vortex to the edge of the hereafter opened.

The orange glow of the sun faded, the room spun, and I found myself on the brink of the hereafter.

CHAPTER 14

What I'm about to show you, few have seen. Eric pressed against my side until his body blended into my ghost. *This is the hereafter.*

We stepped out of the vortex, and the spinning ceased. Closing my eyes, I waited until the swirling lights stopped. When I opened them, the circling of the vortex hadn't finished, and my gaze focused on a new source of twirls. The air in front of me rippled like waves radiating from a gallon-sized drop of water that had plunged into a giant glass. No, a mirror—larger than three football fields and reflecting back the images of Eric, Mira, and Xander. My ghost appeared as an empty space between my evil-bender and the siblings.

We stood in a cave as imposing as Aseret's grand hall. The dust disturbed by the vortex floated as motes in the moonlight shining through an oval hole in the apex of the ceiling; it reminded me of the vent hole at a volcano's peak.

The dust settled and covered footsteps of a circular perimeter marked with a knee-high stone wall. Within, where we stood, there were no visible prints.

"You need to remain between us, otherwise your ghost will be sucked into the hereafter," Eric warned.

"Great, and if that happens?" I asked. Eric and the siblings wordlessly looked at me; it was the only answer I needed. "Stay between you. Got it."

To our right, Mrs. G, Xela, and William stepped out of another vortex. My husband carried a body—Miranda's! He laid the limp corpse on the ground and shifted to his vampire form. Usually, he only shifted when he expected to use his strength. Fear ran through me as my ghost vibrated. William shouldn't have come, and I wished he'd remained with our parents at the cabin. It would only take Aseret one strike to kill, and I'd only gotten my husband back, after thinking he was dead. I couldn't lose him again.

William released a growl from the back of his throat as his incisors lengthened. He stood in front of the witches, knees bent, ready to spring.

What are you sensing that I cannot see? I scanned the room.

Mrs. G and Xela joined hands. Their eyes blackened as the witches began chanting. I listened to the words but didn't understand the ancient language. Only a few syllables resonated, reminding me of the spell I'd recited to free my mother's wrists.

As soon as I thought about my mother, her ghost appeared in front of me along with Aunt Helen's. "Mom, Aunt Helen. What are you doing here?"

Mom's embrace soothed my trembling. Aunt Helen smoothed my hair behind my ear. "Our bodies have been found," my mother said.

"They have?"

"Yes. Eric has gone through a great deal to ensure we can pass to the hereafter. We must join our hosts now, before Eric begins bending. I will not be able to see you after you have your body."

I shook my head. "No. I just found you. Please don't leave me. Don't you want to see Crystal and Ayer grow up? And Dad needs you too. I saw your connection. You can still be with him as a ghost. Please, Mama." I leaned my ghost's frame against her, partly stepping out of my friend's hold. Even if I didn't have a physical heart, I knew it would quiver with sadness.

My mother held me, and Aunt Helen squeezed my hand saying, "It's better this way, for you and for us. We'll always watch over you. You must remember who you are for this to work." She looked at Xela in my body who was lost in a trance. "Trust in the love of your family."

"I do. I always will." Everything I'd done was for my family and for the welfare of others. I'd sacrifice everything for them to be happy.

"They cannot flourish without you," my mom added. "Love yourself as much as you love us, and everything will work out."

"I will. I promise."

My mother and aunt stepped back, then flew into a side tunnel, their essences following them like another set of glowing ghosts that wrapped their silhouettes.

Eric wiggled his fingers, and blue light appeared underneath everyone's feet. "Once the portal to the doorway is opened, it will get nasty," he explained when I raised my eyebrows.

"But how will you fight?"

"Fighting isn't always physical. Leave that to us." Xander stood with his feet apart, taller than I remembered. His hands were thrust in front of him, palms out. Mira held the same stance.

"They'll be here soon," Eric whispered.

"What's that?" I pointed to the gleaming light at the bottom of the mirror.

"The point in between the now and the hereafter," Eric answered. "That's where Aseret needs to be locked up."

I grimaced. "That doesn't tell me much."

"A portal to another dimension. A one-way ticket," Mira supplied.

The light glowed brighter, holding greater meaning. "So, how exactly do we do this?"

"You worry about staying with us. You're doing your job by luring the warlock here. My sources say he's furious with you," Eric said. "Aseret can only be killed beside the portal, so his spirit can be pushed in. Otherwise, he'll escape and roam as a ghost until he finds a suitable host."

"Sounds like you know what you're doing."

"I've done it once. I can do it again." He winked. "Except this time, his culprit witch will be locked away with him."

"Right."

The wind whistled through the tunnels before it gusted into the cave. The current increased, carrying with it the stench of rotten eggs and dirty socks. Seekers spilled into the cave like a disturbed colony of ants. Once in, they moved to hug the walls, holding onto rocks and tree roots. Their cloaks fluttered uncontrollably in the wind. It looked like we were in the eye of a tornado and the seekers on its edge.

Behind them, Aseret floated in, his cloak trailing on the dirt floor. His gaze drifted for a moment toward my husband, and Aseret paused mid-step before resuming his drift. Miranda's ghost hovered at his side. Both held their heads high, but the witch visibly struggled not to look at the body in front of William. Her focus fell on Xela's and Mrs. G's joined hands, and her spirit vibrated. Twenty feet in, the witch and the warlock stopped. Movers and freezers crossed in front of them, creating a pyramid formation, protecting their lord. Aseret did not to step over the threshold in a stone wall that would put him in the same area of the hereafter as us.

The blue light under my family's feet disappeared, but they didn't move an inch. The hall was silent, except for the electric buzzing of the ripples in the mirror.

"Silly, silly creaturesss," Aseret drawled in his monotone. "What worked once, evil-bender, will not work again."

"We're not here to bind you," Eric lied. "Why don't you leave and let us do our job?"

"Don't insssult me," the warlock hissed, turning his head aside to hide a grimace, as if he'd lost the ability to control his emotions. He looked forward again. "Hmm, and you'd leave the twins by themselves? Silly to leave your family without protection."

Eric didn't say anything, just stared at Aseret.

"Ahh well, I shall sssend sssomeone to keep them company at the cabin."

Three seekers and a handful of freezers and movers left through the door behind Aseret.

My family! I said to Eric.

Don't worry. They're safe. Try not to talk. It makes my job a bit more difficult.

Spikes of flesh extended on Eric's neck; they'd also thickened. Calmness swept through my body, the same as when Crystal touched me. I scanned the room but couldn't see her. I almost tasted the twins' lemon-honey aroma on my tongue, though.

"Let's get this over with." Aseret lifted his arms, and his cuffs slid down to his elbows as his translucent hands prepared to beam fire, his strongest choice of magic, from his twig-like fingers.

"Let's." Eric lowered his head and reached right through me to take Xander's hand.

"You'd better hold on." Xander looked at their gripped hands inside my ghost, then squeezed Mira's hand on his other side.

Their energy flew through me. The waves of Eric's bending made my ghost flicker like a broken lamp.

"You have no way of taking me down. My essence is a hundredfold greater," Aseret said, gathering his first blow in his palms. Red fire circled his wrists before enveloping his hands. "You will all end up there, looking at me from beyond as I rule your species." He threw his hands forward and streams of light zipped through the cave, changing into flame, crackling like fire. One flew toward us, the other toward William, Mrs. G, and Xela.

Staying between Eric and the siblings as they'd asked, I closed my eyes before impact.

It should have reached us by now. I opened my eyes.

It never did. Instead, both streams of light slowed their blast and bounced off invisible shields similar to the one I'd created with William in the underworld when we faced off against Aseret.

The warlock pressed the attack, this time with fire, trying to break the invisible hold.

On the side of his neck nearest me, Eric's fleshy spike ripped open. Blood streaked down his neck and body.

You're hurt.

It's all right, he answered without moving. *Let me concentrate.* The spikes vibrated again, and I smelled honey and lemon.

A yellowish mist wafted down from the ceiling like flower pollen. Before it touched the ground, the pollen concentrated in two spots and materialized into my children. Crystal and Ayer stepped out of the golden powder, beaming their aura.

"Impossible!" The warlock slid the hood off his head.

"Love your decorative scars, Aseret." Xander sneered at the warlock's orange glowing marks on the face and neck.

"You afraid to come closer?" Eric taunted. "You've been waiting for this. They're here. Come and get them."

What are you doing?

It's all right, Mama. Stay still, Crystal whispered.

"Tempting, but I'm not stupid, bender." Aseret's gaze flew from my children to Eric as he licked his lips.

"We'll see." Eric smirked.

Seekers crawled around the wall and attacked Mrs. G and Xela. William protected them, clearly stronger than any other time I'd seen him, even in Aseret's hall.

Her ghostly face a mask of determination, Miranda sped toward my children. Charging like a raging bull, she flew right through the twins. The witch stopped and whirled around to try again but bumped into an invisible wall before reaching Crystal and Ayer. She circled to the side and found an unseen barrier there, as well. Miranda zoomed upward like a rocket, then crashed down to the floor.

All the time, Mrs. G and Xela continued their chanting. Each time Miranda hit an invisible wall, Mrs. G's and Xela's arms bruised. Miranda halted, changed direction, and flew straight at the witches, only to hit another wall. She was enclosed in an invisible box, her soul captured.

"Ssstupid witch," Aseret hissed, wiggling his flat nose.

"You will help me, warlock. We're bound by blood." she called, excess saliva slurring her words.

"You're getting old, witch. It's the second time you've been tricked today." Aseret looked at me, unphased by her threat. "Fend for yourself."

"Your blood ties your fate to mine!" she bellowed.

"You have no body, witch; blood ties aren't honored between the realms."

Miranda tilted her head back and released a howl of frustration that rose to the opening in the roof of the cave and never came back. Foaming at the mouth, Miranda turned her back to Aseret and began humming a spell that sent waves of energy at the enclosure. Mrs. G's and Xela's muscles tensed as the blasts from Miranda's chant struck the barrier, but their black eyes remained rolled back in their heads.

"One breathes, ssso does the other. One crafts, ssso does the other. One dies, ssso does the other," Aseret repeated Mrs. G's words.

My ghost trembled.

"That'sss right, Sarah. I will get the twins. Only one crafter will do to end you all. Their essence will be enough to rule beyond any ruler." Hatred flared in his orange eyes.

He can see me, I whispered in my head.

Sarah, don't listen to him, Eric warned, but his cautious tone sounded as if it were coming from another planet, and once again, I felt like the warlock and I were the only ones occupying the cave, the same way when he spoke to me the first time I'd met him.

"Sarah, you can ssstill save your children. Come." He beckoned me with his twig-like index finger.

"Liar!" I yelled. "I will not fall for your tricks, and you will not touch my children."

"Look at them." He waved his hand. A red fog billowed forth, creating a screen. An image of Crystal and Ayer appeared, my children on their knees, bound by the light ropes. Aseret sat on his throne as they cried out in pain, bowing at his feet, except

their voices were locked in their throats as their lips had been sown together. "Is this the future you want for them?"

"I know my children's future, and you are not in it!" I escaped from between Eric and Xander and floated toward the warlock. Somewhere in the distance, I heard muffled voices, but all that mattered was getting Aseret.

As I passed my children, my ghost was yanked toward the hereafter. My family's and friends' feet were locked in place, but I was a ghost. No magic could keep me from being pulled. Now I understood why Eric had warned me to stay with him. Being connected was the only way to keep my ghost from entering the hereafter.

Eric, what's happening? I asked.

But my evil-bender kept his eyes closed. The spikes on his neck lengthened, vibrating with his effort to bend. Another spike burst, pouring blood down his shirt. His skin had paled. It wouldn't take before he was drained of energy. As they let Eric draw on their connected essences, Mira's and Xander's faces were taking on a greener shade.

Fighting the dragging sensation that drew me closer to the nearing hereafter I focused all my energy on escaping the gripping draft. It didn't help. I was about to pass William, Mrs. G, and Xela. Once there, only few feet would remain. My husband's brows narrowed in concern, eyes darting from the haul on my soul to the seekers he continued to shove to the ground, protecting the body that lay at his feet as well as the two witches behind him. His fangs gleamed, and veins swelled in his face, creating a bluish cast.

Aseret resumed his blasts at the invisible shield in front of Crystal and Ayer. My children stood still and waited like patient hunters. Miranda threw her own magic spells at the wall of the box that trapped her soul, bruising Xela and Mrs. G. Her ghost darted from one corner to another, growling and chanting relentlessly.

As I passed Miranda's corpse I remembered Xela's words: "*It takes three witches.*"

Was this where I was needed?

I grabbed Miranda's body by the legs, my hands connecting like a fly to a glue trap. Holding on, I crawled along the corpse and entered her body. My lungs filled with the stench of rotten eggs and dirty socks, but I welcomed the air. My chest expanded, and the breath was disbursed through the body. The heart I remembered from four years ago began beating. Blood circulated through the veins, and warmth returned to the flesh. My eyes opened, and I saw my family for who they were. I was no longer a ghost.

"That's my body!" Miranda rushed toward me but was stopped again by the magical wall.

Mrs. G's face and arms became more mottled with purple. Surely the rest of her body, as well as Xela's, matched the bruises on her face and limbs.

I sat up like an automaton. My new arms and legs pushed me up, and I took Mrs. G's other hand. Her chants flew to me through our connection and spilled out of my mouth. My eyes were open, but I knew they'd become fully black orbs, just like the witches'. Through these eyes, I saw the outline of the box holding Miranda captive.

"No! She's not a witch," Miranda screamed.

Maybe not, but my ancestors were.

Miranda's ghost fell to the floor. As we chanted, her enclosure drew along the ground toward the hereafter. She pressed her back against the far wall. "You can't do this to me. Aseret, help me!"

The warlock's focus didn't falter as he continued his failed attempts at the twins. Crystal and Ayer waited patiently.

A few steps closer. I heard Crystal whisper to her brother.

Aseret neared the threshold of the stone wall. His face contorted, its usually emotionless expression twisted and tightened as the warlock ground his teeth and bit his lips until blood and saliva streamed from the sides of his mouth.

Crystal and Ayer's tattoos danced around their wrists as if they were alive. The spheres spun energy that radiated outward to William, my watchers, and the protective shields.

The seekers stopped attacking William, who walked closer to the hereafter, toward the twins. The blue light under his feet alternated with each step. He looked like he was walking in gravity boots that held him grounded.

The spell I chanted with Xela and Mrs. G overtook my body, and I could only make out portions of the twins' battle. Dust swirled behind Aseret when he stepped over the threshold that protected my family from his streams of fire. A grin stretched across his wrinkled face. The warlock lifted his arms. Sparkling energy encircled his entire body before gathering into one bulk at his front. He released the blow at the children. Crystal and Ayer caught the stream in their hands, absorbing Aseret's wrath, and returned his blast in the form of a spell.

The warlock's body trembled and morphed, reshaping itself, shrinking its contours, until his soul escaped. As the limp corpse thumped to the ground, the children refocused their stream of electricity on Aseret's soul. The ribbons of light twined between their fingers, then flew at the ghost. Aseret ducked out of the way, but one strand of energy caught his wrist. Crystal pulled the stream in as if it were a rope, then whipped the warlock overhand toward Miranda's box. The warlock's spirit yelped and thrashed as it hurtled through the air.

"Now!" Ayer instructed.

William rushed to Aseret's corpse. He picked up the body and threw it into the rippling mirror. Its flesh sizzled when it hit the hereafter.

Another strand of light from Ayer twined around Aseret's left shoulder. The twins yanked, throwing his ghost into the magical box.

On her knees now, the Miranda looked at the warlock with hate in her eyes.

"If we work together, we can break through," he said to Miranda.

"Our ties are cut. We are no longer bound by blood, remember? Your oath has been broken," she said, all will gone from her soul, for the witch had to realize they were no contest to a triple threat of witches.

"You will not betray me!" he screamed at the witch as Eric, Xander, and Mira extended their hands forward and pushed the box toward the in-between.

"You have no choice. You are no longer a warlock. You are powerless and will soon be bound with no one to help you." Miranda laughed as the invisible box slid toward their doom.

Eric fell to his knees, bleeding from all of the two dozen spikes on his neck. The seekers slowly backed out of the doorways, looking from side to side, then finally fixed their gazes on Crystal and Ayer before they left. Chills ran down my new spine. The twins each had a new streak of gray hair woven into their auburn curls.

"We'll hunt them down," said William.

"We will." I turned to my husband.

The witch who seemed so strong a few minutes earlier no longer fought our chant. Her cackles and Aseret's hiss were the last of them to leave the cave as their spirits and the magical box began sinking into the in-between.

Before he'd left, I thought I'd heard Aseret say, "Silly, silly creaturesss. It's not over! His time has come." but Miranda's laugh vibrated louder than his words.

Aseret and Miranda melted into the ripples of the mirror.

CHAPTER 15

A week had passed since our ordeal, and my family and I were taking some well-deserved time off.

"Cannonball!" Ayer tucked his knees up to his chest before plunging into the water.

Crystal followed her brother off the rock face into the emerald pond. The water from her splash hit my face.

I sat on the ledge of the mountain, in Miranda's old body. It took a while to hike the back of the mountain, then repel on the ropes down the side of the cliff. With William's help, it didn't seem that difficult, though I was sure I'd fall into the pond had he not been holding me. I missed my vampire abilities and my old body that Xela still had. I hoped Xander didn't lay a hand on it until she got her own host back.

Each time I tried to speak, my tongue caught on the nicks and chips of Miranda's uneven teeth. Even with a quick makeover from my daughter and Mira, I still resembled a witch.

"How are you feeling?" William asked.

"Like I can finally live in peace."

"Good. There's only one thing left to do." William twined his fingers into mine.

"I don't think Eric is strong enough. You may be stuck with me this way for a while."

"I don't mind."

"I know. But I'd love for the upheaval to settle down. To have a normal life." I looked at the twins jumping out of the water like dolphins, flipping onto their backs.

William laughed. "I doubt we'll ever have a normal life."

"At least we're still the only ones who can disappear under the water." I pointed to Crystal's silhouette as she streaked along underwater like a mermaid.

"Not until your body's returned." William placed his arm around me.

"Yeah. I really think Eric will be too weak to bend for a while." I took a deep breath. Today was perfect—except for my new body, of course. The cloudless sky reflected turquoise in the water below. The smallest of the fish couldn't hide in that water.

"This feels nice," William murmured, shifting closer.

"It does." I rested my head on his shoulder.

"Sort of like a family picnic."

"Less the food."

"Says who?" William pulled on a rope hanging over the cliff, lifting a basket into view. I tried to smell it, but Miranda's nose wasn't nearly as good as my vampire one.

"When did you do this?" I asked.

"Well, one thing that hasn't changed is your need to know everything."

"I do not!"

He cocked his head.

"All right, I do," I admitted. "I guess I may have some control issues."

"Some?" he teased.

"Fine, a lot. I like to do things by myself and my way." Frowning, I crossed my arms.

"And that's why I love you." He kissed the tip of my nose.

Crystal and Ayer sprang out of the pond like penguins and sat beside us, one on each side. Water dripped from their dangling feet into the ripples below. They seemed to prefer remaining in their late teens.

"I figured you'd smell the food." William laughed.

"Yup. What you got there?" Ayer wiggled his nose, dug into the basket and pulled out a grilled chicken sandwich. Three bites, and the sandwich was gone.

"Three for each of us," William warned, passing me an apple.

"What am I, chopped liver?" I asked.

"Nope, I have something special for you." He placed a container on my lap.

I opened the lid. "Pancakes! Thank you, thwank wou," I mumbled around the forkful I'd shoved into my mouth.

"Hold on!" William pulled a bottle of maple syrup from the basket and poured it on top of the stack in my lap.

"Where did you get the recipe? These taste just like—"

"Your Aunt Helen's?"

"Yes!"

"Now the recipe has been passed down to you." He handed me a booklet. "Xela put in her goulash recipe, as well. Just in case you need to bribe Xander."

"I have to memorize that one." I let out a laugh.

Crystal took the fork from me and speared a piece of pancake. "Yummy."

Ayer leaned back, resting against the rock. "We'll need to leave for a while."

"When?" I asked.

"After you're bent back," Crystal mumbled, chewing her food.

It seemed natural for the fledgling casters to go into the world to explore and fulfill their duty. I remained unusually calm, then noticed Crystal's hand resting on mine. "Are you soothing my emotions?"

"Yes." My daughter's warmth oozed through me.

"You don't need to." I leaned against her shoulder.

"I thought you'd be upset we're leaving." Her head rested on top of mine.

"Sad, yes. Upset, no. I'm pretty sure you can handle anything."

"We can," she said. "It won't be long. And we'll visit."

"You'd better." I smiled as she sat up straight. "Your home will always be here for you."

"We know, Mama."

"Where will you live?" I asked the twins.

"We have some cleaning up to do. Aseret managed to build sects of demons all over the world." The excitement in Ayer's tone reminded me of William's. "We will take up Uncle Eric's home for a while."

"I wish you weren't the ones to clean up Aseret's mess," I said, my voice flat.

"It's not just Aseret. The keepers need us. Don't be sad, Mama. We'll visit often." Crystal placed her hand on top of mine again.

"Anything you need, we're here," William said.

"What I need right now is a swim." I looked down at the reflection of four pairs of dangling feet. Miranda's bulkier body released sweat in places I wasn't used to. Drops trickled down my back, and today's breezeless air didn't help.

"Let's go, then," William encouraged.

"I'm not sure if this body can swim." I felt the chill in my spine "What are you doing?" I exclaimed as Crystal took hold of my elbow and William the other.

"Taking you for a swim!" William laughed.

"No!"

But it was too late, and I hit the water with my behind. The sting of the contact singed my buttocks, and I found myself struggling to breathe. Miranda's lungs weren't as full as my vampire ones. William lifted me to the surface.

"A little warning next time would be nice," I said wryly when we emerged.

"What, and ruin the surprise?" He laughed as he helped me out.

"I can't wait to have my own body back," I said.

"I can't wait until you have your body, too." William's lust shone in his eyes.

"Sh, the kids."

"Mama, we're crafters, not kids," Ayer yelled from above before plunging past us into the water. "Cannonball!"

"You will always be my kids." My voice bounced against the cliff.

For the first time since I could remember, I actually had a family day to enjoy. Though not in my own body, I felt as comfortable in this skin as in my own. I treaded the water, enjoying its cooling effect as I tipped my face back to soak up the sun. Floating on my back, I outstretched my arms and closed my eyes. Stray clouds wandered across the sun, shading the glow behind my eyelids every few minutes. William held my hand, floating at my side, the partially submerged parts of his body invisible, the same way mine would have been if I had my half-breed body back. I heard the twins finishing their lunch up on the cliff.

"I have a surprise for you," William said.

"Another one?" I opened my eyes and turned my head to the side.

"Yes, but you'll love this one. We need to get home."

"Now? I'm really enjoying this." I squinted when the sun hit my face.

"I know you are, but you'll enjoy your gift even more."

"I'm intrigued." I picked up my head and looked around. "Is the surprise at home?"

"I'm not saying anything."

"Hmm, you're cute when you're secretive. Now I really want to know." I faced my husband's bopping torso.

"Then let's go."

William lifted me over his shoulder and swam to the shore. He set me down and jumped over the wall of shrubs while I lifted a towel from a bench and wrapped it around Miranda's black hair.

"OK, I'm ready." I stepped from one foot to the other.

"Home, Sarah, home." William took a step and disappeared.

"Are you forgetting I'm still human?" I shouted after him.

He reappeared at my side just long enough to say, "Not for long."

I used Miranda's legs to run as fast as they could go. The muscles ached, complaining with each step. My lungs wheezed, feeling they could work at only half capacity, and by the time I got to the clearing, I was heaving louder than a marathon newbie. I sat down on the front steps and stuck out my hand. William handed me a water bottle.

"I will never take being a half-breed for granted again." I gasped before pressing my lips to the tip of the bottle to suck in water.

William handed me another one.

"Why is your Hummer parked there?" I pointed to the center of the clearing.

My husband shrugged. "I let Ekim take it for a spin."

I finished the second bottle. "Okay, I'm ready for my surprise," I announced, wiping drops of water off my chin.

"You will have your half-breed body soon enough," Eric said as he stepped out of the cabin. The siblings and Xela followed.

"I really do miss my senses." Sweat dripped down my back as I pushed myself up. If I'd been in my own body, I'd have my abilities. Then my friends wouldn't be able to surprise me. It must have been a week of sneaking and whispering. Even the twins were acting as if they were hiding something, I realized now. At least I wasn't a ghost, though I missed my mother, the same way I'd missed her my entire life. Willow often stepped in to comfort me when I thought of her.

"Change first, then come back out." William motioned me inside. "And, Sarah, take your time." He winked.

"Like I could move quicker than a turtle." I rolled my eyes and walked to my room.

My hands swept through the clothes in my closet, and I looked for a comfortable skirt with an elastic waist. Fitting Miranda's body into my wardrobe and trying to care for a neglected face turned out to be a challenge each morning. William had bought a few necessities, though I didn't want much; I'd rather hold onto the hope that it wouldn't be long before Eric could exchange my soul with Xela, who still possessed my body.

After a few unsuccessful outfits, I pulled one of William's t-shirts over my head. *What seems like a fast change for me must seem like an eternity for my husband and my friends,* I thought, not happy with my outfit, but it was the best I could do. I left the room and headed back out to the porch.

The twins had changed and shifted to younger selves to play rock, paper, scissors in the doorway. They looked like they'd been at the game for a while now, two nine-year-olds as carefree as I remembered them. It made me happy to know they could lose themselves so easily. I stepped between them onto the porch, squinting into a setting sun.

William sat in a lounge chair, sipping a Bloody Mary. A Fuzzy Navel waited for me on the table. Mira swung on the hammock Eric had installed, one end attached to the stump left after Ayer took the tree down. Xander and Xela relaxed on the lower step of the porch, his arms wrapped around her. I still had a difficult time getting used to seeing Xander's arms around my body and wondered if it bothered William.

William read my expression. "I know who you are. I always will." He pulled me onto his lap.

Willow was at the end of the porch, reading through a new gardening book. Atram and Ekim had moved the loveseat from the solarium to a corner of the porch and were now discussing their plans for tomorrow. My father said he'd join me on my trip to the prison, to meet up with an acquaintance in Pinedale.

"I'd like to come along my friend," Atram said to my father.

"Not a good idea this time. It'll be dangerous," Ekim said.

Before I had a chance to question him, my gaze found the center of the clearing.

I gasped. "How did you . . . when did you . . ."

The Hummer had been moved back to its usual parking spot at the side of the house. In the spot where the last of the evening's rays streaked through the lower canopy, a garden bloomed. I remembered stepping out of William's Hummer for the first time to feel the tickle of the freshly mown grass. Now the blossoms of orchids I had never seen before bloomed here, their stems swaying with the breeze as if they were dancing. With William at my side, I walked toward heart-shaped bed of flowers.

"Happy birthday," William whispered.

"I forgot."

"I know. You remember everyone else, but not yourself." He wrapped his arms around me from behind. "We want you to know you're not forgotten, and never will be. Everyone helped."

"Thank you!" I threw my arms around his neck.

My family lined up behind William, and instead of singing Happy Birthday, Crystal, Ayer, and Eric shot sparks from their palms that exploded above the canopy like fireworks. Their crackling sounded just like the song.

I watched the display in delight. "I've never seen anything so beautiful."

"I have," William said, holding my gaze as he set me on the ground. "There's one more thing." He motioned Eric forward.

"We're ready to switch your souls." My evil-bender looked from me to Xela.

"I thought you said you couldn't do it yet."

"Not by myself, but I have some help now." He pointed to my children, who had already shifted to their caster age of seventeen. I never noticed when they managed to change. The shifting came so naturally to Crystal and Ayer, it seemed they were born with the ability. *Because they were,* I reminded myself.

I examined Eric's neck. "You're still bleeding. I can't ask you to do this."

"He's strong enough." Xander slapped his hand on Eric's shoulder, then gripped it, digging his fingers in deeper than I liked. A red spot blossomed on the bandage around Eric's neck as one of his spikes oozed fresh blood. Xander lowered his eyes, taking his grip away. "Sorry. It's just been a long time, and I have needs."

"Xander!" Xela smacked him on the back of his head, the way Mira would have.

"I just want you." He placed his hands on Xela's hips and pulled her in.

"I know exactly what you want, but the more patient you are, the better it will be." Xela leaned into her soul mate. The scent of estrogen and testosterone blended with the evening air.

"Okay, you two." Mira stepped between them and turned to Eric. "You better do this soon, or I'll throw up."

"I'm not doing this for them. I'm doing this for Sarah. She needs to finish her work at the prison, and I'm sure William has had enough of her being away from her body."

"You'd do that for me?" I asked.

"I am bound to you, aren't I?" Eric smiled. "Consider it a birthday gift."

"Thank you, Eric." I wrapped my arms around him in a tight hug. He squirmed, and I saw a scab on his neck rupture. "What does it mean for you?"

"It means someone else will need to wait a little longer to get his soul mate back. Xela will take over this body for now." He tightened our embrace.

"I already have her back," Xander said.

"So, can you do something about this?" I spun in front of my evil-bender.

Eric locked gazes with Xander. "If I do, I won't be able to bend for a while."

"If we can borrow your ruby until Eric recovers, that would help." Xander winked at his witch.

"You only think about one thing, don't you?" I rolled my eyes at my friend.

"I try. Do you know how difficult it is to concentrate with the extra blood flow?" He raised his brows.

I shrugged. "Then why don't you help yourself get rid of it?"

Mira burst out laughing, and water sprayed out of her mouth in a fountain from the sip she'd just taken. "You've got perfect timing," she sputtered.

"I may not have my vampire hearing back, but I can still hear you," I said.

"I know." She forced a laugh and returned to the hammock.

"I don't want Xander looking at someone else when he's with me. No offense," Xela added to me.

"None taken," I said.

"I only see you." Xander's eyes mellowed as he consumed Xela with his gaze. It was as if he were seeing her for the first time. Love shone from his face like it hadn't in decades. "But out of respect for Sarah . . . this has to be done."

"Then done it shall be." Eric motioned to Crystal and Ayer, and the twins moved to stand on either side of him.

Xela came closer to me. She squeezed my hand.

"You really want to do this?" I asked. "You'll be stuck in this body."

"You've done enough, Sarah. It's time for you to enjoy the life you were meant to live."

When she said things like this, the black witch that'd I glimpsed in her once in a while disappeared.

"Besides, Xander likes role playing." She winked.

Eric held the twins' hands, and the swirling in my stomach began, the same sensation I felt before entering a vortex. The treetops ruffled their leaves as the wind picked up; the moon rose higher in the darkening sky, quicker than it should. I wasn't sure if the time passed for me differently than the others, but I'd never seen the moon rise this way.

"What's going on?" I asked, but I couldn't hear my voice.

Don't worry. We need to draw energy. Eric's voice in my head soothed my worries, though the sound coming out of his mouth vibrated. The red dots on his bandaged neck enlarged.

The body hosting me weakened as my soul was sucked from it. I hovered above its head and exchanged a nod with Xela's spirit. Her black curls flowed down her back and chest, toward an hourglass waist, framing a pale face. Golden eyes like those of an eagle glowed as her ghost floated toward me, hands gesturing gracefully for us to trade places. *No wonder Xander fell for the black witch.* She was better than any woman Xander had ever dated, at least in my lifetime.

Our bodies stiffened and stood still, waiting like mannequins, frozen in time. I floated above my head as Xela's spirit drifted toward Miranda's host. Before I sank into my flesh, I looked at Eric. His face showed strain, and his neck bled more heavily. Crystal and Ayer were supporting him, their banded tattoos whirling around their wrists the same way they had in the underworld, channeling the keepers they'd told me. Mira dropped to her knees. I never saw my best friend cry before.

I drooped lower. As I touched the top of my head, the colorful jungle went black.

* * *

The undeceiving aroma of William's scent mixed with mine wrapped around me when I woke up in my bedroom. The birds chirped outside, and my freshly washed linen drapes fluttered in the open window. The intoxicating blend of fresh blossoms from my flower garden brought a smile to my face. No other nose than a half-breed's could be sensitive enough to identify each kind of flower. Hearing the murmur of voices, I perked my ears like a cougar's.

"Her heart rate's changed. She's waking up," William said in another room.

I grinned.

"It's about time. It's been three days," Xander said.

"Cool it," Mira warned.

"Switching bodies is a big deal. It takes a lot of energy," Xela explained.

"I know, I know. Are you two ganging up on me?" I imagined him throw his hands up.

"Let's go." My father's voice but, of course, William was the first to enter the room.

"Hi." He leaned in to kiss me before sitting beside me. The brush of his lips felt like our first kiss. I tasted warm peppermint tea.

"Hi." I smiled, savoring his touch.

"You all right?" asked Xander.

Mira bounced on the other side of the bed.

"Yes." I sat up. "How is Xela?"

"I'm fine too." She stepped from behind Xander.

"You don't have your body," I noted.

"No, that would really take a lot of bending. Eric isn't strong enough, and it's a little complicated to bend a black witch." She pointed to her neck while raising her brows. I assumed my bender's spikes hadn't healed yet.

"Everything is always complicated. Where's Eric? And the twins?" I listened with intent, but couldn't hear them, or their breathing anywhere in the house.

"They're fine. They're resting." William took my hand into his.

"I drained them?"

You didn't drain anyone, I heard in my head. *I'm fine, the twins are fine, but we can't come right now.*

Where are you?

It's not important. Rest. I can't speak too long; it takes a lot. But trust your senses—your children are all right. I'm all right.

Thank you.

Just doing my job.

Eric's humble attitude never ceased to surprise me. When he spoke in my mind, I felt his presence, even though I knew he might be on the other side of the planet. Our exchange took seconds.

"You didn't drain them." Mira took my other hand. "Just make sure you're strong and know you're back to your normal self."

"That's right. You just relax." My father tapped my shoulder as a suggestion to lie down.

"I'm fine, you guys. You don't have to treat me like an invalid." I pushed myself up again.

"Good, because you have some work to do. A message came from the warden with the latest sample. He has the papers ready to sign," William said.

Did I hear a tremor in his voice? Why would William's nerves peak, and why was he trying to hide them?

"Perhaps she should wait a few days," my father cautioned. I noticed him kick the side of William's leg.

"In a few days, he may change his mind. Now is the right time," William insisted.

"William's right. I need to get back to work as soon as possible." I paused. "Plus, I want to make sure the warden is feeling well after Aseret's possession. William's right. We don't want him to change his mind."

"I'll come with you," William said.

"No, you're behind on your work, too. I'll be fine." I sat up higher, stretching my arms to the side.

"What if—" William passed me a bottle of water.

I held the container between my palms. "There is no 'what if.' No seekers or demons would follow after seeing what happened to Aseret."

"She's right," my father said. "If there was ever a safer time, it is now."

"Good." I swung my legs over the side of the bed. "Because I'm ready to live my life, the way we were supposed to."

After a hearty breakfast and a hunt, I packed my suitcase, then reread the paperwork. The warden's prison, one of the last to be bound by the agreement, would become an execution-free facility. Once done, we'd be able to receive blood donations from the prison in exchange for security.

I left for Huntsville the next morning. This time I'd travel like a human—William had made arrangements for a car to be ready in Sao Paulo. In less than ten hours, the warden's signature would seal the deal. And humans and vampires will be one step closer to coexisting peacefully.

CHAPTER 16

The door to the warden's office pushed open with ease. I wondered how many times Aseret had stolen the warden's body in the past and used it to stalk us. How many times had he used information from the fragile man with a cane to hunt us?

The warden sat hunched behind his desk, the bulk of his upper body outlined by the glow from the window behind him. Dust had settled into in the curtains' creases, and cobwebs laced the window's corners. The warden's hands rested relaxed on his desk; his cane was propped by the chair. He looked at me from below his unibrow and smiled. It reminded me of a teacher welcoming students on the first day of school.

Instead of the confusion I'd expected after being posessed by Aseret, the warden seemed relieved to see me, as if he felt the time to sign the papers was long overdue. He gestured with his hand for me to come in, his fingers longer than I remembered; the skin paler, as if he'd had his tan from a week ago surgically removed from his flesh—or perhaps he'd forgotten to apply his makeup. His nose appeared shrunk, as well.

I pulled out a chair, placing my folders on the desk in front of me, and sat down. A tall candelabra at the side of the desk held melted candles. The wax that fell before hardening had left a splattered, solidified puddle on the hardwood floor. The room had an odd smell to it, one that reminded me of a blown-out match, the scent mingling with that of ancient paper. I peered at the bookshelf on my right. The leather-bound books looked hundreds of years old, the few pages sticking out yellowed, the red ribbon bookmarks faded to a sickly pink. They were crammed onto the shelves any which way. *What an odd way to keep books,* I thought, remembering my parents' neat collection in the basement before it burned, all of the books arranged by genre and height.

My scan for titles instead found strange markings and symbols on the spines. I recognized not only the water mark and the sphere on a few, but also an orchid identical to the one on my left wrist. Out of sight below the desktop, I wrapped my other hand around my tattoo and felt the mark heat. My gut was warning me, but I wasn't sure of what. When my gaze found the last tome, displaying the mark the twins had received on their wrists, shivers flew through my body.

The warden's unibrow had softened, and he looked like a puppy, although I didn't think I'd want a puppy with his face. I sat still in the leather chair across from him, warily scanning his desk for the papers I'd come to sign, but all I saw was a map. An odd map, not the city or country type I was used to. Multi-layered diagrams of hollow tubes, tunnels, and mazes in two-dimensional layers criscrossed the paper. My thighs stiffened as the pounding in my chest became more pronounced. But why? Aseret and Miranda were gone for good. What was the warden's business with the underworld?

"What is this?" I pointed to the map.

"Ah, the time has come." His pale hands remained flat on the desk, nonthreatening.

A red stream of light zoomed from the warden's mouth and hit my chest. I lost consciousness.

* * *

A swaying light bulb within a cheap shade dangled above my head when I woke up, its white glow searing my sleepy eyes. The shadow cast by the lampshade relieved the blinding effect of the illumination, but my heavy eyelids closed anyway. A buzz of electricity circled the room. Moving was impossible as restraints on my wrists and ankles kept me immobile. What material would be strong enough to hold me down? Me, a half-breed vampire. My back lay flat against a metal surface, and my arms were stretched out to the sides, as if I were attached to a cross. I wanted to open my eyes again, but they objected. My chest ached.

As I twisted my arm, the restraint burnt around my wrist. The smell of fresh blood forced me turn my head and open my eyes. The burgundy liquid trailed from a cut on my arm. My head fell to the right, and I looked at a mirror. Something inside me whispered that it was a two-way mirror, covered by a curtain on the other side. I tried to remember where I'd seen a two-way mirror before, and the memories flooded back. *The prison. I'm in the draining room.*

My head lifted forward again, and I closed my eyes to the dimming and brightening flashes behind my eyelids. The left side of my head throbbed, from my eye to the back of my head. *A headache?* Impossible. The stabbing pulse cut like a razor. I squeezed my eyes more tightly shut, hoping it'd stop, but hope was all I had.

An odd smell of peppermint and garlic entered my nostrils. I didn't recognize the strong scent that seemed to camouflage the owner's identity. To the left I saw a tall man's back. Beneath a long black hooded cloack, his shoulders were padded and squared like in the eighties. He was taller than the seekers who'd chased me in Pinedale. His upper body proportions suggested someone shorter so he might be wearing platform shoes. I hadn't seen a seeker this tall yet. All seekers should have been dead or in hiding anyway. Was he a demon?

He threw a piece of paper into the garbage pail beside the table, then stood by the door, his arms folded into the cuffs of his cloak, the hood drawn low over his eyes and nose. A cracked lower lip tightened when he noticed me looking at him.

I slid my gaze to the table set up on the wall where he'd been working, meant to hold the usual utensils for an execution, and saw not only syringes and needles but an electric saw.

The man's mouth curved. He couldn't be a seeker. Seekers did not express their emotions.

For some reason, my heart didn't begin pounding at the thought this could be a demon. In fact, the rhythm of my pulse was weaker. My heart *couldn't* pound. *Why am I so weak?*

The door opened, as slow as all the other movements common to creatures from the underworld when they weren't fighting. The warden wobbled inside like a penguin, turned and locked the door, then reached out and touched the teeth on the saw. The blade cut his finger. He wriggled in pleasure, put the finger in his mouth to suck the blood off, and focused on me.

"Who are you?" I mumbled, feeling the effect of the toxin inside me overpowering my blood flow. The corner of my lip cracked when I spoke.

"For a half-breed vampire, I thought you'd be more perceptive," he rasped, then cleared his throat as if trying to find his voice.

"Who are you?" I repeated.

"Ah, Sarah." His speech was no longer sluggish or slurred. His shoulders broadened, and the hump on his back disappeared as he straightened. "You've done me a great favor." He examined the way my body was positioned before shifting the cross table I lay on half an inch to the left, licking his lips. "Tsk, tsk, tsk," he murmured, his tongue sliding in and out like a lizards'.

"He looks at you as if you're the next in line to go into that room," I remembered my father saying.

"What favor?" My tongue touched my cracked lips. My throat was sore as well, making my voice scratchy.

The warden looked toward my feet. I lifted my head as far as I could and saw an expressionless vampire standing against the wall. The vampire's skin was not as pale as most, but smears and streaks revealed that that was due to carelessly applied makeup, similar to what the warden had worn before. He bore an identical cloak to the warden's, the hood also shadowing his eyes and nose. His lips were slightly parted, revealing an extended overbite; this vampire was waiting for his meal.

The back of my head hit the steel bed again as pain lanced into my chest.

He can't hurt me. The vampire can't hurt me, I thought, doubting that was true. Cuts on my skin would heal, but I was still half human. What would happen if he drained my blood without leaving a drop to keep my human heart alive?

Something stung at the crooks of my elbows, embedded in my skin. *Needles?*

I used my remaining strength to look down to my arm. Four-inch needles extended from my veins to clear tubing, emptying my blood into two half-full buckets, one on each side. Now the dryness in my throat and my near lack of a pulse made sense.

They're going to drain me. I wiggled again, trying to work my way free, but the ropes holding me down singed me, frying my skin. *How long will it take?*

"Who are you?" I grated.

The pain shot through my head again. *How much blood have I lost?* I concentrated on the drops flowing into the bucket; their momentum slowed.

"Ah, Aseret hadn't mentioned me, had he? Smart of my older brother." He grinned. "Very smart."

"Your brother?"

"Yes, we had different views of how the world should be. Though he promised to spare a few vampires and humans, having you all to myself now is much better. You took care of the underworld; I will take care of this one." He tested the end of a tooth on the saw again. When it cut his finger, the warden hopped from one foot to another. "You'll make a good meal for the wolves."

"My family will find me," I said.

"Perhaps. In pieces." His gaze slid to the mirrored window, then back to me.

My spine froze. Was he planning to spread the word of a dead half-breed vampire as a warning? I panicked, but the beating of my heart remained sluggish, dying. I closed my eyes. "You will not get away with this," I said, my voice faint.

"I think I already have. Your family is busy. They cannot help you. Your husband is dead, I hear. Too bad the lava bestows quick death. So unlike what you'll face." He looked at the saw again and laughed freely. The bellow reminded me of Aseret. Even his speech, now that it was not disguised, was slower, with pauses between words, though the tone was much more confident.

The warden didn't know William was saved after he fell into the crevice.

Eric, help me. My head throbbed again. The room spun. What had the warden given me?

"The connection you have to the twins is more than that of motherhood," he continued. "Your connection is magical; after all, they were conceived because of magic. You don't even know the strength of your own blood."

I had a different theory about how my children were conceived, but I wasn't abot to share it with him.

"You hold power over the casters. When you die, they will be weakened. In fact, it may be just enough to push them over the edge so they'll join me. I'll recreate the underworld on Earth, the way it should have been, the way my brother never agreed to. The keepers themselves will dance in the palm of my hand."

"They will kill you. I'll make sure of it. If not from this world, then from the next."

"I let you take care of my business; I couldn't have Aseret stand in the way. See, whereas my brother thought humans and vampires should die, I disagreed. Why waste such a good resource? Slavery will be redefined when they all serve me. I recognized your strength the minute you shoved me against the wall." He focused on the viewing room again. "I couldn't compete with the power of your essence. So why bother?" He shrugged. "Let the strength come to me. And you have. Now, you die, the twins die, and I collect all your essence, including the one the keepers are channeling to the twins."

"You're more delusional than your brother," I whispered. All strength had disappeared from my voice. Just moving my lips had become difficult. My breathing was shallow. The room began to haze over.

Eric, where are you? The pain in my head flew from my left eye to the back of my skull again. My eye twitched.

"No one can hear you. You didn't think I'd leave such an important detail overlooked, did you?" he mocked as if he knew my thoughts.

I focused on his drooping face, which looked less wrinkled than before. He wasn't lying. I was on my own.

"See, my brother's calculations may have helped him to build a following before the prophecy, but he didn't consider failure. I have. And where he failed, I'll gain."

"He never mentioned you."

"Of course he didn't. I let him think he used me to get to you. I knew a prophecy to destroy him couldn't be stopped. After all, it was a prophecy."

"You're forgetting the prophecy was to stop the extinction."

"And you have. Like I said, I have no reason to waste the essence of billions of humans and who knows how many vampires." His laugh was less annoying than Aseret's. "Now, don't you think you've wasted enough strength? Save it for me." He lowered his head closer to my face, and I saw his sharpened teeth, below a flat nose which, unlike Aseret's, didn't twitch. His breath reminded me of the grossest dumps I'd scouted for rats before I knew who I was, back in Pinedale.

"You searched for me," I said, remembering seeing the warden in Pinedale.

"And with Aseret's help, I found you; I made you seek me out."

My arms felt limp, and I imagined that the vampire against the wall was William. Oh, how much I missed William! I fixed my gaze on his face. Each time I blinked, the contours of his jaw intensified. The vampire lowered the hood off his head. The turquoise eyes struck me. His cheeks and forehead morphed, readjusting other features that grew more identical to my husband's every second.

"William. You're here," I whispered, or I thought I had, because the voice that escaped me was barely composed of a breath. My eyes closed. My concentration flew to my right hand which I thought I lifted toward him. "Help me. Please." I opened my eyes, but my hand was still tied to the table.

The vampire against the wall had his hood lowered over his eyes, down to the tip of his nose.

It took all the strength I had in me to turn my head the other way, to not see this monster, to try to rationalize that it was a hallucination.

The warden backed toward the door, nodding to his demon and vampire.

I took another shallow breath. Was this the end? I shouldn't have discouraged William from coming. I should have listened to him. But we were so sure it was safe, that no one would hurt me.

Drop after drop, the buckets filled. The vampire waited, I didn't know what for, but he seemed indifferent. I wasn't sure if I'd lose consciousness before I'd die, nor how long it would take before my heart beat for the last time. Would anyone hear it?

The sound of a hundred hooks sliding along a rail in the distance reached my ears as I began to drift off. It reminded me of someone scratching their fingernails on an old chalkboard.

My head fell to the right as I tried to locate the source of the sound.

I didn't want the warden to be the last person I'd see, and he wouldn't be. As I looked at the two-way mirror, I realized my last memory would be much worse than seeing the warden.

The viewing room curtain was open. Any hope I had vanished. Seated in two rows were my family and friends, all staring at my body like a bunch of drugged zombies. Eric sat at one end, my children beside him, then Xela, the siblings, Mrs. G, my father, and William's parents. Their faces showed no fear, no pain, no emotion. They were bound hand and foot with magic ropes, their hands behind their backs, their legs to a metal bench that had replaced the chairs I remembered.

This isn't happening! I shut my eyes, trying to shed a tear as a human should, but my body was nearly drained and no drop could escape.

I didn't want to give up, but how couldn't I? This was even worse than any nightmare I could have had. How I wished it was only a nightmare! It wasn't like me to lose faith, but I had no choice or control over my physical body and its response to the loss of blood. Lifting my arm was impossible, as was swinging my head to the other side; I was forced to look at my family.

My eyelids drooped lower and finally closed. My last thoughts were directed to my husband and children. *I love you.* Perhaps someday, those words would reach them. Though I didn't want to admit it, I knew I'd see them soon, in the hereafter.

The world went black beyond my eyelids, then lightened.

My soul detached from my body. The rip away from my flesh was quick, feeling like a continuous papercut across all my limbs. Confused, I hovered above my corpse not wanting to float any farther. I'd stay near my body until someone dragged me to the hereafter. Would I join my mother? What about my aunt? When I thought about the hereafter, I wanted nothing more than to live longer. My wish was to stay here, in the flesh. Just when I'd finally gotten my life figured out and accepted who I was, I'd lost it again.

I had looked forward to spending time with the twins at the emerald lake when they visited. I'd zip through the canopy, William holding me from behind when we went to collect fresh orchid blossoms. I'd linger in the sun as it warmed me while I pulled fresh weeds out of my new garden. These were dreams now impossible to fulfill. I was a ghost. And soon, once my body was cut and mangled, there'd be no way to return. He'd feed the pieces to the wolves.

The vampire at my feet strode to the table and fiddled with some switches. The other demon blocked the doorway when the warden stepped closer to see.

I didn't want to die.

The electric saw started up.

I wouldn't let go. I couldn't. I grabbed my legs and pulled myself along the corpse until my soul was sucked back into its body. I closed my eyes, bracing for the sawed flesh and cracked bones.

CHAPTER 17

A face hovered below mine and I wanted to scream but couldn't. The hollow eyes were darker than black with depth that reached into the pit of hell. The unibrow was gone, along with all the other features I remembered. Had he walked down the street, I would have not recognized the contorted face. The angles of its cheekbones shifted with every expression. The face of a murderer, thief, rapist and a con man: each time the warden grinned, he resembled one of the inmates I'd seen when I passed the cells in the prison. Somewhere in between the shifts, the face of a demon lurked. It was unlike any I'd seen, close to what I'd imagined Lucifer himself to be.

Shivers run through my body. A cold chill climbed from the bottom of my spine.

"This is not the end," the warden slurred. He sucked back on the saliva that hung out of his mouth. He bellowed a ghostly laugh and focused on a body that lay face down on the floor. The legs bent and black cloak rose up, revealing platform shoes.

One of the two vampire guards.

That's when I noticed the empty metal bed and me hanging over someone's shoulder. The grey linoleum floor turned crimson with splattered blood. Lightheaded, I knew I was on the brink of death. If I'd only close my eyes, my soul would find a way out of this body. The sound of a hacking chainsaw behind me rung in my eardrums. My limbs bopped up and down in the motion of calculated swings. The shaking of my captor's shoulders vibrated mine, and I didn't want to turn to see what he was doing. I smelled burnt flesh and dead blood.

I tried to pick up my head again but couldn't. It would take too much strength so my gaze remained on the lower part of the room. The warden's ghost flew toward the corpse lying on the floor. I saw his smirk, and just before he reached for the new host, I closed my eyes, choosing to leave my body. When the limpness returned, my ghost hovered over the table where I'd been tied a few moments ago.

One of the two guards held my loose body over his shoulder while cutting the warden to pieces. The vampire's head was still covered with the hood, his arms and cloak drenched in blood.

His guards turned on him. The thought elated me for a moment, but this only meant we faced a new war against the vampires. How could I find the strength to fight my own kind?

Below, the warden began to enter the lifeless body on the floor but bounced back. Confusion swept his face as he examined the corpse and pushed toward it again.

"No, you don't." I rushed at his ghost with as much speed as I could. My hands found his neck, and I pushed him off the body, through the wall, then the floor. My feet pressed harder against the floor, taking us below ground. New energy circled me. I smelled honey and lemon as yellowish mist enveloped me, and I wasn't sure whether I smelled it or my body back on earth did. As a ghost, I felt oddly connected to the realm above.

As I tightened my grip, we passed earth, rocks, and an underground river before falling into a hall in the underworld. The landing broke my hold on the warlock, but we ended up exactly where I wanted us to. I backed toward the wall, letting my ghost disappear into it.

The warden leaped at me, but I moved out of the way and followed him into the room behind me that he fell into. Before he gathered himself, I shot up to the rooted ceiling and pulled out Miranda's book of spells on the top of the table. The pages flipped by themselves, opening to a spell.

The warden's ghost hovered back and forth in front of me, and I recognized confusion on his face. His gaze skimmed from me, to the book, then back to me again.

"This is a witch's lair." He circled around me, scanning the room, but I ignored him, knowing he'd figure out a way to recompose his thoughts. I couldn't hesitate. The fireplace roared with fury, welcoming me back.

The letters on the opened page in the spell book glowed blue, and I read them.

The warlock launched at me again but was stopped before he reached me. His spirit faded from translucent to barely visible. I connected to my inner witch ancestors, continuing down the page. A gust picked up the dust in the room, spinning five tornadoes around the warlock. Each time he tried to grab me, his ghost vibrated until the magic spell tied his ghost to the ground.

"Silly, Sarah. This isn't over. It has just begun. I will find a way to get your essence. After all, you're all connected to the keepers," he threatened.

The page of the book flipped, and I read the next glowing paragraph. Light flew out of my mouth toward the ceiling of the lair. It collected into an oval above the warden's head and opened a portal.

As I finished the spell, the five funnels around the warden merged into one, spinning him upward, until he was sucked into the warp.

The dust settled. I lowered my shoulders.

The book shut, and I exhaled an unnecessary breath, making a mental note to remember to come back and get the book for Mrs. G.

In the far distance, I heard familiar voices reciting the same words over and over again. I hid the magic book back up in the roots. The chant became louder and louder, and I felt my ghost being pulled back up to earth. Giving into the hymn, I let my spirit follow the witches' mantra, their repeated words beckoning me back to the prison. My ghost slammed into my slouched body, cradled in someone's arms, and everything went black.

* * *

I opened my bleary eyes and stared at the blurred colors of what I recognized as the Tiffany lamp in my bedroom. My head no longer throbbed. I listened to my pulse as the heart in my chest thumped—my heart, as strong and vibrant as if I'd fed on ten mountain lions. I focused on my arm and the purple bruise on the bend of the elbow. A similar bruise was on my other arm. I sniffed the air.

"William?"

"Stay still." He touched my shoulder.

I lowered my head back to the pillow. It felt so heavy it would sink between the feathers. I turned to the left to see William at my side, though he and almost everything else was still hazy. There was a fresh scar on his upper lip and another one on his brow. "What happened?"

"Nothing to worry about. It's all been taken care of."

I tried to remember what had happened at the prison, but nothing made sense. Had I been dreaming? Because lying here in my bed with William at my side seemed too good to be true. I expected to be dead. But the bruises on my arms wouldn't lie. William had saved me somehow.

"They were all tied up. And drugged. Crystal and Ayer and your parents. Mira and Xander. They were all . . ." My pulse sped as if I'd run from here to Pinedale.

"Sarah, calm down. It was an illusion. He didn't want you to have any hope." He placed a wet cloth on my forehead. The coolness liberated the pulsing inside.

William's soft words sounded like a fairy tale. *Was I dead?* He took my hand into his, the touch rejuvenating me.

"Illusion? You weren't in the viewing room?"

"No." He shook his head. "I was in the execution room, with you."

"What?" I tried to remember, but my faint memory only provided me with the vampire who stood at my feet, waiting to use the saw to kill me, and the other demon. "I'd have smelled you."

"No. You were drugged. And I ate so much garlic with peppermint leaves, it emanated from my pores. It's a good thing the warden's sense of smell was nonexistent." William swooshed his tongue in his mouth, making a face as if he'd just eaten dirt.

"Was?" I perked up.

"He's gone. He'll never hurt anyone again."

Never say never. My quick thought evaporated as the pounding in my head began all over. "How?" I asked.

"We knew his plan. Crystal and Ayer had known about his scheming for some time now. They've been the only ones aware of his presence, even more so than his own brother, Aseret."

"They couldn't tell us?" I massaged my temples.

William pulled open a drawer beside the bed. "Here. Codeine. It should help." He handed me two pills.

"Thank you." I dipped my head back, swallowing them without water.

"If the warden sensed any kind of trouble, he'd flee. Finding him would have been more difficult than defeating Aseret. He was the smarter brother and would never give us the opportunity Aseret had given us. It'd be impossible to kill him. We had to trick the warden. The children had to send me away whenever he came close. In the clearing, when Aseret took his body, they couldn't risk him seeing me up close, even through Aseret's eyes. Otherwise we would never be able to infiltrate his prison. I've been working there for months now."

"Months? And I didn't know about it?"

"I'm sorry." He lowered his head. "It was necessary at the time. I'd been instructed to keep it a secret so that our plan would work."

My head still hurt. "And it worked? What day is it?"

William shook his head. "Relax, sweetheart. It's been five days. The warden kept his business under lock and key, like his prisoners. And his planning and communications were more modern, unlike Aseret's. Most of his dealings happened online."

I had an insight. "Your iPad?"

"Yes, I was tracking him. With the twins' help, we were able to devise a plan to destroy him. Something he'd never suspect." He tapped his finger on the tablet in his lap.

"Did it have to come so close to me being dead?" I complained.

"He needed your soul. He wouldn't show his true form unless there was a chance you'd be dead. It was the only way to make him transform into his demon form, something he had to do to take your essence away."

A memory of Lucifer flashed in my mind, but the pain in my head took it away too quickly.

"Did he transform?" I asked.

"Yes."

A vision of the warden's soul zoomed through my mind, and I closed my eyes. Something about the mention of his soul stroke a chord inside me, but I couldn't remember. My head throbbed.

"His soul. Has it been destroyed?"

"No." William shook his head. "Mrs. G and Xela tried to find it, but somehow his spirit flew away from the prison too fast. And you were weak. Eric and the twins vortexed us back home."

"So everyone is okay?" I asked.

"As well as they can be, yes."

He was hedging. His heartbeat remained steady, but his delivery came too quickly, too smoothly; he had to have practiced what he'd say when I asked about my family.

I sat up. "You're hiding something."

"We'll go see the others, but only if you're feeling up to it."

"I feel fine. Stronger than I should be." I licked my lips, tasting the residue of the blood they must have fed me. Its iron tang covered the inside of my mouth. It sated me more than any other animal's blood had in the past. Something between a baboon and perhaps an orangutan . . . But I was sure it was a different mammal.

Xander knocked on the door before peeking into our room. "William, it's time."

"Let me help you." William put a supporting hand under my arm.

"Time for what?" I asked.

"If I tell you, you'll panic. You need to see; it's better this way." He helped me off the bed, and I slipped my feet into the warmed slippers.

"What is?"

My heart raced. The thumping in my chest increased as I stepped out of our bedroom into the living room of our cabin. On my left, Mira sat in Eric's lap on the arm chair, checking his bandaged neck. The red spots on the white fabric reminded me of an albino fly agaric mushroom. Mira's face told me not to ask. I was more curious about the woman sitting on the couch beside Xander anyway.

"This is the real Xela." Xander took her elbow, beaming with pride, as if he were presenting his bride.

Xela smiled with her original face, a genuine smile in a genuine face. She appeared younger in person. Life radiated from her, mostly toward Xander. The same black curls tumbled down her back and chest, a full chest in a tank top small enough to fit my daughter.

I looked to Crystal, absorbed in flipping through Mrs. G's medicine notebook. Her eyes scanned each page, as if she were memorizing one after another. She wore a tank top that was, thankfully, right for her size. Ayer touched her shoulder, and I thought I saw words flow from Crystal's arm through to Ayer's hand. The mesh of black print travelled along their skin so quickly only they could read it.

You're all right, Mama, I heard them whisper in my head.

Everything will be all right now, Crystal added, trying to soothe my feelings without touching me. It worked.

Atram sat on a corner of a bed that must have been dragged in from another room. On it, Willow lay on her side, her eyes closed, her skin pale. I rushed to her side, almost tripping in my haste. William caught me and helped me sit at her feet.

"She'll be up soon," my father-in-law whispered.

"Her heart isn't beating," I blurted, my voice high with panic as I touched her cold knee. That's when I saw a puncture on her wrist which dangled off the side of the bed.

Atram picked up her hand and set it on the mattress.

"She's not human?" I asked.

"No," Atram said calmly. "A vampire. Still learning to adjust."

"How?" I asked, then I saw a dark drop, the size of a pinhead, on her hand. I leaned forward and took a whiff, detecting the same iron tang I'd had in my mouth. "You let me drink from Willow? I killed her?"

"No, she's alive." Atram smiled. "Well, not the kind of alive you were used to, but she'll be with us for a long time."

I stood and swayed on my feet. William supported me as I stared at the faint smear of blood on her chin from a recent feed. How could they allow me to take a life? My insides twisted, and I fought against the urge to throw up my recent meal. My first human kill was my mother-in-law.

"She saved your life. You'd lost too much blood in the prison," Atram explained.

"You let me feed on Willow?" I repeated.

"You would have died, Sarah. And human blood is still more potent than any serum we could invent," William whispered in my ear.

I couldn't stop looking at Willow's pale skin. I blinked as my sight hazed and the room spun. William pushed an ottoman under my knees and I sat. "What happened? I saw everyone behind the mirror."

"It was merely a magical illusion," my husband reminded me.

"You weren't there."

"I was there, Sarah. Just not where you thought." William held me tighter.

My hands started to tremble as the memories came back. More memories than I'd bargained for. "Ayer and Crystal knew."

"Yes. The children brought you back home. Their knowledge as casters limits their physical abilities. They cannot meddle too much. The balance needs to be kept."

Thank you, I said to my children.

Always, Mama, they replied. *Always.*

"Eric heard your faint plea for help and insisted on coming," said William.

"You saved me? You brought Xela and Mrs. G to connect me back to my body." I looked at my evil-bender. "And you're hurt."

"I sensed your soul far away. I didn't save you, but I do have to stop bending, for a while, at least. The spikes need some rest." He pointed to his neck, then turned to Mira, tightening his arms around her. "I'll need to rely on you a bit more, sugar."

"I don't mind at all." Smiling, she stretched her neck up and kissed his lips.

"So who was it?" I closed my eyes to remember. What had happened came back to me in flashes. Just before the saw touched me, someone had picked me up. His hood fell back, and my nose pressed against his hair, and I inhaled a woody musk scent. The sleeve of the black cloak slid up his arm, revealing part of a tattoo on his wrist. A scream rang in my eardrums— someone screamed as if they were being skinned like a wild rabbit. Then splattering blood. The sting in my arms as the titanium needles were ripped out. Then the screaming stopped, ending as a gurgle. And William's voice, ringing through the room, "No!" followed by "I'm sorry." A mist smelling of wildflowers swirled around me, overpowered by honey and lemon . . .

I faced my husband. "William. It was you. You held me."

"I did what I had to do."

"I didn't recognize you."

"Some props are helpful." He dangled a set of porcelain teeth on his finger. "And you weren't supposed to recognize me."

"The warden thought you were dead." I squeezed William's hand.

"He needed to think you were helpless. You couldn't have felt any hope, or he'd have been suspicious."

"Right." I wasn't going to argue. If it weren't for William, I'd be dead. "You had it all planned out, didn't you? That was the secret you were keeping. For months."

"Yes."

I looked around the room. "You all helped. You all saved me, saved the races." My eyes welled up. Not only was my family here with me, but we worked together, had one another's backs when in need. They never left me, even in a time when I had felt lost and alone. Did I deserve to be so fortunate?

"We're a family, aren't we?" Atram gave me a genuine smile, and I knew he'd never accuse me of killing his wife.

"Of course."

William embraced me. His arms felt more comforting than hot coco on a cold winter day. I closed my eyes, savoring the feeling of an innocent touch, one I'd thought I'd never feel again.

"Can we promise each other we'll never break our promises again?" I said.

"How about we leave out the promises and let our instincts guide our lives?"

"Couldn't agree with you more." I leaned into him.

Willow moved her head. I waited for her body to thrash in pain, but she opened her eyes, then closed them again without any other movement.

"I've never seen a human change," I said.

"Fortunately, it's not as dramatic as Hollywood tries to make it." Xander laughed from behind me.

"Willow will be a vampire, just like you." I looked at Atram.

"She will. You may not see it yet, but it's better this way. I know it's selfish, but I won't need to worry as much."

"And my father . . . where's my father?" I scanned the room, then looked behind Mrs. G who sat in a wicker chair, her hands held together in her lap.

Mrs. G held my gaze. Her witch persona today reminded me more of a caring mother, and I her child, much as I had been in Pinedale.

"The book!" I remembered stashing the spell book in the tangled roots of the ceiling in Miranda's lair—just before I freed my mother. Or perhaps it was another time? The memory blurred. "I know where to find the magic book you were looking for."

She showed a kind smile. "In do time we'll get it. Now, your father, darling..."

I stood up. "He should be here. I can feel it," I insisted, taking small steps forward.

"Sarah, the warden was strong." William paused, trying to find the right words. I let him think before he spoke. Care and concern mixed with apprehension tinted the shade of his eyes, and I knew what he wanted to say was important. He, too, didn't want me to be hurt. "And even vampires aren't immortal." His shoulders drooped.

"Where is my father?" I asked again as a lump formed in my throat. Tears streaked down my face.

William's expression mellowed. "Sarah . . ." My husband's apologetic face told me what he couldn't.

I closed my eyes and remembered the saw again, as well as the demon who stood beside the warden. It hadn't been a demon. It had been my father in those platform shoes.

A new memory flashed, and my body twitched. The saw flew from my father to the warden. The warlock ducked, grabbing the handle away from my father and swung at me and William. My father threw himself in its path . . .

"He says she can handle it," Ayer's soothing voice interrupted.

"You can see him?" My eyes flew open, wiping my nose with my sleeve. I whipped my body around until my gaze rested on my son.

Ayer nodded.

"He can only show once, then he has to move on," Crystal explained, standing beside her brother.

"I don't want him to move on." My voice shook. "I just got him back. I want him here. With me." I sniffled and inhaled like a two-year-old, all stuffed up.

Ayer shook his head. "You've done what was needed, Mama. You accepted him as your father."

Crystal's hand was on my shoulder; I wasn't sure when she'd moved to my side.

I regretted the years that had passed when I didn't know him, when I'd hated him for creating me. I looked around the room, from my best friends to my in-laws to William and my children. Love all around me. If it weren't for my father, I wouldn't have my family; I wouldn't know the devotion of a friend and a watcher; I couldn't experience motherhood and understand unconditional love. My father had protected me when I didn't know him; even when I rejected him and despised him, he always loved me. I owed him my life, and he shouldn't have sacrificed his for me. Somewhere inside, I understood, for I would have had done the same, if it was my child whose life was threatened.

"Why only once?" I looked at Eric.

"The balance is restored. Souls will no longer be lost."

"He was reunited with his body?"

"He didn't need to be. His final breath came when he turned to ash. He will not be able to see you again after today." My evil-bender sighed. "I'm sorry."

"Eric, please . . ."

Ayer's hand found my other shoulder.

"He shouldn't have jumped in . . ." I was nearly panting as William swooshed the ottoman under my buckling knees.

And then he was there. My father's ghost, as vibrant as he was in life, floated toward me. The fierceness of his ghost, stronger than when he was a vampire, had been softened by the joy in his eyes.

"It makes me happy to see you alive," my father whispered.

I jumped to my feet and wished for my ghost back, because I wanted nothing more than to wrap myself in his embrace. He placed his arms around me as if he was corporeal, and the warmth of his soul's essence soothed my pain. Though I hugged an ephemeral form, I imagined the pressure of his arms as he squeezed me. He smelled of jasmine and wildflowers, just like my mother and the bouquet I always imagined her holding when she collected blossoms on the day she met my father.

"And I would do it again to make sure you live the life you were meant to live—with William and the children. You're a parent. I'm sure you understand what I had to do."

Sobbing I nodded, and tightened my embrace.

"Don't worry, I'll be all right." He smiled as he let me go.

I believed him, because my mother's spirit stood beside him. For the first time since her death, they were truly reunited.

My father took my mother's hand. Energy vibrated between their souls. His eyes glowed with happiness as he looked adoringly at my mother, who looked at him like she hadn't seen him in decades. The way they stared at each other reminded me of how much William adored me. My husband's love flowed with every glance.

Even though I'd lost him, my father had gained what he'd missed for the last few decades—his true love. He'd be happy in the hereafter, and so would my mother.

My heart warmed, and stability returned to my legs for the first time since I'd woken up.

My parents placed their arms around me. The pain in my chest eased as they kissed my cheeks, the gestures as gentle as if fog had streamed in a blanket around me, taking away worries and pain. I felt swaddled in love, like a newborn baby.

"It's time we moved on, Sarah. Eric has been kind enough to let us say our goodbyes together," my father said.

"Does this mean I'll never see you again?"

"Never say never." My mother winked. "You're in good hands here. They," she nodded toward my family and friends, "would give their lives for yours, just as you would for them."

"I know." I wiped my wet cheeks with the sleeve of my sweatshirt.

"It's time," Eric whispered. The red dots on his bandaged neck had increased in diameter.

"I will miss you," I said to my parents.

"And we'll watch over you, always. Your Aunt Helen, too. She says hello but can't be here. She's holding the doorway for us."

I nodded, mouthing, "I love you" as they drifted backward. Their souls glowed, not because they were souls or ghosts, but because their essence vibrated with more love than I'd seen in a long time. The sun shone through the front window, illuminating their spirits. The energy around my parents tightened, shrinking. The streaks of sunlight beamed through them with increasing intensity until they disappeared in a white flash.

* * *

I lay with my hands under my head, watching the stars fall from the sky. The canopy had shrunk enough to expose the universe; drought neared.

"Do you think we're the only ones doing the exact same thing right now?" I asked William.

"Watching the sky?"

"Yes, from a tree house, in a jungle, happy." I smiled.

"I hope not." He turned his head toward me.

For the first time in four years, the comfort I'd felt while at his side was the same as the first time we'd come to the tree house. The scents of the blossoms wafted around us, the pollen twirling in oval patterns. I'd become used to the high caused by the flowers; my body controlled the intake of their gifts.

"If we were, it'd be a shame." He exhaled. "I can't imagine anything better."

"I can." I smirked.

"Hmm, if I could read thoughts, I'd guess yours were the same as mine." He propped his head on his elbow. I felt the heat of his stare.

"I can't believe how much I missed this." I turned on my side to face William.

"Me too." He regarded me, pulling me closer. "You're back. You're finally you."

"I know. And I'm never leaving again."

He looked at me from below his brows.

"I am not leaving again," I insisted.

"Good, because we need you. *I* need you. And the world needs a selfless leader like you."

"You're talking like I'm going to be the next president."

"Never say never." He laughed. "Why don't we start with something more fun."

"Oh yeah? What's that?"

William pressed his lips to mine. The connection was as electrifying as the first time he'd kissed me; shock waves coursed through my body. He let me control him as much as he controlled me; after all, we were no longer two halves, but two equals. The rage I'd missed when Miranda first stole my body returned as passion, and I shifted into a vampire. With William at my side, I could only think of one way to express it.

Straddling his hips, I pressed William to the floor. He shifted as well, sitting up to hold me tighter, losing himself in my body. I didn't notice when the clothes flew off. His kisses dropped to my neck as I dug my fingers into his back. I looked up and saw a series of falling stars and thought, *Today is the first day of the rest of our lives together, as two equals.*

BONUS MATERIAL

William's Secrets

Hopeless wails drifted through the recovery ward of the prison. The cells quieted as William passed, keys dangling off the loop in his slacks. Overhead lamps dangled in the flowing drift. Some bulbs flickered as their light began dying; other had just been replaced and shone too bright, blinding the inmates who'd covered their heads under the sheets.

"I'm coming." He comforted each prisoner, making his way toward the far end of the hall. William's daily task to check on all inmates took him just over an hour. The warden's schedule had been reserved for scheming, which allowed the half-breed vampire to work at the prison long enough to earn the warden's trust as a worthy employee, yet not run into the warlock too often. When the right time came, infiltrating the facility would be easier.

The key clicked in the metal hole, and William pushed the first gate open. A paled body rested on the bed in the corner. Red streaks flowed out of his arms onto the blue sheets. William shook his head at the warden's carelessness.

How does he expect these prisoners to donate blood once per week if he doesn't take care of them? And where is he sending the blood if we haven't signed the agreement yet?

William opened the bottle of water that rested on the metal stand and sat at the bedside. The inmate didn't even have strength to twist the cap himself; none of them did.

"You need to drink." He held his arm under the back of the prisoner's neck, tipping the bottle toward the mouth.

Water covered the inmate's cracked lips, and the frail man began sucking on the plastic opening as soon as the liquid entered his mouth. Like a dehydrated hiker who'd just crossed a desert, he couldn't get enough. None of them seemed satisfied when William had helped with their recovery. The warden's orders drained the inmates of too much blood. Drops flowed down his chin and neck, soaking the pillow.

"Slow down." William pulled the bottle back. "Don't waste it."

The prisoner's hands flew to the container, holding it against William's strength. The half-breed let him finish.

"Richard, open your arm," William instructed.

"More." The prisoner's raspy voice was barely audible as he reached out for the empty bottle.

William pushed on the inmate's wrist to open the inside of his arm. Blood still dripped. The half-breed let out his fangs and bit the tip of his own finger. The cut would heal in seconds, but it was enough time to cover Richard's wounds with his own blood. The hole where the needle had been inserted for way too long had closed.

He took the empty bottle and stood. "You'll feel better soon. You can't drink too much at once. I'll be back tomorrow."

"Thank you," the man whispered before his head plopped down on the hard mattress and he passed out. Richard was one of the few whose kind words William appreciated. Most of the inmates here came from a life of treachery and pain. The warden had used this transfer facility as his own blood factory. William promised himself he'd put a stop to the blood smuggling. The thieves the warden hired probably didn't care for the right serums to be mixed in. Thousands of vampires had been found dead, and no one could explain the cause. William suspected the warden was the source of the problem.

He continued the routine down the hall, picking up his pace. Eric would vortex William back to the Amazon in less than an hour, just before Sarah returned from following Xander to the cave where he'd kept Xela hidden.

William had tried to limit the days Sarah saw the warlock, but he also knew that soon he would have to face his greatest fear. He'd need to let his wife come alone to the prison, when the warden would be ready to kill her.

Shivers ran through William's body, and his fangs sprouted on their own. The risk of letting the warden think he captured William's wife successfully seemed too great, but it was the only way to kill him. The warlock would never face off against them in a true battle, the way his brother Aseret has in the underworld. The warden's wisdom and conniving had been his strength. Pinpointing his weakness had proven difficult. After all, someone who could disappear in a blink would need to be ambushed. Even then, to kill him, they would have to strike without him knowing. A good distraction was key. And William's wife was the bait.

* * *

The stars fell down from the sky more often lately, as if the night sky cried. William hid secrets from his wife, but sometimes the most important secrets were the ones that had to be kept from those closest to his heart. The guilt ate him from inside. Each lie felt like a prick that stopped his pulse. But William knew he wasn't the only one who lied. He closed his eyes.

Why would Sarah give up her body again without telling me? He thought. *Or did she?*

If what he sensed was true, it would take all his strength to keep this secret as well. Why didn't they want him to know? *Were we being tested by the keepers? How long would it take for us to be torn apart into two halves again?*

William was certain Sarah would tell him the truth if she could, but he also knew that his wife was the most honorable and trustworthy person he'd ever met. Her decisions, though quick and stupid, were always on instinct, and her instinct trusted him enough to forgive him for not recognizing her when her body had been stolen by the witch.

She must have a good reason to keep her secret.

A breeze rustled the leaves above. William's eyes flew open. A stray cloud passed over the tree house, dimming the stars for a moment.

"Why do you seem to be here when you're not?" he whispered.

Even when Sarah wasn't with him, he sensed her presence. The memory of her kisses warmed his lips. William wanted nothing more than to keep his wife in his embrace forever, when in truth, he knew her wild spirit would roam, finding a way to better the world. Any time they spent together was precious.

William's lips warmed, and his pulse raced. "Come back to me safely." He hoped the words would reach her soul, wherever she was. For now, he had to pretend the witch who possessed his wife's body was married to him, but he knew it was for the better. Sarah would want it that way.

It wouldn't take much for William to strike and release the secrets he held. If Xander didn't keep his distance, it would push William over his threshold. Even if the soul wasn't Sarah's, the body still belonged to her. He couldn't let Xander touch his wife's body and wasn't sure why the shifter was drawn to the witch.

"I'm not sure I can deceive you," he thought aloud.

The half-breed vampire wondered if perhaps keeping secrets from each other was what made them stronger and independent.

The decisions they'd made were on instinct, not emotion, and it guided them both well in life.

"To keep a secret so big . . . how can they ask me to do this?"

The aroma of aloe and vanilla floated through the treehouse. William's eyes flew open.

I wish we could work together on this. It will test everything I believe in and who I am.

"But it's for the best. Otherwise, we'll never be safe. I have to protect you." He closed his eyes. "I love you so much. Come back to me, Sarah."

As much as he'd felt her presence with him in the tree house, it disappeared too quickly.

* * *

Having Sarah again as his wife, even as a ghost cursed to be in flesh, rejuvenated William beyond his expectations. The hour they'd spent in Xela's old lair making love and finding each other had given him the strength he'd need to lie to his wife. He'd said as much as he could to ensure she remained strong when he passed, but still, Sarah's unpredictable nature had him worry.

William wished he didn't have to be dishonest, but faking his death had to seem as real as possible. It had to be believable, and he couldn't think of a better way to sell the act than a mourning wife. The only question that remained was whether Sarah would let him go.

Will she ever forgive me?

William and Sarah stood on the half-burnt bridge in the underworld. Miranda's curse on Sarah's ghost almost ruined the plan, but with the ruby ring in his pocket, he still had a chance to pull it off.

"Put it on. If it works, you should be a ghost again. Go," William whispered, sliding it onto her finger.

Her hands disappeared along with the rest of her body.

"What about you? We need to get to the dungeons," she said.

Though William controlled his breathing and kept it shallow, beads of sweat rolled down his temples. It wouldn't take long for the seekers to recognize his smell. If he could only make it to the end of the bridge, the spot he and the twins scouted before, the plan would work.

"I'll follow soon. I just have to deal with them." He nodded toward the seekers.

"I won't leave you. You cannot do this by yourself," Sarah insisted.

It was like talking to a wall—an invisible wall that was his wife.

You have to. I'm so sorry for doing this to you.

"I can't fight them if I have to protect you, too," he motioned his gaze toward the end of the bridge. "Now go."

"I don't need protection. I will *not* leave you. Stay still," Sarah's ghost whispered.

After a minute, William heard a loud echo of a rock cascading down one of the entrances. The sound drew the seekers away from the bridge and William zoomed toward its end. Once on the cliff, a few yards away from the crevice, William didn't care to be quiet. His objective was to ensure the seekers attacked him, instead of following his wife. Sarah now waited for him in the staircase, probably anxious to see how her husband would sneak by the hurdles of seekers.

William brushed the tip of his shoe a little harder against the rocky footing. The seekers turned around like a tidal wave in an auditorium. They took one big inhale, and William wondered whether there'd be enough of the rotten air left for him to breathe. For a split second the hall fell silent, followed by yelps and screeching as Aseret's army attacked.

The half-breed vampire braced against the assault, shoving one seeker after another down into the flowing river of lava below. They pursued, and even when their comrades fell into the boiling river below dying, the others didn't falter. The demons watched from farther away. William knew they would be the ones to spread the word of his death.

The heat behind William increased as he neared the brink of the crevice. The flowing lava in the river below bubbled upward, sending its spits higher each time he peeked. Seekers struck at his front.

Aware that Sarah would be able to pass into the dungeons eased his worry only a little, for he was aware that his death could potentially send his wife over the edge herself, and that's the last thing he wanted. At least she didn't have a body to burn, but with Miranda's curse, who knew what could harm her fleshed ghost.

"If you don't remember me, you will now," he growled, shoving the seekers into the lava-filled crevice.

William would have no problem overtaking the seekers to pass through the dungeons to help Sarah look for Miranda's body. But that wasn't the plan. He agreed with his children the news of his death had to reach the warden. Aseret's brother needed to think Sarah had no hope; otherwise he'd never show his true form and they wouldn't be able to kill him.

Two more seekers approached from the side, and he smashed one into the other, sending both down into the burning pit. A third one fell victim to gravity when the other two pushed off against him. Their bodies burned before they hit the flowing magma. Black ash wafted upward on the waves of heat like feathers, along with the fresh stench of dirty socks and spoiled eggs.

William heard Sarah throw another rock to grab the seeker's attention, but he knew it wouldn't work. He hoped she'd continue the way he'd asked her. It was their only chance against the evil warlock.

One more step and he'd fall into the pit of hell. The heat almost burned his back. The seekers reached and grabbed at his skin, their talons slicing the flesh like scalpels. Although William's skin would heal in seconds, the sear stung like salt poured on fresh wound.

The camouflaged yellow mist in the void below indicated the time to die has come. William's toes balanced on the ledge of the crater, his heels wobbling his body until William couldn't control his balance any longer.

Be strong, Sarah. You need to go on.

William tipped back and fell toward the burning river, and time seemed to slow. Looking up at the ledge of the crater, William saw the seekers throw their hands up in a screech of victory, then went back to their work. The spits of lava surpassed him, and William could only hope the twin's plan wouldn't fail. He trusted them with his life.

The aroma of honey and lemon filled William's lungs, and the yellow mist opened a vortex below him. No one would be the wiser, including his wife. For effect, the twins had added the smell of burning flesh and woody musk as leftovers. Sarah would think he died.

Aware of the sorrow he was subjecting her to, William's heart ached for his wife. She'd blame herself for his death, thinking she failed her entire family. Could she go on? Would Sarah overcome her grief and find Miranda's body? Inside, William knew she would. He trusted his wife's inner strength. Her ability to make the right decisions, even when they seemed wrong, would triumph. *Stay strong, Sarah.*

The heat intensified near the mist, and before his flesh began to burn, William found himself flying through a vortex Crystal and Ayer had prepared. The orange glow of the underworld turned into fresh greens and blues, all blending into one color. The smell of falling water filled the spinning funnel. When it stopped, William stood in an immaculate bedroom where the back wall was a waterfall.

Crystal and Ayer knelt on a plush carpet in the middle of the room, facing each other, their buttocks resting on their heels. Air spun around them like a tornado, flapping Crystal's hair like Medusa's. Ayer's hands clutched as he contained the sparkling electricity within his fingers. Jolts of power flowed around their bodies. The children raised their arms above their heads, connecting at their wrists. A final flash of lightning spread from the point of contact toward their torso and down to the ground.

The havoc settled, and the twins opened their eyes.

"Is she safe?" William asked, stepping closer.

The casters stood. "Yes, but she's devastated. It's out of our hands now."

"We shouldn't have done this." William shook his head, roaming his fingers through his hair.

"It was the only way, Father. The news of your death had to seem real. She won't give up on us." Ayer placed his hand on William's shoulder. "She won't mourn you for long."

"In the meantime, let's go steal a body." Crystal winked.

William's mouth dropped open. "What body?"

* * *

In a cave eerily familiar to Xela's, pervasive shadows flickered along the walls, cast by the glow of the fireplace.

"Uncle Xander set up the cave." Crystal explained. "He thought it'd help him find the witch he once loved."

"The witch in Mom's body." Ayer added.

"That's why he's drawn to Sarah." William wiped the sweat off his forehead.

He and the caster twins rushed toward the slumped body in the chair. William and the caster twins rushed toward the slumped body in the chair.

"Untie her hands," Ayer instructed as he crouched and began to loosen the knots at her ankles. William's fingers danced with the rope, pulling on ends like an experienced sailor.

Crystal stood tall, her arm stretched out at her front as her hand maneuvered to hold a vortex open on the wall.

"Done." William straightened.

The witches' arms flopped to the side, and William caught her before gravity pulled her to the floor. Ayer had finished with the lower ropes, and William lifted the corpse, cradling it against his chest. He knew this was the body Sarah would soon possess. It was the only body they had for her, for now.

Ayer pulled out his palm. In it rested Eric's blue sphere from Xela's lair. "It will take you back to Uncle Eric's home. Leave the body there. We will open a vortex for you when the time is right. Mom should be there by the time you return." He handed the glowing ball to William.

"Thank you for your help. I don't know where you get your strength from." William backed into the vortex Crystal had opened in the wall.

"From you and from Ma," the twins said together.

Crystal closed the portal after her father had stepped through.

SNEAK PEAK AT BOOK FOUR IN THE SERIES

EVIL-BENT

A TWO EQUALS NOVELLA

The demon's fireball flew through the arctic air toward me. It sizzled, cutting the frozen space with heat that would disintegrate my body. Bracing my legs against a sheet of ice, I shot a field of energy out of my arms in defense. It swallowed the sphere, blasting another sound wave through the white plains and lifting fresh snow for a fresh tumble roll.

You have an order to kill, I repeated the keepers' mantra in my mind. *All of Aseret's servants shall die.*

The ongoing task to hunt the strayed creatures had kept me away from my family and friends for over a month now. My only companion was my love Mira, whose shapeshifting abilities could hide her in any situation. She has been at my side for almost three decades.

The job became easier each time I bent their evil spirits out of this realm as I had direct power to bind the underworld demons to the hereafter, a portal no being could escape. But the temporary gift from the keepers was also my doom. Once my job was done, the power would be taken away, along with my immortality and my memories. I had no choice in the matter. My water mark forced me to kill; the keepers' powers transferred through my soul.

The demon smirked. From the way his palms twitched, I knew he prepared to send a new blow my way. Spheres of cold fire manifested in my hands, and I threw them at the demon's chest, one after another. They flew at light speed with blue tails of electricity. The demon fell back, then pushed upright as if an invisible force had helped him.

How did he do that?

I released a shot, followed by a firmer one. The whizz of the fireballs released an electric smell of lightning.

Somehow, he stood up again. This one was strong.

More energy flew through my veins, its voltage shaking my body as if I'd been dipped in water with a floating toaster. The current spread across my skin in waves. Pain disguised as ecstasy stretched the fleshed spikes on my neck, extending them like a bulldog's collar. The burning reached its maximum. To me, the next best thing to an orgasm was bending.

An aura of power enveloped me. Purple hue hugged my body. I gathered the energy and pushed it to my front, aiming it at him. The fiery orb consumed the demon as soon as I released it.

He had no time to yelp. His body disintegrated on contact, and the soul was sucked into a void I'd opened with the snap of my fingers, another ability the keepers had bestowed upon me. The demon's spirit was now bound to the hereafter.

Ashed mist floated like feathers in the light breeze, spreading the demon's signature stench of dirty socks and rotten eggs. This monster possessed more power than I'd seen in a while. I followed the drift of his remains spreading across the skies, then falling back to Earth. My gaze connected to each wafer as it touched the snow, dissipating within the white plush.

A long held breath escaped my lungs. My new skills drained the strength out of my body to the brink of my own death. But the order had to be fulfilled and once my job was done, I'd be no one, stripped of my supernatural gifts for defying the keepers. My choice over a month ago to help a witch marked with a sphere sealed my fate. The keepers, angered by my decision, had punished me. Soon, I would be a mere human, unworthy of the love of my life. Mira would no longer be part of my future.

Mira and I had followed the demon for three days, apprehending him in the North Pole this morning. His black cloak was easy to spot over the fresh snow, like a drop of black oil in a cup of milk. He was one of the last to survive our month-long quest to exterminate those who followed Aseret. They were always given a choice to change—I could bend their sphered mark and the evil away—but the demons had been scarred too deep to make that choice and preferred to fight. Their souls had been enveloped and murdered by Aseret's black magic beyond rehabilitation.

My soul mate insisted on helping, her shapeshifting abilities useful to apprehend other shifter demons. But she didn't know where her help would lead.

Three more demons and my job would be done.

My powers would be taken away.

My life spared, but at what cost?

The throbs stopped, and I knew my eyes returned from a full purple to their natural blue hue. Lowering my shoulders, I relaxed. The spikes sunk back into my neck to rest. I twisted my torso to the right, and the vertebra cracked, one disk after another in a sequence of piano keys.

"That felt good." I closed my eyes again to relive the threshold I passed. The pleasure of bending could never be explained to anyone. A necessity I needed, like air. A life without my powers was unimaginable, yet closer to reality than I wanted it to be.

"You can shift back now," I called.

Mira crawled out from under the snow. Her white ears shrunk, and the paws spreading evenly over the snow to support her bear's body lengthened into delicate fingers. Hinds remained a bear's until she stood up, only then magically transforming into thighs and calves I longed for every day. For a second, before her clothes shifted to cover her, I had a glimpse of a naked caramel goddess, most vulnerable in her shifting state. My soul mate.

"Wow." Mira brushed her fingers through her hair. "You look like you enjoyed it better than—"

"Don't say it," I warned, "or I may have to prove you wrong, sugar."

Perhaps she knew me better than I thought.

"Sex." She smirked, grazing across the snow toward me.

"Tease."

"You know it." She squeezed my hand and nuzzled her nose into my shoulder, pressing her front against me. I wrapped my arms around her and tried to remember a past when she wasn't with me every day. It was difficult to picture.

Mira's body warmed mine, and I realized I was shivering. Part of her shifting nature allowed her to adjust body temperature, sometimes in more beneficial ways than other, like now. The iced aroma of forget-me-not blossoms mixed with her pheromones into an intoxicating blend. That's why I referred to her as "sugar." As I recalled the sweet taste of her skin, blood rushed through my veins quicker, filling the lower part of my body first.

"Here?" My brows rose as I scanned the barren plateau. Even my sight couldn't find anything beyond the infinite snow and ice, and my sight was almost infinite.

She nodded, biting her lip and pushed the remaining white strand of hair behind her ear. It darkened into auburn. Only my soul mate knew what made me tick.

"You may not feel it, but it's freezing," I noted.

"I'll warm you."

Mira's breath left a trail in the air between us. It flowed from her mouth and touched my lips, curling around my cheeks as I breathed her in. My inhales shortened, and heart sped up. She drew her hands up to my hair, tangling her fingers until their tips touched my scalp. My goddess drove me to the point of ecstasy in seconds. No other woman could ever make me this crazy, and we haven't even kissed. I ran my hands under her shirt, stroking her spine on the way up, the way she liked it.

A quiet squirm escaped her mouth, and before I knew it, Mira's lips covered mine and her tongue danced in my mouth. My muse captured my soul with each deepening kiss. I closed my eyes and felt as if I were spinning. Tingles flew through me, and with a pinch, my flesh extend around my neck into Mira, breaking when they touched her skin.

I winced.

She pulled back. Her eyes held mine, and I blinked to clear a sudden blur in my vision. Mira went out of focus again, and the Arctic begun to spin behind a fog. I smelled the iron tang of my blood.

My knees buckled, but Mira caught me before I hit the ground and sat beside me on the snow. The sky stretched its infinite clarity.

"This is really taking a lot out of you." The concern in her voice trembled with worry and anger. "Lie down for a moment."

I couldn't argue: my legs wouldn't hold me up for long.

"Let me see your neck," she whispered, tugging at the bulked turtleneck under my chin. Her fingers brazed the broken skin that covered my spikes. "They're bleeding again."

"They'll heal." I took her hand away from the burgundy dots I imagined dripping down my neck, remnants of my fleshed spikes that ruptured during bending, then kissing.

"You cannot keep doing this. Why don't you speak with the keepers again," she pleaded. "Perhaps I can talk to Father."

Castall, Mira's father, was one of the three keepers who watched over humans, vampires, and warlocks. She'd felt guilty about his harsh decision, but I had a feeling my friend didn't have much choice in the matter. The keeper of warlocks who used to protect and guide me had been overruled by his partners, Drake and Gabriel. I saw it in his eyes each time we spoke of the inevitable.

"You know the deal. Unless I bend the mark back to Xela's wrist, they won't help." My eyelids grew heavier each time I blinked.

"Talk to Xander," she almost begged, the same way she had each time I weakened. "My brother will understand. Xela will too. I'm sure he doesn't mind her having the sphere."

"She'll hurt him if she gets it back. She won't have a choice, and I'll have to imprison her." I removed a thermos from my backpack, opened the canister with hot tea, and sipped. "I cannot risk to cause you pain. Your brother's turmoil would hurt you too. Besides, removing Xela's mark was the right thing to do. I wouldn't even want to change that."

Mira tightened her palms and stood up. Steam rolled off her skin as if her entire body breathed. "And you'll just do your job for the keepers and be stripped of your powers. They're using you. It's not fair. You didn't do anything wrong."

It was odd to see Mira standing in front of me in shorts, sneakers, and a thin blazer when I had bundled up in an arctic coat and boots. Made the seriousness of her words soften. Each time she tried to argue against what needed to be done, my heart ached, as I had no choice in the matter. Mira and Xander's appeals to their father didn't help. My relentless shifter wouldn't give up on me.

"I took off a mark. In the keepers' minds, I'm a traitor. The only reason they let me continue is because of my history of serving them."

"So? Where is it written that you can't take off a mark? You're an evil-bender. If it's not allowed, then no one should be able to do it!" Now, steam seemed to come out of her ears more than the rest of her body.

"It doesn't have to be written, sugar. I didn't ask the keepers' permission. That's all that matters."

She pouted, dropping on her knees in front of me. "You'll be mortal. That's not enough time for us. I can't lose you."

"I will still love you. I will always love you," I lied. I was the only one who knew my punishment included more than stripping the powers of an evil-bender or shortening my life span. I hadn't found the right moment to tell her. Maybe there wasn't one.

"That's a bit harsh, don't you think?" she asked as if she'd read my mind, and pulled on my hands. "Stand up, nice and easy."

I pushed up to a crouch. "The keepers won't compromise. In their eyes, one step away from your duty means you'll turn to the dark side. They don't want to take that chance."

"You're not like that." Squatting, she held my hands between hers. I didn't need gloves with Mira around.

"I know."

"They know it, too. They're just being stubborn." She furrowed.

"Funny how that's exactly what I love about you but hate about the keepers." I smiled.

Her brows rose, but Mira didn't argue.

I must seem weaker than I thought.

"Are you strong enough to vortex us?" she asked.

"I think so." I let go of her hands and packed the thermos into the back pack.

"I hope we don't bump into the other demons. Xela's reading showed the last ones will hold magic beyond our understanding. I don't think you can face them in this state." She grabbed my hand to help me up. I used her strength to pull myself and leaned against her.

"Me too."

Secretly, I didn't want to face off against a demon for a different reason. If I killed the last three, I may as well have committed suicide.

Mustering strength, I twirled my finger to release the energy of a vortex: a time hole which could take us back to her home in the forest where I'd moved in. I no longer stayed in my waterfall room in Monasterio de Piedra where I used to live. Too close to the keepers. Too close to those responsible for my doom. Besides, the caster twins, Crystal and Ayer, had been living there for the past month.

The air swirled, lifting the snow. The flakes drifted up and down in a sequence of twirls which reminded me of angel halos. The doorway opened, beaming green from within. The aroma of rosemary and peppermint, Mira's home, enveloped us as we stepped in over the threshold. The peaceful snow and ice left behind reminded me of the loneliness I'd soon experience. My memories would soon be wiped away.

About the Author

Marta lives with her husband and two kids in Cambridge, Ontario. A great skier (in her kids eyes), she loves the outdoors and quiet mornings on the porch with a cup of coffee. She can often be found creating new worlds in front of her computer. She has a sarcastic sense of humor and those very close to her know that she can make a joke out of almost anything; but she would suck as a comedian. Her favourite colours can all be found in nature.

If you enjoyed Two Equals, please consider leaving a review. All authors depend on the support of their readers to find an audience.

Books by this Author in the Two Halves Series:

Book 1: Marked: A Two Halves Novella
Book 2: Two Halves
Book 3: Two Equals
Book 4: Evil-Bent: A Two Equals Novella

Connect with Me Online:

Twitter: http://twitter.com/martaszemik
My Blog: http://martaszemik.blogspot.com/

Acknowledgments

As always, I am grateful to be surrounded by many loving people who support me, my fantasies, and my writing.

First and foremost my family, without whom this novel would never be in the hands of my readers. Thank you for your continuous support, faith and encouragement.

Mom, your go getter attitude has rubbed off on me.

Dad, your humour is infectious.

Mike, "all you need is love".

Maya and Alex, you are who I live for. You are my life.

I am grateful to my editors Marg Gilks and Nicole Zoltack, and my reader and editor friends for their invaluable input, critique, support and love. A big thank you to Robin Ludwig Design Inc. for the beautiful book cover.

"Never say Never" is a quote I've lived by for the past twenty years. It takes me beyond what I think I'm capable of.

CPSIA information can be obtained at www.ICGtesting.com
Printed in the USA
LVOW050013151212

311627LV00002B/27/P

9 780987 877253